The Oxford Conspiracy

In 1836, what you don't know can't hurt you; what you do know certainly will…

Robert S Birch

ISBN: 978-1-0687635-3-3

Published by RSBirchBooks

Dedication

For Julie

Acknowledgement

My heartfelt thanks must go to my wife, Julie, for all her ideas and for producing the artwork.

Radcliffe Infirmary 1770-2007

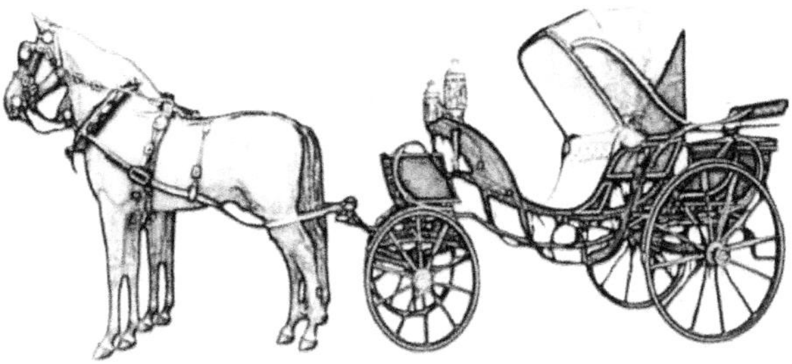

Barouche

Gig

Contents

Chapter 1

The Box

When John Crosley's leg came off and fell into the basket, there was a collective sigh of relief from the observers in the gallery. It was not as though amputation was an unusual procedure, but in the days before anaesthetics, it was always a dramatic moment when a struggling patient surrendered their limb to the surgeon's saw. It had taken six men to restrain Crosley while his leg was removed; each with a different role to perform in a drama that was horrific to observe and unspeakably brutal for the patient.

For House Surgeon Samuel Ansell, it was a particularly satisfying moment because his mentor was smiling his approval, and the patient was still clinging to life. Both surgeons knew that capital surgery imposed great stress on the human body, and there was always a risk of the patient dying from apoplexy before an operation could be completed. As Sam waited for the detached limb to be taken away, he glanced down at Crosley. The man was delirious with pain, and he lay there muttering his discontent with a pallid face that was damp with the moisture of shock, fear, and blood loss. In 1836, amputation - especially at the thigh - was a dangerous operation of last resort, reserved for those occasions when death was otherwise highly likely. Limb removal had saved many lives, but it had ended many too, and so it was a procedure chosen only after careful consideration. However, on this occasion, it was not the choice of surgery that made Crosley's case so unusual; it was what the man had claimed when he first arrived at Oxford's Radcliffe Infirmary.

It was a Sunday evening at the end of June, and a breathless runner had arrived to warn the infirmary staff that a cart was bringing a gravely injured man for urgent treatment. The porter had summoned Sam from his room, and he was already waiting on the ward when the patient arrived. He could see at once that the man's leg would have to be removed. Crosley had been run over by the iron wheels of a heavy passenger coach resulting in a compound fracture of the femur and severe soft tissue injuries to his upper leg. The fractured bone was protruding from his breeches, and he was losing blood at an alarming rate. This type of accident was common enough in the city, but it was not often that a patient claimed they had been pushed off a coach intentionally, and that someone at the infirmary was behind it.

It was an astonishing allegation, and Sam had initially wondered whether Crosley was delusional from the shock of his dreadful injury. His speech was certainly slurred, and he was babbling incomplete sentences which were difficult to understand. However, his underlying terror had been unmistakable, and Sam understood enough of the man's hoarse protestations to recognize that Crosley's fear stemmed from the knowledge that he was being treated at the Radcliffe Infirmary rather than his anticipation of the surgeon's knife. Sam had been about to question the man about it, when a nurse began to remove Crosley's clothes. It reminded Sam that he needed to prepare for surgery, and he had decided to set the matter aside until his patient was back on the ward.

Back in the operating room, the basket containing the leg was out of the way, and Sam put down his saw and set about tying off the man's blood vessels and tidying up the stump. He frowned as Crosley's accusations once again intruded on his work. Why was the man so frightened? Indeed, what could be more terrifying at this infirmary than being held down by six strong men for an amputation? Next to him, Consultant Surgeon Charles Wingfield noticed his protégé's momentary hesitation and mistook it for complacency.

'Now, Sam. That was very nicely done and at an excellent pace too, but you need to keep up your concentration and avoid relaxing before the job is complete. I have sawn through many a limb successfully, only to lose a patient while I am completing the stump. Shock can be insidious and accumulative.'

Sam nodded; he knew Wingfield was correct, so he forced himself to focus and redoubled his efforts. After tying off all the vessels, he stretched flaps of muscle, soft tissue, and skin over the sawn end of the femur to create a pad to cushion the stump. He was using the latest techniques recommended by the great London surgeon, Robert Liston FRCS who declared that speed was of the essence. It was well known that Liston was in the habit of starting an amputation by producing a watch and calling out to the gallery: "Time, gentlemen, please!" It was said that his record from first incision to limb removal was less than 30 seconds. Sam was unable to match that, but he did understand the requirement to be swift in order to spare the patient distress and to minimize blood loss.

A few minutes later, the operation was complete, and Sam was able to wash his hands in a bowl of warm water. His apron was thick with congealed blood from the toil of a busy weekend, and he was relieved to exchange it for his frock coat which was handed to him by a waiting orderly. He watched as Crosley was taken away on a stretcher. Sam had directed that the patient be treated with a mixture of laudanum and alcohol, but he knew that it would offer Crosley little relief from the excruciating pain that he would face in the coming days. He hoped his friend, William Perks, the House Apothecary, would take pity on the poor man and give him an extra strong dose - even if it bordered on being a dangerous quantity. Beside Sam, Charles Wingfield was pleased with the outcome and clapped him on the back.

'Excellent work, Samuel. That patient is very weak, and we may yet lose him, but you have given him the very best chance of survival. All we can do now is pray to God and hope that Matron and her nurses can restore him to good health.'

Sam bristled with pride. Wingfield was a popular and talented surgeon. He was a surprisingly large man for one with such manual dexterity, and he had a booming voice especially when he laughed. He had arrived in Oxford twenty years earlier and established a busy private practice from his home in Broad Street whilst supporting the infirmary as one of the two surgical consultants. The Radcliffe Infirmary was a charitable endeavour established in 1770, and it was supported by subscribers who paid an annual fee to gain access for their servants and workers. One of the perks of subscribership was the entitlement to vote on the appointment of key personnel including the governors and some of the senior medical staff. Wingfield's appointment as a consultant had been controversial because he had won the ballot by a single vote after there had been a string of new subscribers in the run up to the election. Some of the unsuccessful candidates were unhappy with the outcome and had voiced their discontent in the local paper. However, the surgeon had been a popular choice in the city, and the complaints soon dried up, and the matter died away.

The controversy was a measure of the intense competition that existed for hospital appointments even though they were unpaid. A hospital consultancy greatly enhanced a surgeon's professional reputation and increased the popularity of their lucrative private practice. Sam's route to the infirmary's operating room was a little different, however, and he owed much to Wingfield's patronage.

Samuel Joshua Ansell came from a humble background. His mother had died in childbirth and his father was a cloth merchant whose modest, but profitable concern was situated by the Oxford Canal. After Sam's mother died, his father's sister came for a short visit but never left. Aunt Winifred brought up

Sam and became his surrogate mother. She made a loving parent who held firm views on how the baby boy should be raised, despite having no children of her own. Material riches and social advancement meant nothing to her, but personal qualities were important, and she insisted on consideration, good manners, and a sense of duty. It was not a religious quest; Aunt Winifred just believed that spiritual health spilled over into all aspects of life and were prerequisites for contentment. She was a tolerant woman who Sam loved, and he was saddened that she had recently become a little infirm.

While Winifred worried about Sam's spiritual wellbeing, Sam's father was concerned with more practical matters. He saw education as the key to advancement, and he had invested heavily in his son's schooling. From an early age, Sam was fascinated by medicine and the workings of the human body, and he had declared his intention to become a surgeon even as a youth. His father was slightly disappointed that Sam showed little interest in the family business, but he had nonetheless done his best to pay for his son's medical education. Sam did well at school, but a university education was just too expensive, so he had continued his medical studies whilst articled to a surgeon apothecary in a practice in Oxford.

Eventually, he caught the eye of Charles Wingfield who was impressed by the young man's enquiring mind and dedication. It was a time when surgical training was by apprenticeship to a practicing surgeon who would take on trainees for a fee. The apprentices paid for the surgeon's instruction and attended ward rounds, lectures, and anatomy classes. The more affluent were able to learn about human anatomy by paying a substantial fee to perform dissection. The trainees were initially known as pupils who took on menial tasks and observed the surgeon's work. Later, they would become dressers, trainee surgeons working under supervision. Once an individual had assembled a portfolio demonstrating their learning and experience, it was presented to the Royal College of Surgeons which could grant a fellowship and official recognition. It was a costly education, and it was difficult to find a surgeon willing to take someone onto their books at an affordable price. Sam was therefore extremely fortunate when Wingfield offered to accept him as his apprentice for a token fee that Sam's father could afford to pay. More recently, his mentor's kindness had extended beyond instruction. Wingfield had bolstered Sam's submission to the Royal College of Surgeons with a glowing testimonial, and he had lobbied the Board of Governors on Sam's behalf to get his freshly qualified protegee appointed to the new post of House Surgeon. In truth, Sam owed a great deal to Wingfield, and he looked to him with a great deal of affection and gratitude.

As the two men left the operating theatre, Sam considered mentioning Crosley's accusations, but Wingfield was hosting a dinner party and was already rushing outside to his waiting carriage. Sam decided not to trouble him, and after bidding Wingfield goodnight, he returned to his room, resolved to ask Crosley about it directly the following day.

***

The next morning, Sam was served breakfast in the

doctors' parlour, a small room reserved for the house doctors and Matron. Shortly after sitting down, he was joined by his friend, William Perks. The House Apothecary was a few years older than Sam and had been the sole house doctor until Sam was appointed. As a surgeon with a fellowship, Sam was technically senior to Will, but he respected the older man's experience and trusted his clinical judgement.

Sam's respect was well founded because apothecary blood ran deeply through Will's veins, and his extensive knowledge reflected generations of family experience. He grew up in Banbury where his father owned an apothecary's shop that had been in the family for over a hundred years. During that time, the name Perks had become well-known locally, and the practice was widely recommended for its medical expertise and the quality of its treatments and service. Will had been articled to his father and had achieved a Licentiate of the Society of Apothecaries which was the highest professional qualification available at that time. That had placed him in a strong position when he applied successfully to the infirmary for a house appointment.

One of Will's responsibilities was to see all new patients to decide whether they should be treated as outpatients or admitted onto a ward. The governors were constantly trying to keep down costs by minimizing admissions, so the apothecary found his clinical decisions under the regular scrutiny of infirmary secretary Absolom Whiting. Will seemed untroubled by the constant interference, and Sam admired the way that his friend was somehow able to retain his humour and clinical independence whilst keeping Whiting at bay. Will's diplomacy had recently been acknowledged by the Board who had finally agreed to provide him with an assistant to relieve a growing workload.

As the two friends tucked into bacon, eggs and haddock, the conversation inevitably turned to the events of the previous night.

Will sawed at a piece of tough bacon. 'I saw that you had a nasty one last night, Sam. I'm referring to John Crosley, the patient with the thigh amputation.'

'Yes, it was yet another coach accident. I do wish they would slow down; the number of casualties seems to be getting worse. Crosley was very weak when he was returned to the ward. Did he live, do you know?'

Will wiped his lips with a starched napkin and pushed the hospital bacon to one side after capitulating in his battle to halve it.

'Well, he was alive at three o'clock this morning,' he replied. 'I was called to see a patient on the ladies' ward and popped in to see Crosley while I was up. He was very weak, as you say, and in a great deal of pain. I gave him laudanum as requested and topped him up again in the early hours. Hopefully, it hasn't finished him.'

Sam looked at his friend. He did not want to sound foolish or alarm him. 'Will, was Crosley speaking at all? Did he say anything to you?'

Will shook his head. 'Goodness me, no. The dose I gave him would have felled a horse. Why do you ask?'

Sam decided on partial disclosure. 'There's no particular reason. It's just that he was making some extraordinary claims when he was brought into the infirmary. Some of it was rambling and made no sense, but he seemed to be alleging some kind of foul play. He said he'd been pushed off a coach. I just wondered if he added anything else when you saw him.'

His friend shook his head. 'No, I'm afraid not.'

'Oh well. If he's awake when we go down to the ward, I'll ask him about it there.'

Will nodded and glanced at a large grandfather clock in the corner of the parlour. 'Well, it's time, Sam. We don't want to keep them waiting.'

The two men rose and made their way down to the first ward which was on the ground floor. On the way, they passed by the dead room. Will looked inside and shook his head at Sam. The wooden tables were empty and the shrouds on them were flat, like tablecloths. Nobody had died during the night.

By 1836, the Radcliffe Infirmary could house 130 patients. It was run much like a large house with a matron acting as a form of housekeeper who was responsible for most of the non-medical staff working inside the building. Her workers included the nurses who were typically middle-aged to elderly widows who would otherwise be without an income and were willing to tolerate the horrors of the foul-smelling wards. The women were not medically trained, but most of them had nursed children or their sick husbands. Their pay was tiny, but they lived for free in the infirmary as members of the house staff. Considering that most of them were supposed to be in mourning, they were a flirtatious bunch who loved to tease the two house-doctors, though when they did, they were always careful to ensure that neither Matron nor the chaplain were within earshot.

Waiting for them at the entrance to Bagot Accident Ward for Men was Nurse Catherine Wallace.

She was a woman whose confidence was matched by her good looks and voluptuous figure. She was unruffled by the seniority of the two doctors, and when she spoke to either of them it was always with the unspoken suggestion that she had more to offer than conversation. There was no doubt that of the eight hospital nurses, Wallace was the most flirtatious nurse of them all.

'Good morning, gentlemen. I hope you slept well and had the sweetest of dreams,' she smiled coquettishly, leaving the two men in no doubt that such imaginary dreams included her own active participation.

Sam cleared his throat and blushed. 'Er yes, thank you nurse, I slept extremely well…er…thank you.'

Nurse Wallace laughed at his discomfort. 'Well, I'm very pleased to hear it, Sir. I slept exceedingly well too,' she teased. 'But that's enough of my nighttime adventures. We're all ready for you,' she added before leading them into the ward.

Bagot Ward was usually reserved for men who had suffered accidents, although when the infirmary was running short of beds, it would sometimes house medical cases too. That was the case on this occasion, so both men had patients waiting to be seen.

Whenever he entered a ward, Sam was always hit by the rancid smell of disease and ill health which clogged the air and seemed to linger in his clothes long after he had departed the cramped rooms. The ventilation was terrible, and the light was poor, giving the impression of a crypt for the dead rather than a sanctuary for the living. The beds ran parallel to the wall and were separated by oak partitions which rose from floor to shoulder height. Sam had always thought it was an inefficient use of space that limited patient examinations to one side of the bed. Bagot Ward was away from the street on the quiet side of the infirmary. However, inside the room the silence was punctuated by the sound of human suffering and unpleasant bodily functions. Sam pitied those forced to live there for more than a few days.

Will left Sam's side and went to the first bed which was occupied by a man, probably in his thirties, who had a hacking cough. Sam thought it was certain that he had Phthisis which one day would become known as Tuberculosis. It was untreatable and the biggest killer of all the chronic diseases that presented at the infirmary. Ahead of Sam, a movement caught his eye. A man was kneeling on the mat at the side of a patient at the other end of the ward. Sam recognized him at once. It was the Secretary, Absolom Whiting, and lying in front of him was Sam's patient, John Crosley.

Though Sam was an amiable man, he had taken an instant dislike to Whiting. The secretary was a tall, lanky character with the personality and cunning of a weasel. He was forever chasing patients for money - either directly or from their relatives. It was a job that had to be performed by someone otherwise the infirmary would quickly become insolvent. However, Whiting was often hectoring, and he was quite content to bully sick patients with dire threats of expulsion. He was also highly manipulative and seemed to have the governors wrapped around his little finger. He knew everything and everybody, and he loved telling people what to do.

As Sam approached, he could see that Whiting

was trying to rummage through the contents of the patient's wooden effects' box under the bed. He was using one hand to lift the lid and the other to fumble around inside. As he drew closer, Whiting became aware of Sam's presence; he withdrew his hands from under the bed and stood up.

'Good morning, Mr Ansell. A pleasure to see you on this fine day,' he said, trying to sound pleasant.

Sam studied him carefully for signs of guilt but found nothing in the man's face. 'Good morning, Mr Whiting. I see you've been to see my patient here, Mr Crosley.'

'Yes, I was just asking him about his next of kin and whether he had a subscriber to support his treatment. He seems to be having some difficulty in answering.'

Sam was unconvinced. Routine patient admissions required subscriber sponsorship whereas emergency cases, like Crosley's, were always accepted regardless of a patient's status or ability to pay. It was a practical and humanitarian policy which attracted strong public support and much goodwill. Whiting knew this, but he was trying to hide the fact that he had been caught with his hand inside the patient's possessions.

Sam glared at the secretary. 'I'm not surprised this man isn't answering you. He's had an extremely traumatic ordeal and is heavily sedated. Look, Mr Whiting, if you don't mind, I need to examine Mr Crosley's stump. If you are looking for details of his next of kin, then you are more likely to find them in the Admissions Register than in the patient's effects' box.'

Whiting flushed with anger. 'I don't know what

you're suggesting. This infirmary is a charity, and we must save every penny. It's for the good of everyone in Oxford. It's my responsibility to the Board of Governors,' he added as indignance was replaced by pompous self-importance.

Sam recognized the implied threat and decided that he had baited the bear for long enough. 'Look, Absolom, I have a busy day ahead of me and I need to attend to Mr Crosley. The Apothecary gave him a big dose of laudanum, and until that wears off you won't get much sense out of him. If you come back in the late afternoon, then you should find him in a better condition to answer your questions.'

The use of the secretary's first name had the desired effect. Whiting thought that it signalled capitulation, and he strode out of the ward after bidding Sam a haughty good morning. It was not capitulation, however, because Sam had lied. As soon as he had glanced down at Crosley, the surgeon recognized that his patient was dying, and that the man's life would end very soon. The blood loss from the injury, followed by the shock of an amputation, had been just too much for the man. Crosley's breathing was laboured, and he was staring up at Sam with glazed eyes that would soon close for the last time. Sam was certain that by the time Whiting returned in the afternoon, Crosley would have departed for a better place.

He pulled back the sheets and examined the dressing. Blood had continued to ooze from Crosley's stump, but there was no sign of a flood, and he replaced the bed covers. It was time to let nature take its course, and Sam rose to leave. As he did, the man's hand shot out and grabbed the surgeon's arm. It was a strong grip for one whose remaining time was almost exhausted.

'Listen, Mr Ansell. Please listen to me.'

Sam was startled and quite surprised that his patient was able to speak. 'Good morning, Mr Crosley. You've had a terrible accident, and I'm very sorry to tell you this, but I had to amputate your leg.'

'It was no accident,' he whispered. 'You see, I was pushed off the coach by a stranger sitting next to me outside on the top level. I believe he was working for somebody in the infirmary, and I think it might be the man that was just here. He was trying to ask me about it.'

Crosley tried to sit up which served only to make his breathing more difficult, and he flopped back onto the horsehair pillow. His life was ebbing away.

'In my tunic... the notebook. It's the canal you see…' He tailed off, exhausted, but he had strength for one last request. 'Call the chaplain, Sir, please, for I am nearly done. And Mr Ansell… tell my wife I'm sorry… I tried.'

Crosley's hand fell from Sam's arm and his eyes closed. He was still breathing, but he had spoken his final words, and it was pointless to press him on the matter. Sam was about to ask Nurse Wallace to summon the chaplain when he paused. He looked around, and after confirming that he was unobserved, he lifted the lid on the box under the bed and completed the job that Whiting had attempted earlier. Crosley's tunic was folded up under his bloodied and torn breeches. The notebook was in a side pocket. It was small but beautifully bound in brown leather. Crosley's name was embossed on the front cover along with the name of the firm of solicitors that employed him. At first sight, it looked quite unremarkable, but inside were the seeds of a conspiracy that would shake the very foundations of the British establishment.

Chapter 2

The Ledger

The main surgical ward rounds took place after lunch, three times a week, and were led by one of the two consultant surgeons. They were a peculiarly regimented affair that were conducted with military precision under the watchful eyes of Elizabeth Strickland. She had been the Matron at the Radcliffe Infirmary for nearly twenty years, and she patrolled its wards and corridors with unceasing vigilance as she searched for anything or anybody that was out of place or lacking proper employment. Deeply religious, she had never married because she was happily wedded to her work which she regarded as a vocation. The staff knew better than to err and then attempt to dissemble, because Matron was well-versed in the school of workplace excuses and could probably quote each one verbatim. Those who felt sufficiently brave to contest her inquisition were likely to end up feeling the lash of

Matron's tongue which could strip away a miscreant's armour in seconds, leaving an offender in fear of holy retribution or worse.

The Radcliffe Infirmary was run according to strict rules laid down by the Board of Governors, and Matron was a key enforcer. The regulations covered a wide gambit including finance, admissions policies and standards of behaviour - not just for the staff - but for the patients too. If a patient stepped outside a strict moral code, then they could be expelled and their entitlement to further treatment rescinded. That day, the ward round was led by Mr Cleobury, the other consultant surgeon and a good friend of Charles Wingfield. Matron had ensured that everything was ready for him and took up her usual position just behind Cleobury and ahead of Sam.

As the entourage made its way around the wards, Sam was itching to look inside Crosley's notebook, but the day had been so full that he had not yet found an opportunity to inspect it. As anticipated, Crosley had died before lunch, and by the time Mr Cleobury reached Bagot Ward, Crosley's bed was already vacant and ready for its next occupant. Nurse Wallace caught Sam's eye and beamed a smile that spoke of her usual promise. Sam looked away quickly, but when Mr Cleobury became involved in a detailed discussion with a patient, Sam took the opportunity to ask her quietly whether the chaplain had been reached in time.

She nodded. "Yes, Mr Ansell, The Reverend Savage came to administer to Mr Crosley just before he passed away. We then moved him up to the Dead Room.'

Sam realized that Crosley's notebook had

become a liability, and that he would struggle to explain why it was in his possession if he was challenged. He was particularly concerned that Crosley might have repeated his accusations to the chaplain and mentioned the book before he died.

'Did he wake up at all after I saw him this morning?' he asked.

Wallace looked at Sam quizzically. 'No, Sir, I don't believe so. The chaplain would know, though.' Sam was slightly reassured and was about to ask more when Matron became aware of the whispered conversation behind her and swung round with a glare that forced an early end to the exchange.

***

An hour later, the ward round had ended, and instead of taking afternoon tea in the doctor's parlour, Sam broke his routine by rushing to the privacy of his room to read Crosley's record. On the way, he glanced inside the Dead Room and saw the chaplain administering to the corpse of a woman who was laid out on one of the tables. The position of infirmary chaplain was paid for by the university, and candidates were subject to an election by the colleges. The chaplain's duties included pastoral care for the patients and the funeral arrangements of the dead, including the occasional interment in the infirmary's burial ground. The Reverend Savage was a small, middle-aged man who had an unsightly disfigurement on one side of his face. He had commenced his ministry as an army chaplain, and despite being a non-combatant, he had been wounded at the Battle of Salamanca when a stray musket ball had grazed his cheek and removed a sizeable amount of the soft tissue. Sam was a little wary of the man who, despite a cheery disposition, always seemed to interfere in other people's business. Will and Sam referred to him as 'Whiting's Snoop' because whatever the chaplain unearthed always seemed to find its way back to the secretary.

Savage noticed Sam and ended his prayer. He rose from the dead woman's side, replaced the shroud over her face, and smoothed down his surplice. 'I was sorry your efforts last night turned out to be fruitless,' he said, gesturing to a shape beneath a shroud on the table next to the woman's.

Sam shrugged. 'Crosley was very badly injured,' he replied. 'We did our best.'

Savage hesitated. 'You haven't seen any of the man's possessions, have you?' he asked. 'I was told he might have been admitted with a notebook or something similar. Apparently, it contains confidential information from his workplace.'

Sam shook his head as the book in his pocket seemed to treble in size. 'No, Reverend, but you could try Mr Whiting. He seemed to be searching for something when Crosley was still on the ward.'

The Reverend nodded, recognizing that it was a circular enquiry, but making little effort to disguise his disbelief. Sam noticed his scepticism, and thought Savage was about to press him further on the matter. However, the cleric seemed to change his mind, and he said no more about it. Instead, he wished Sam a good morning and turned to resume his work with the dead. Sam left him at prayer and continued to his room. Crosley's notebook was causing quite a stir.

Sam's accommodation was a small but comfortable room with a bed in one corner, two armchairs near an open fire, and a desk at a window facing the grounds at the rear of the infirmary. Sam sat at the desk and opened the notebook. Crosley's writing was clear, concise and extremely neat. Inside the front cover there were two addresses. One was for Mayhew Brothers, a well-known firm of solicitors in central Oxford. The other was Crosley's private address on New Inn Hall Lane. The company address included Crosley's name and recorded his position at the firm as being Chief Clerk. Inside, Crosley had chronicled the details of a wide range of legal matters that he had clerked for the partners. It was not a full record, just the particulars of his contribution to the firm's casework. As Sam flipped through it, he could tell that some of the entries concerned several well-known individuals within the Oxford establishment. Much of it was routine, but some of the entries looked quite sensitive, and in one case Crosley had recorded all the lurid details of a particularly notorious divorce that had played out in the newspaper. It was clear that he must have been an employee who was greatly trusted by the partners. However, this was a book that would normally be locked in the firm's safe, and not one that Crosley should have taken home with him. But why had he?

As he studied some of the casework notes, Sam reached a section concerned with the firm's business clients. One of them stood out because it was so detailed. It was a complete record of dividend payments made on behalf of the Oxford Canal Company. Sam immediately recalled Crosley's final words to him on the ward. He had mentioned the canal. Was this what he had been referring to? He looked at the list of names. Some of them were very well known and included the Duke of Marlborough and Lord Kirtland, both governors of the infirmary. Even the church was a beneficiary, with the Bishop of Oxford and his Diocese represented by Canon James Marshall.

Sam knew that many years earlier the Oxford Canal Company had been involved in a major financial scandal. The company had issued some new shares which were heavily promoted and sold at an inflated price during a frenzy of buying. However, almost immediately after the sale, it was announced that a competing canal was to be built from the Midlands to London. Unfortunately, the new canal would bypass the City of Oxford, leaving the Oxford Canal as a backwater servicing local trade only. The value of the new shares in the Oxford Canal Company plummeted on the news, and many holders of the stock were still sitting on huge paper losses many years later. That said, Sam knew that many local businessmen, including his own father, relied on the canal for their trade, and so the Oxford Canal Company was still reasonably profitable and paid a respectable dividend.

As Sam studied the entries, he noticed that one of the long-term shareholders was the Radcliffe Infirmary which owned a holding worth nearly £1000, far less than the £5000 that had been paid to buy the shares. The annual dividend payment of £98 was also shown, but Crosley had underlined it several times with large exclamation marks next to it as though there had been a mistake. Sam put the book down on his small writing desk. Was this what Crosley had been rambling about? Had there been a financial mistake or perhaps even a fraud? Why had Crosley been seized by this entry? Had his curiosity really cost the man his life?

Murder seemed an extreme response to silence a clerk but, on the other hand, Crosley had been adamant that he was pushed off the coach deliberately.

As he pondered the matter, there was a knock at his door. Sam put the notebook back into the desk drawer and opened the door to find Will standing there.

'Hello, Will. Are you finished for the day? Please come in.'

Will advanced into the room. He was a lanky individual with thinning hair and glasses that made him appear slightly owlish. He flopped into a tired armchair. 'Apothecaries never finish their work,' he declared. 'Unlike my part-time surgical colleagues!'

Sam laughed. 'Your patients remain here too long, Will. Our patients are either cured quickly or pass away. Would you like a glass of sherry by the way?'

Will nodded. 'That is certainly true. I've been making up a tincture containing echinacea for a man with erysipelas of the arm. It took me an hour to get the necessary ingredients from Edward Little and a similar time to make up the preparation. At least you can deal with your patients quickly, though I still maintain that surgery is little better than butchery,' he added, half joking.

Sam laughed. The apothecary certainly worked hard and relied greatly on William Little, the gardener, to supply the necessary herbal ingredients for his treatments. At the rear of the infirmary was a patch of land extending to four acres. The far end of it, where it bordered with Walton Street, was walled off and enclosed the infirmary's burial ground. The remaining land was let out to the gardener who could grow whatever he wanted so long as it included the list of herbs required by the apothecary for treatments. It was an arrangement that had worked well until the Board imposed punitive rents. Since then, there had been a constant stream of gardeners who found that they were unable to turn a profit. Little was just the latest to attempt the impossible.

Will took a sip of sherry. 'Talking of passing on, did you ever get to the bottom of Crosley's accusations before he died?'

Sam looked at his friend and decided to relate the whole story. When he had finished, he walked over to the desk and removed the notebook. He handed it to Will who was momentarily silenced. Eventually he spoke.

'Well, that is an intriguing account, Sam. The Oxford Canal scandal was many years ago, but it's famous because so many local people were caught out including some well-known figures. I had no idea that the infirmary lost money too. It's meant to be a charity, for goodness' sake.' Will's face darkened as he absorbed the implications. 'Think of the times we've asked for new equipment only to be told that there's no money. Now we learn the Board has been speculating and losing on stocks.'

Sam waited for his friend to vent his frustration. When he fell silent, Sam said, 'but there's something else very wrong, Will. Look at the notebook. Why did Crosley underline the dividend payment? Is the amount incorrect? And why did somebody attempt to kill him?'

Will shook his head. 'I don't know why he was killed, but I do know how we can check the payments. There will be a record of the accounts in the Annual Report of the infirmary which was published last month. There's always a copy of it available for public inspection within the ledger kept in the foyer near the porter's room. Wait a moment, I'll go and check it.' He leaped up and returned two minutes later. Instead of looking inside for the information, Will had brought the whole book for inspection. The 1835/6 Annual Report was gummed into the ledger and was the last entry to have been made. They found the accounts section at the beginning of the six-page report.

'Well, well, well,' Will said triumphantly. 'Somebody has been skimming off money. Look here.' He pointed to the relevant line on the income side of the balance sheet. 'Thirty pounds, but Crosley's notebook says that ninety-eight pounds were paid by the solicitors. Where did the rest go?'

Sam grew cautious. There might be more at stake here than they realized.

'We must tread carefully, Will,' he warned. 'Somebody was willing to kill to conceal this fraud. Until we know who's behind it, we'd be advised to keep this between the two of us.'

However, their discovery had angered Will. He was outraged that the infirmary's funds were being misappropriated, and it took several minutes of argument before he finally agreed to keep the matter private.

'Very well,' he eventually grumbled. 'But how then should we proceed?'

'Well, before he died, Crosley asked me to visit his wife. He asked me to tell her that he had tried. I have no idea what he meant by that, but Mrs Crosley might be able to shed some light on the matter. I propose to visit her on my half day off, tomorrow afternoon. Until then, promise me you won't tell anybody else.'

Will agreed, and after a further glass of sherry, they took to the parlour for supper where they ate with Elizabeth Strickland. The two men had been dreading the start of July because it meant that they had to listen to Matron's regular bible reading which took place in the parlour, after supper, on the first Monday of every month. The readings lasted for an hour, and both doctors usually struggled to remain awake, especially if they were worn out after a busy weekend on duty. It was a tiresome event, and both men would stare intently at the fire, willing it to die down sufficiently to allow them to make polite excuses and retire.

Chapter 3

The Widow

Sam planned to make two visits during his afternoon off; the first to see Mrs Crosley, and the second to see his father who lived only a further ten minutes beyond the widow. Sam left the infirmary using the rear exit and picked his way through William Little's market garden towards the rear gate leading to Walton Street. Just by the start of the path, he passed by Jack Rance who was known as the Donkey Boy. The young lad was aged about twelve and was employed to mind the infirmary's donkey. Twice a day, the animal was attached to a huge circular windlass that was used to pump water up from the well to two large cisterns housed in the roof of the main building. The unfortunate animal spent much of its life going round in an endless circle. Rance's job was to keep it working and to tend to the animal overnight when the infirmary relied on the water stored in the roof for its supplies.

As Sam passed by, he nodded at the boy who smiled back, flattered that he had been noticed by one of the infirmary's gentlemen.

Further on, the path entered the burial ground. The graveyard had been consecrated by the Bishop of Oxford in 1770 and was reserved for those who could not be buried in their own parish, either through lack of funds or because they had died whilst travelling through Oxford, but far from their homes. The Governors were proud that every patient was guaranteed a Christian burial, but they had been forced to issue strict rules after the burial ground had started to fill up at an unsustainable rate. Patients who had been admitted under sponsorship were expected to be buried in their own parish and at their own expense. To ensure this rule was not abused, the Governors insisted that subscribers lodge surety funds in case a patient passed away and had to be buried at the infirmary's expense. In practice, most of the interments in the burial ground were of paupers. The chaplain made the arrangements, purchased coffins and delivered a brief service. None of the graves were marked with a headstone which meant that they were dug rather haphazardly and sometimes on top of each other, close to the surface. On a hot day, there was occasionally an unpleasant smell in the graveyard, and Sam would have avoided it by choosing a longer route from the front of the infirmary. However, the weather had been unseasonably cool, and he left the grounds by the rear gate on Walton Street without having to hold his breath.

Twenty minutes later, Sam arrived at a modest townhouse situated on New Inn Hall Lane, near the prison. Sam knew the area quite well because he had grown up nearby. John Crosley's house was in an ordinary neighbourhood where the town houses which opened onto the street provided attractive homes for the respectable middle classes. However, life was very different behind these buildings. A network of dark passages led to backyards that were surrounded by overcrowded, ramshackle dwellings for the poor. The sanitation was dreadful, and the air was thick with the stench of blocked drainage and overflowing cesspits. There were other dangers too, and after dark, the filthy alleyways became home to footpads who lurked silently in the shadows waiting for the lost or the foolhardy. Even though it was daylight, Sam was extremely relieved to find that Crosley's front door opened from the main street rather than a back alley.

The Crosleys had no servants, and the woman who came to the door was dressed in a black dress suggesting recent loss. She looked to be of a similar age to the surgeon, and if Sam had somehow been able to wipe away the grief that was etched on her face, he would have revealed a most attractive woman.

'Mrs Crosley?' Sam enquired. 'My name is Samuel Ansell. I'm the House Surgeon at the Radcliffe Infirmary. I treated your husband after…well…after his accident.' The woman looked at him, and for a moment a shadow passed across her face. Sam was unable to tell whether it was fear or renewed sadness.

'I have spoken to you already,' she said quietly. 'I have nothing to add.'

'Spoken already? Why? Has someone else from the infirmary visited you?'

'Yes, that man, Mr Whiting. He came around very early yesterday morning to tell me that my husband had been involved in an accident. Then he returned in the afternoon and told me John had passed away. I really have nothing further to say,' she added, defensively.

Sam knew this was not a conversation that should be taking place on the doorstep, but after he suggested they continue talking inside, the woman became agitated and looked frightened. Sam wondered if Whiting had threatened her.

'I'm sorry, Mr Ansell, I can't say anymore. I just can't,' she cried, confirming his suspicion.

Sam decided that honesty was the best approach. 'Please Mrs Crosley, I genuinely want to help, and it was your husband who asked me to come and see you. I don't wish to shock you, but I believe that John might have been murdered and that somebody at the infirmary is involved, possibly Mr Whiting.'

Mrs Crosley searched his face for the truth. 'Did John really send you?' she asked.

Sam nodded. 'He did, and he asked me to tell you that he'd tried.'

A cloud passed over her face. 'No,' she said. 'What precisely did he say? His exact words.'

Sam realized that entry to her property might well depend on the correct answer to this strange request. He paused for a moment as his mind returned to the ward, and he ransacked his memory for Crosley's last words.

'Your husband was talking in incomplete sentences by that time. I think he said: "Tell her…I tried." No, wait that's not quite correct. No, it was, "tell her…I'm sorry…I tried."' Then realization dawned. Crosley had been trying to frame a single sentence and had shortened it as exhaustion overcame him. Sam looked at Mrs Crosley.

'That's it,' he told her. 'Your husband was trying to say, "tell her I'm sorry *that* I tried." He was wanting to apologize to you for trying to do something. Does that make sense?'

It did, because though a tear fell from Mrs Crosley's eye, she stood aside and let Sam enter the house. He followed her into a small sitting room that was slightly faded, but clean and comfortable. She looked at him as he sat on an armchair opposite her.

'Please call me, Mary. I need to be quick because I am expecting our family to visit at any moment.'

She took a deep breath. 'You see, it all started when John found some evidence that somebody was stealing funds from the infirmary. He told me that it was something to do with the dividends paid by the Oxford Canal Company amongst others, and he made a note of it in his company notebook. When he told me about the fraud, I warned him not to take it any further, and to my regret our final words were exchanged harshly in anger.' She paused, struggling to contain her grief.

Sam smiled to comfort her. 'I'm sure John would have understood. What did he do?'

'Well, I was concerned that John might lose his job if he interfered, but he told me the senior partner, Mr Richard Mayhew, was a man to be trusted, and John insisted on going to visit him at his country residence on Sunday rather than wait until after the weekend. He was always dedicated was my dear John. And a good husband too, which is why he kept his final words for me. Thank you for telling me them,' she added, as grief interrupted her account.

Sam wanted to reach out and take her hand, but he knew she would misunderstand his intentions, so there was a brief pause while she regained her composure. Sam eventually broke the silence.

'So, it was Whiting who told you about John's accident? What did he say?'

She dabbed her eyes with a handkerchief. 'Well, when John didn't come home on Sunday evening, I sat up all night hoping and praying for his safety. I suppose in my heart I knew that something bad had happened to him. Then Mr Whiting called. It was early on the following morning, and he told me that John had fallen off the coach. He was at pains to make sure that I knew it was an accident, and he asked me about the notebook.'

Sam's curiosity twitched. 'He knew about the notebook, even then?'

She nodded. 'I lied and said that I had no knowledge of the matter except that it was something being handled by the partners at John's firm. I told Mr Whiting that John had taken a book with him when he went to see Mr Mayhew, but beyond that I knew nothing.'

'And then he came back?'

'Yes. Later, in the afternoon, I was getting ready to visit John at the infirmary when Mr Whiting returned and told me that John had died. He also told me that they had failed to locate the notebook during a search of John's possessions. He said it was important because it contained sensitive information about a great many cases handled by the partners who wanted it back, and he again pressed me on its whereabouts. I repeated that I didn't know anything else about it, so he contented himself by warning me to keep quiet about the matter. He threatened me by saying that I could end up with a large hospital bill if I broke his confidence which was why I was unhelpful when you first called.'

Sam was shocked by her account. It appeared that Whiting was at the heart of some kind of scheme to defraud the infirmary, and that Crosley had been murdered after raising questions about it. Sam was fairly certain that Whiting was acting alongside others, but he had no idea whether the secretary was a general or a foot soldier. The notebook was clearly important, but Sam knew it had become a liability that could cost him his job if it was found in his possession. It was lying in his unlocked desk and needed to be hidden urgently before someone came looking for it. He considered Mary Crosley. Was she in danger? He thought it was unlikely, but he could not be certain.

'Look Mary, I think you'll be safe here. You did the correct thing by denying any knowledge of the notebook. I believe that Whiting will leave you alone now, and he's more likely to look for the notebook at the infirmary rather than bothering you here. If you're still worried, perhaps you have family that you could stay with for a few days?'

She nodded. 'Yes, my sister-in-law lives on the other side of Oxford. I think I'll stay there until John is buried and things have settled down.'

Sam smiled his approval and stood up to leave. Mary Crosley rose too.

'You've been so kind, Mr Ansell. And I'm very grateful to you for trying to save John's life, and for helping me, too.' Sam nodded and told her that she should send a message to him at the infirmary if she needed any further help or information. When Mary smiled, it was as though a curtain lifted and revealed a beautiful woman who was once thought to be missing but actually had been there all along. It was quite unsettling, and Sam felt a little bashful as he shook her hand and left the house.

***

Ordinarily, Sam would have returned to the infirmary, but as his father lived only ten minutes away - and it had been a few weeks since Sam had last seen him - he decided to pay him a quick visit. The house was on Titmouse Lane at the western end of the castle, and from the street, it looked conventionally middle class. However, it was slightly unusual because on one side of the building there was an archway over an access to the rear of the property where a large warehouse stood alongside a wharf on the Oxford Canal. As a cloth merchant, it was an ideal arrangement for his father. Goods were brought in on the canal, stored in the warehouse, and sent out to his father's customers who were mainly the city's tailors and proprietors of haberdashery shops. The proximity of the house meant that his father was always on hand to iron out problems although Sam's aunt complained that it encouraged her brother to work longer hours than he should.

When Sam arrived, he was met by the housekeeper, Mrs Seddon, who told him that his father was still at work in his office at the warehouse. Sam asked after his aunt and was saddened to learn that she was too poorly to see any visitors. He asked Mrs Seddon to pass on his best wishes and walked down the access road to spend an hour or so chatting with his father.

Mr Ansell was always pleased to see his son, and he was immensely proud that Sam had been awarded his fellowship of the Royal College of Surgeons. He was a thoughtful man who was careful never to give any indication that a bit of him wished that his son had followed in his footsteps. Over tea, they talked about some of Sam's recent cases with Sam being careful to respect his patients' confidentiality by leaving out any details that might identify them.

'There was a very nasty case the other night, father,' he said eventually. 'And it's a little bit concerning,' he added. His father looked at him over the top of some reading glasses.

'What is it, Samuel?' he asked, and then sat in silence as he listened to his son tell the tale of a male amputee and his notebook. As Sam gave his account, his father's expression darkened, and concern ploughed deep furrows across his brow. At the end he sighed.

'I think you should leave this well alone, Samuel. Stick to your medicine. You've spent years getting to where you are now, and you did it the hard way without a silver spoon in your mouth. We are all so proud of you. If you meddle in this, you risk losing it all. It's just not worth it. Is there nobody you can tell? What about the chairman, The Reverend Thomas?'

Sam observed his father's concern and immediately regretted telling him about the incident. As the man had grown older he had become more cautious and always looked for a way around an obstacle rather than confronting it. It had not always been that way, however. When Sam was a child, his father had shared the business with a partner who had embezzled company funds and brought the firm to its knees. Sam could still remember that it was a time of family austerity where the rooms were always cold and there was little food on the table. Fortunately, his father had detected the fraud before the company became bankrupt, and he had eventually confronted the man. Sam knew little about the fight that ensued, but he knew there had been violence and that his father had walked with a limp ever since.

Twenty years later, Sam thought about the bravery and determination his father had displayed as a younger man, and he wondered why he was now urging such caution. Perhaps it was just old age, he concluded. Sam's aunt had brought up her nephew with a deep sense of right and wrong. Now, as Sam reflected on his father's advice, it felt wrong to ignore the hospital fraud and absolutely correct to confront it. His determination was fuelled by his upbringing, but also by the knowledge that the diversion of infirmary funds was directly affecting patient care, and that felt outrageous and worthy of challenge.

Sam looked at his father and decided to ignore his advice. He tried to placate him by telling him that he would consider who to consult, and he promised not to do anything that would risk his job. He was pleased when the worry lines on his father's face melted away with Sam's reassurances, and he was glad that the visit was ending amicably. With the exception of this short exchange, it had been a pleasant hour, but it was time to leave, and Sam rose and shook his father's hand.

The shadows were lengthening as Sam set off back to the infirmary, so he decided to stick to the busy main roads. It was a longer route, but it felt like a safer one, and he needed to stretch his legs. He enjoyed the exercise, but Sam would have felt quite differently had he noticed the stocky man walking along the same route but 100 yards behind him. Twenty minutes later, he entered the infirmary using the front entrance and went up to his room to find Will pacing up and down the corridor.

Chapter 4

A Narrow Escape

'Well?' Will demanded after Sam had unlocked his door and they were sitting in the two armchairs. Sam liked his friend. Will was always considerate and loyal, but he was also impetuous and easily fired up. Crosley's death seemed to have stoked an inferno of outrage, and Sam was worried that his friend might act hastily and maybe even endanger the two doctors. Sam knew that his news was likely to make the man's anger even worse, but there was no holding back.

'It's certainly a conspiracy, Will, and I'm sure that Whiting is at the heart of it,' Sam said as he described his visit to see Mrs Crosley. When he had finished, Will was enraged.

'The rat!' he thundered. 'Picking on a grieving widow on the very day of her husband's death. Has that man got no morals?'

'I think not,' Sam replied, alarmed by his

friend's outburst. 'But there is a bigger question here, and that is: who else knows? When Whiting first went to see Mrs Crosley early on Monday morning, he already knew that her husband had been in possession of a notebook. How did he know that? He must have been sent an urgent message by Richard Mayhew and instructed to recover it from her. It was after Whiting returned from his first visit to see Mary Crosley that I caught him rifling through her husband's effects' box.'

Will frowned. 'If they accept that the book is not at Mrs Crosley's, and that it came to the infirmary with John Crosley and now it is missing, they will assume that someone here has taken it. And that means both of us will fall under suspicion because both of us treated Crosley before he died. I don't suppose they would suspect Nurse Wallace. Perhaps we should act first and raise the matter with someone on the Board of Governors?'

Sam thought for a moment. This was what his father wanted them to do. Will was correct: the two doctors would be the first line of any enquiry into the missing notebook, but who could they trust to pre-empt such an investigation?

'We don't know how far this extends, Will. It's possible that it's a straightforward fraud organized by Whiting purely for personal gain. That would be easy to deal with, but the involvement of the senior partner at a firm of solicitors makes me think that there might be something a bit more complex taking place. Who could we confide in? Even some of the governors might be involved. Either way, we do need to hide that book quickly because someone is going to come looking for it very soon.'

Will nodded. 'I agree. Look, I was once trying

to hang a picture in my room, and I discovered a loose wooden panel which is covering a small cavity in the wall. I could hide the book in there until we decide what to do. I'm certain nobody could find it unless they already knew about the cavity.' Sam signalled his approval, and it felt like a weight had been lifted from his shoulders as Will left the room to conceal the book.

Later, the two men ate dinner together, and in Matron's absence, they continued to discuss who they might approach on the Board that could be trusted. They were few in number, and by the time the two doctors retired, they were still undecided. However, as is often the way with such things, the matter was soon taken out of their hands.

***

The Board of Governors' quarterly meeting always started early. Even as Sam and Will were eating breakfast, a steady stream of carriages was already starting to arrive at the front of the building. Waiting to greet the visiting officials and dignitaries was The Reverend Vaughan Thomas, Chairman of the Board. Thomas was an irritating little man who interfered in everything. He was a stickler for the rules and had once discharged a patient for reading a novel on the ward. He had berated Matron for allowing such behaviour and insisted that bibles should be the only reading material provided to patients. He was also a bit of a sycophant who loved grandstanding with the senior members of the board. The quarterly meeting was ideal for this, and he always met each governor personally at the top of the steps, shook their hands warmly and directed them upstairs to the conference room. The board had a core membership which met weekly. However, each quarter and annually there would be a full board meeting where the senior patrons would also gather. It was ostentatious and designed to attract maximum publicity – not just for the infirmary – but also for those individuals who graced the charity with their great beneficence. The meeting would go on all morning with decisions presented to members by the secretary and then mostly rubber stamped. Matters were always completed before the governors adjourned for a first-class luncheon.

It was as this lunch was ending that Sam committed an act of selfless bravery. Will was still working, and after taking lunch alone in the doctor's parlour, Sam had gone for a short walk in the grounds at the front of the infirmary. A stream of carriages had started to gather to collect the visitors who were milling around on the steps and bidding their farewells to each other. Sam could see the Duke of Marlborough and Lord Kirtland shaking hands at the front of the steps. He recognized Lord Kirtland because he always brought along his daughter, Anne, who was a few years younger than Sam and beautiful in body, and especially so, in mind.

Anne was a most unusual young woman for her times as she was educated in matters that were usually the preserve of men. It had all started a few years earlier when Lord Kirtland had employed a tutor called Mr George Harmer to prepare his son, Thomas, for boarding school and university. By then, Lady Kirtland had instructed Anne's governess to give Anne an education befitting her station. This included reading and writing, but also ladylike activities such as needlework, music and drawing. For Anne, these were pleasurable enough hobbies, but they did not really tax her mind, so one day she crept into one of her older brother's classes to listen to his academic studies. She was captivated by what she heard and had sat quietly at the back absorbing everything. Harmer noticed the girl's interest and allowed her to stay. On the next occasion, Anne came equipped with writing materials and started to contribute; one lesson became two which soon became a routine. Thomas, in the meantime, was sworn to secrecy

Harmer noticed that Anne was an unusually talented mathematician who also showed a real interest in natural philosophy and engineering. After several months of clandestine lessons, he went to Lord Kirtland and nervously told him what had transpired. He explained that Anne was particularly gifted, and he asked if the lessons could continue on a more formal basis. Lord Kirtland was unusually forward-thinking and, in the face of angry opposition from his wife, he had decided that his daughter should be allowed to learn whatever she liked. He even managed a wry smile when he found Anne reading a copy of Mary Wollstonecraft's '*A Vindication of the Rights of Woman.*' Kirtland was certain that somewhere there would be a suitor who could hold his own against his emancipated daughter. In fact, he had smiled to himself, it might even be a rigorous test of a young man's suitability.

Anne's studies were important to her, but she always made time to accompany her father on his visits to the infirmary. Whilst he was engaged with board meetings, Anne Kirtland roamed the wards to visit patients, sometimes reading to them, and offering comfort to those who were suffering from their ailments. Sam and Anne often met and exchanged words on these occasions, and Sam went to great lengths to contrive even the briefest of encounters. Anne knew that Sam admired her, and her warm smile seemed to offer him encouragement and a hint of future promise. Sam was surprised that she was so knowledgeable and confident, but far from being intimidated, he found they had much in common. He enjoyed their discussions on science and natural philosophy which were animated and conducted without any hint of awkwardness. In fact, familiarity and friendship had gradually started to change into mutual attraction, and it hung over their discourse as a great unspoken truth. Whilst Sam enjoyed these encounters, he held some deep reservations about the future. She was the aristocratic daughter of a nobleman, and he was a mere house surgeon, the son of a cloth merchant. It didn't sound a very promising match. He had spoken with her father, Lord Kirtland, on a couple of occasions but had never met her mother. Sam really liked Anne, but he was doubtful that it could ever amount to more than friendship and secret admiration.

On this occasion, Sam had been unable to talk with Anne because he had been working through a long list in the operating room. As he watched her father chatting on the steps, Sam noticed that Anne was nearby sitting in a Barouche that was attached to two large horses who were fidgeting impatiently at the front of the queue of carriages waiting to depart. He walked towards her, determined to engineer a quick exchange of smiles, and noticed the driver stepping down to attend to a strap that had come loose at the rear of the carriage.

It was unfortunate that on the day of the

governors' meeting, the south wing of the infirmary was undergoing some repairs to the roof, and the workmen were in the process of building a tower of wooden scaffolding to reach the damaged area. As Sam made his way towards Anne's carriage, there was a shout followed by a tremendous crash as a piece of timber slipped from its cradle and fell to the ground. The loud noise caused the near-side horse to panic, and it reared up causing the carriage to lurch to one side. Sam could see the fear in Anne's face as she clung to the side of the seats to avoid being thrown out onto the hard ground, several feet below. The situation deteriorated, however, as the offside horse also started to panic, and together the two snorting animals set off at pace dragging the driverless carriage towards a ditch that was being dug alongside the drive. Sam acted instinctively. He knew that if a wheel entered the ditch at high speed, then the Barouche would tip over and Anne would be flung to the ground or even crushed. He had to prevent it, and so as the horses sped towards him, Sam stepped out into their path and grabbed the dangling reins. As the carriage careered to an abrupt halt, the near side horse reared up. It towered above Sam, and the Barouche lurched to one side precipitously. As the hooves fell, the last thing Sam remembered was Anne's face, wide-eyed in terror, as she fought to stay within the passenger compartment. Then an iron-clad hoof came down on his forehead and darkness fell.

It was late afternoon before Sam started to come around. At first, he heard distant voices. These seemed to get closer and eventually became attached to some blurred faces. Complete consciousness followed soon after, and it was heralded by the realization that he had a headache to match Mount Vesuvius. Sam groaned, and the face of Charles Wingfield hove into view.

'Ah Samuel, you have rejoined the living. Thank the Lord. You have suffered a nasty blow to the head. I have stitched it for you, but we must be vigilant in case there is an effusion of blood on the brain. As you know, it can develop even hours after a head injury. For the moment, you must stay in bed and try not to move about too much. I will send for some beef tea to keep up your strength. Tomorrow, I will look in on you first thing in the morning, but in the meantime, there are some visitors to see you.'

Wingfield left the room, and moments later there was a brief knock, and Lord Kirtland and Anne walked in. Sam struggled to sit up, but Lord Kirtland waved him back.

'Mr Ansell, please don't move on our account, we are deeply indebted to you. My daughter was determined that we shouldn't return home until we knew you were going to be alright.' Beside him, Anne's eyes filled with tears as she absorbed the vicious line of stitches on Sam's forehead and the dark bruises that were staring to develop on his face.

'Oh! Mr Ansell. I see you are grievously hurt and on my account, too. I'm so grateful to you, and I will pray for your recovery; I believe you may well have saved my life.' Sam tried to smile but succeeded only in providing her with a tortured grimace.

'I'm sure I will mend eventually, Miss Kirtland,' he managed. 'Mr Wingfield is an excellent surgeon, so I am in good hands.' Anne's father was seemingly oblivious to the depth of his daughter's concern.

'I must tell you, Mr Ansell. That was the

bravest thing I think I've ever witnessed. That carriage must weigh nigh on two tons. If you had gone under the wheels, you would not be here with us now. I am eternally grateful to you, Sir. When you are better, you must come to High Cross Manor and meet my wife, Lady Kirtland. We will never be able to repay you for your chivalry today.'

'Thank you, My Lord, that is very kind of you.' Sam was about to say more when the door opened, and Matron appeared with some beef tea.

'I'm very sorry, Lord Kirtland, but we must let Mr Ansell rest now, on Mr Wingfield's instructions.'

Lord Kirtland nodded. 'Yes, we will leave you to rest, Samuel, if you will permit me the use of your first name?'

Sam indicated his approval, and Lord Kirtland walked to the door. As he pulled it open, Anne stopped and glanced back to reward Sam with the very smile that he had been seeking to engineer outside the front of the infirmary. He smiled back causing her to blush as she turned to follow her father. Beside him, Matron had noticed the silent exchange.

'Now, Mr Ansell. Remember your place,' she said after the door had closed. Sam groaned inwardly. He had been caught flirting, and he knew he would face an extra-long reading on the perils of fornication at Matron's next bible evening. He turned to look at her and was astonished to see the barest of smiles on the woman's face and a slight twinkle in her eye. Contrary to hospital myth, it seemed that Matron had a heart after all.

***

Once he was alone, Sam grew restless and wondered when Will would appear. While he waited, he returned to the question of who they might approach on the Board of Governors to notify them of the fraud. He decided that if they spoke to anyone too senior, like the Duke of Marlborough, it was likely that the matter would be referred straight back to the secretary. The chairman was an obvious choice, but Sam thought The Reverend Thomas would fear the adverse publicity and would probably try to cover up the matter. He could think of several other governors who would try to distance themselves from a public scandal, leaving only a handful of members who might be willing to act decisively. As Sam started to run through a list of potential names, there was a knock at his door. The face of Nurse Wallace appeared around the door, and she held up a finger to her lips to silence him. She was taking a great risk by entering his room.

'Nurse Wallace…,' he began.

'No, Sir, please be quiet. I have been asked to deliver a note to you from Dr Perks. It's very secret.' She saw the wound on his forehead, and her face crumpled with concern. 'Oh, Mr Ansell. That looks very nasty. Are you alright, Sir?'

Sam nodded. 'Yes, it's not so bad. But listen, Catherine, if you are caught here alone with me you will lose your job, and I might lose mine too. We must be quick.' She advanced into the room and withdrew a small envelope from down the front of her dress. She laughed and blushed uncharacteristically.

'I had to keep it safe, and it seemed the best place for it,' she explained as she handed the letter over to Sam. The envelope was unmarked to spare the bearer the risk of discovery if it was intercepted before delivery. As Sam thanked her, she looked a little crestfallen as she realized that she was being invited to leave. Sam knew she wanted to stay with him, and he was tempted to accept her unspoken invitation. It could be lonely as a house doctor, confined to the infirmary without the opportunity to forge close relationships. He imagined it was similarly limiting for a hospital nurse, too. He also knew that Catherine Wallace had been widowed earlier than most of the other nurses, and he wondered if her flirtatiousness was a sign that she missed the physical intimacy of her marriage. On occasions, he had been enticed by her inviting smile and voluptuous figure, and he had been forced to suppress his own physical desires. He knew that he only needed to ask, and she would gladly share her experience in such matters, but he remained silent, and she smiled sadly as she recognized that the moment had passed them by once again. As the door closed behind her, Sam breathed out and forced himself to concentrate on Will's note. Once he started reading it, he forgot Nurse Wallace.

Dear Sam

I am sorry that I have not been to see you, but I have got myself into a difficult situation and I didn't want to get you involved too. You see, after we last spoke, and when I heard you had met with an accident, I decided to approach Sir George Roach, the Board Treasurer about the scandal that we have discovered. I told him that I was told of it by Crosley while I was treating him after his operation on Sunday Night. I did not mention the notebook which remains hidden. Roach told me he was certain it was a misunderstanding, and he warned me not to speak of it to anyone. He said that I should concentrate on my work and let him deal with the matter himself. It sounded like a threat, and I got the impression he might be involved in the plot so tread carefully. At least they think that I am the intruder which leaves you in the clear to get to the bottom of the matter. It's a matter of justice for our patients.

Best wishes, William.

Sam sighed. His friend was so impetuous. Will had promised that he would not act precipitously, and now he had alerted one of the governors. That said, his friend had drawn some of the attention away from Sam, and he could now investigate the fraud with less fear of interference so long as he was discreet and remained linked to Will only in a professional sense.

Chapter 5

First Warning

Sam's injuries required him to stay in bed for a further two days, and it was the weekend before Wingfield decided that the risk of cerebral bleeding had passed. Sam still had a headache, and there was an angry line of stitches on his forehead. However, he had become bored and was relieved when Wingfield asked him to carry out the surgical ward round on the Saturday morning.

Sam rose at the usual time and ate breakfast alone. The place seemed unusually quiet, and as Sam made his way down to start his rounds on the lower floor, there was no sign of Will or the Matron. When he reached the foyer, the reason became apparent. A large group of hospital staff had gathered near the foot of the stairs, and when Sam appeared they burst into loud applause. He was astonished; even his father was standing there clapping with the staff. Then he saw who was behind it when Charles Wingfield stepped forward to present Sam with an inscribed silver tray. It was a handsome gift.

'The Board of Governors has asked me to present this silver tray to you in recognition of your extreme bravery outside this building earlier in the week,' Wingfield began. 'By your actions, you undoubtedly prevented a serious and likely fatal accident without a thought for your own safety. You are a credit to your profession and to this great charitable institution.'

To renewed applause, Wingfield handed the tray to Sam and shook his hand before indicating that Sam should speak. Sam was unprepared, but once the clapping had died away, he managed to blurt out a few words of thanks and encouragement for the staff before the group dispersed and returned to their duties. Afterwards, his father came over and shook his hand.

'Well done, Sam. 'I'm very proud of you. I won't stay because I have work to do, and so do you. Come and see me soon and we'll have a nice bit of supper. Your aunt is a little better so she might join us.' He patted Sam on the back and started to leave. As Sam watched his father step outside the front door, he became aware that Absolom Whiting was watching from the back of the reception area. The Secretary sidled over and stuck out a bony hand which Sam took despite his dislike for the man.

'Well done, Mr Ansell. Praise indeed from the Board of Governors. But I must tell you that The Reverend Thomas wants to see you immediately. Please don't delay,' he added smugly. 'The Chairman indicated that it was rather a serious matter.'

Sam muttered his thanks and left his award

behind the porter's desk for safekeeping before climbing the steps. The Reverend Vaughan Thomas was waiting for him.

'Come in, Mr Ansell. I understand that you have received your award which was well deserved. However, I need to address you about a more serious matter.'

Sam was not invited to sit down so he remained standing, feigning calm. He then noticed that Sir George Roach, the infirmary's treasurer, was present and observing him from a small armchair in the corner. He was slightly overweight, with a red face, and he sat staring at Sam, brooding, with ill intent. In front of Sam, The Reverend Thomas continued.

'Sir George, here, has been made aware of certain allegations regarding the infirmary accounts. Do you know anything about this?'

'Indeed not, Sir,' Sam replied. 'What sort of allegations?'

'That need not concern you, but they seem to have originated from the patient you treated last weekend, John Crosley. Do you remember him?'

'I do. He was the victim of a coaching accident, and I had to amputate his leg. The operation was a success, but he had lost too much blood and passed away during the following day.'

'And did he tell you anything of note, Mr Ansell?'

'Well, I remember he was delirious and rambling a lot when he was first brought in. He seemed to think he had been pushed off the coach, but when I asked him about it on the following morning he told me that he knew nothing of it, so I put it down to the effects of the severe injury he had suffered.'

The chairman was looking increasingly pleased. 'And did he give you anything? A book or some such like?'

'No Sir, he was heavily sedated and incapable of handing anything over.'

'Thank you, Samuel,' the Reverend said indicting that the inquisition was over. 'One last thing though. You are friends with Dr Perks, the House Apothecary, I think?'

Sam thought carefully. He had no wish to abandon his friend, but Will had given him a little space to investigate this scandal, and he needed to play his role in that plan even if it meant that he was forced to distance himself from his friend.

'Well, I would say Perks is more like a colleague than a friend,' he said carefully. 'We eat dinner together sometimes and enjoy listening to Matron's bible readings each month, but that's about the extent of it, I would say.'

The bible readings were a triumph. At their mention, the chairman glowed with pleasure. 'Bible readings,' he said, 'I had no idea. That is excellent, Mr Ansell. Highly commendable.' Then his face darkened. 'I'm sorry to tell you, however, that Dr Perks has acted inadvisably. You see, the cleaner found some laudanum in his room which is strictly against the infirmary rules. I have had to remind him of his responsibilities by docking his pay and suspending him for ten days. I am not accusing you of complicity, but you should treat his punishment as a reminder of the need to comply with the regulations, and to raise any matters of concern with the Board through Mr Whiting. Such breeches of discipline are damaging to the reputation of the infirmary, and in future they will be dealt with by dismissal.'

Under normal circumstances, Sam would have protested his friend's innocence, but he needed to appear distant, and so he merely nodded his understanding and moved towards the door. He had almost made it when Roach spoke in his thick Irish accent.

'One moment, Mr Ansell, did you attend the house of John Crosley and speak with his widow?'

Sam was wary. Someone must have followed him into Oxford. 'I did visit, yes. Crosley spoke to me very briefly when I attended the ward on the Monday morning. He asked me to summon a chaplain to attend to him, and he asked me to tell his wife that he loved her. Given the speed of his demise, I thought that a visit to the man's widow was a Christian thing to do, especially as I had operated on her husband. I undertook the visit in my own time. We discussed how Crosley had fallen from a coach, and I explained why I chose an amputation as the necessary treatment. She seemed satisfied with what I had to say, and she was grateful that the infirmary had treated her husband without any sponsorship. Why do you ask, Sir? Has she made a complaint?'

Roach shook his head. 'No, we just want to understand the facts, Mr Ansell. You may go about your business, thank you.'

Sam left the office and breathed a sigh of relief. Both men had seemed satisfied with his responses, and he hoped that he was no longer under suspicion. That was not the case for Will, however. Sam did not believe for one moment that his friend had been abusing hospital treatments. No, this was a contrived offence, not serious enough to merit dismissal, but sufficiently damaging to call into question Will's professional standards and reputation. It was also a wider threat to others, like Sam, who might feel inclined to question the Board's absolute authority.

Later that evening, after the oil lights had been dimmed, there was a very quiet knock, and Sam opened it to find Will. After they had exchanged their news, Will looked pleased with himself.

'Well, it looks like I have successfully drawn attention away from you, Sam.'

'Yes, but at what cost? Your professional reputation, Will…'

The apothecary smiled. 'These things never last for long. I'm certain it will all be forgotten soon enough, and we cannot turn back the clock. At least they didn't dismiss me. But in any case, how do we proceed?'

'Well, I think you should keep a low profile,' Sam replied. 'They will be watching. Remember, they knew I had visited Mrs Crosley, so I suggest that we do nothing for a few days and let the matter settle.'

Will nodded. 'Yes, I am suspended for ten days, and I think I'll spend it with my family in Banbury. I can't wait around here. Not with Whiting smiling away with such smug satisfaction.'

Sam laughed and wished his friend well; the two men shook hands and Will left the room to start an enforced holiday.

Chapter 6

Hat and Tails

One evening, during the week following Will's suspension, it became apparent that the apothecary's intervention had rattled some cages. Sam had eaten dinner alone and was reading Jackson's Oxford Journal when he noticed a letter to the editor from Absalom Whiting. The Journal frequently published articles about the infirmary, and these were followed closely by the readership. The board meetings were always reported, and the paper included weekly and annual statistics on the number of admissions, discharges and accidents. On this occasion, the Secretary had written to inform the public that a mistake had been made in the annual accounts in respect of a dividend paid by the Oxford Canal Company. He wanted to reassure readers that the error was purely clerical, and that the Radcliffe Infirmary had suffered no loss because of it.

Sam smiled to himself. The two doctors had

scored a minor victory. The fraudsters were covering their tracks, but at least the money was being returned for its original charitable purpose. When Sam was next in the entrance hall, he checked the ledger containing the annual reports and noticed that Whiting had pasted in a handwritten erratum explaining the error. It was clear that the conspirators were leaving nothing to chance.

Sam was pleased that the money seemed to have been returned, but he was reluctant to let the matter lie. How long would it be before the fraud was repeated? he asked himself. He was especially angry at the treatment of Will who worked so hard on behalf of the infirmary and its patients. Neither doctor was particularly well paid, and Will's orchestrated punishment indicated that there were some within the management who took their loyal service for granted. Sam felt undervalued and resentful, and that fuelled his determination to expose those responsible. However, Sam recognized his situation was still a little precarious, and that it would be wise to allow suspicions to subside before taking further action. So, while he waited for Will to return, Sam tried to keep a low profile by immersing himself in his work. There was plenty to occupy him, and despite the daily spectacle of human suffering, some of it was quite distressing.

***

Most doctors try to keep emotionally detached from their patients, but it is not always possible, and later that week Sam dealt with an unpleasant case that would live with him for the rest of his life. He was just finishing his morning rounds, when a nurse ran up to him in the corridor. Tears were falling down her cheeks.

'Mister Ansell, Sir, please come quickly, there's an awful case come in. It's a little girl. She's burned terribly.' Sam followed her to the ward and saw why the nurse was crying. It was a pitiful sight.

Harriet Mills was sitting on a bed holding her arms up in the air so that they would be clear of her sides. The five-year-old was burned badly over most of her body, and she whimpered each time someone tried to touch her or cut away her scorched clothes.

'How did this happen?' Sam asked although he was quite sure he knew the answer.

'Her mother brought her here. It happened at home,' the Nurse replied. 'She's waiting in the reception area,' she added.

It was a common cause of child mortality. Younger children were frequently dressed in long flowing gowns made of cotton. As they played and dashed around the house, there was a constant risk that they would get too close to an open hearth, usually in the kitchen, and set fire to themselves. The cloth was highly inflammable, and though it only burnt for a minute or two, it left some children with pitiful injuries that were often fatal.

With Will absent, Sam was left to deal with the case although he could see there was little that could be done to save the girl.

'Please would you ask the assistant apothecary to attend. And ask him to bring laudanum,' he instructed one of the nurses. 'And while we wait, let's try to cut away the rest of her clothes.'

Five minutes later, the charred clothing was removed, and the assistant apothecary had arrived. He looked at Sam, and they exchanged a silent understanding that the girl was clearly going to die. However, it would have been wrong to have done nothing at all, and they decided they would at least try to dress Harriet's burns, if only for the sake of the girl's mother. They gave her a dose of laudanum and eventually managed to apply the dressings, but it was a ghastly job. The dressings were made from used bed linen donated by the public which was cleaned and cut into strips in the infirmary laundry. They tried to be as gently as possible, but the child cried out each time they lifted or touched a limb to apply a bandage.

Not long after they had finished, Harriet Miles went quiet, and Sam knew they were near the end. He nodded as the apothecary raised an enquiring eyebrow and then dosed the girl with another large dose of laudanum. It would remove the pain, but the side-effects would also suppress the girl's breathing. The two doctors knew the girl was dying from her terrible burns, but they both felt it was better that she passed away peacefully, even if the pain relief shortened her life by an hour or two.

Sam turned to the nurse. 'Please fetch Mrs Mills. Be quick, now.' The nurse nodded, and a few moments later a tearful woman came into the ward and sat on the bed. She looked at Sam who felt wretched as he crushed any final vestiges of hope.

'I'm sorry, Mrs Mills,' he said gently, 'but there is nothing more to be done. You should say your goodbyes now. Would you like the chaplain to attend?' She nodded as the tears fell, and the nurse scurried off to find Savage. A few minutes later, the short life of Harriet Mills came to an end as she passed away peacefully, leaving those around her feeling helpless and more than a little inadequate.

***

It was rare that Sam felt personally affected by a patient, but the Mills case had been a harrowing experience that had left him feeling a bit low. His mood wasn't helped by a pounding headache which had plagued him intermittently since his head injury. After leaving the ward, Sam decided that a five-minute walk and some fresh air might help to lift his spirits. However, as he was leaving the building, he was spotted by the porter, James Moss, who rushed after him, waving a letter.

'Looks important, Sir,' he remarked, looking at the envelope which was embossed with a coat of arms. Sam inspected it but was unable to recognize the writing. Moss was hovering at his side and seemed surprised that a mere house doctor should receive such well-marked mail. Sam knew that the porter was loitering in the hope that he might get a glimpse inside the envelope or an explanation that could be shared with the other infirmary staff when he gossiped about it later. Sam ignored the man's inquisitiveness, but thanked him, and carried on walking while he opened the envelope. Inside, he found a short note from Lord Kirtland inviting him to attend the family's annual ball on the following Saturday. Sam saw that he was also invited to stay overnight as a house guest which he knew was quite an honour. His mood lifted. He was a little overawed at the prospect of mingling with Lord Kirtland's guests who would probably include most of Oxfordshire's dignitaries. However, he was greatly excited by the idea of meeting and maybe even dancing with Anne Kirtland.

Before replying to the invitation, Sam went to see The Reverend Thomas and sought permission to take leave for the two days that he would be absent from his duties. The chairman smiled and seemed pleased that members of the infirmary staff were mixing in such high circles, though Sam also detected a hint of slight envy as the man gave his approval.

Sam faced one problem, however, and that was what should he wear? He was unused to attending formal functions in such lofty circles, and he certainly didn't own anything suitable for a ball. However, his chosen profession had bestowed on him one particular advantage: he knew a great many people who would willingly help him. A few months earlier, Sam had successfully removed a bladder stone from the wife of a well-known Oxford tailor, called Alfred Taylor, who was known colloquially by his customers as 'Taylor the Tailor.' Alfred was an eccentric individual, prone to uttering long sentences that were unfailingly positive. Though Alfred had spoken a great many words in his life, Sam doubted that any of them had ever been cynical or downbeat. Alfred was invariably cheerful and optimistic, even when faced with the most distressing of situations. After Sam had treated Mrs Taylor, Alfred had been effusive in his gratitude and had even tried to pay the surgeon for his services. Sam had declined a five-pound note that was waved in his face, but Alfred had made Sam promise to visit his shop if he ever needed something special to wear. Sam knew there would never be a better moment to call in the man's promise and to seek his expertise.

Sam had the following afternoon off, although he had promised to work in the evenings during Will's absence. The premises of Taylor the Tailor were only a ten-minute walk from the infirmary. As he opened the door to the shop a bell rang, and he was immediately recognized.

'Mr Ansell! Upon my word, Sir! What a pleasure! What an extremely pleasant pleasure!' Alfred had not changed one bit. However, the excited man had noticed the vicious cut on Sam's forehead and Alfred's enthusiasm became fired by his over-active imagination. 'Good Lord, Mr Ansell, what has befallen you? Footpads? Highwaymen? There is a mighty story to be heard, I'll be bound! You must tell us about it. Yes, you must! But first we'll send for tea. Martha, Martha!' he shouted. 'Bring tea, my dear, Mr Ansell is upon us!' Mrs Martha Taylor appeared from the apartment beyond the counter and smiled at Sam.

'It's a pleasure to see you again, Mr Ansell, Sir,' she beamed. 'You have fixed me exceedingly well, and I am completely cured.' She studied Sam's face and frowned when she saw the stitches in his forehead. 'But I don't think you are here to discuss work matters, and you look like you need some tea, so I shall bring it.'

Sam thanked her. It was a pleasure to hear from a previous patient, especially when his work had improved an individual's life. Beside him, Alfred Taylor was bobbing up and down with excitement, and as they sat drinking tea, Sam explained in plain terms what had occurred the previous week at the front of the infirmary. He did not exaggerate, but then there was no need because Alfred added all the necessary colour to Sam's account as he went along. When the surgeon had finished, Alfred was quite beside himself.

'Well, Sir! Such bravery! And did you get the girl? There's always a girl!'

Martha intervened from the counter. 'Alfred! Really! Where are your manners, you great pumpkin?'

Sam almost laughed aloud at her term of endearment. A great well-meaning pumpkin! That was Mr Taylor for certain.

'That's alright, Mrs Taylor. There was a girl in the carriage, and her father is Lord Kirtland. I have been invited as a house guest to their annual ball which is why I have come to see you. I don't know what to wear, and I need to hire something suitable for the occasion.'

Beside him, Alfred was almost in a swoon. 'Ah,' he said. 'Ah!' Then he closed his eyes and was transported to the ball. 'Ah yes. Yes, yes, yes, indeed!' He opened his eyes, looked at Sam and winked. ''Mr Ansell, you shall go to the ball. Indeed, you will, Sir. And we are going to need something special. Very special indeed. Not too fancy, not too plain but something to catch a canary. Yes…a canary, Mr Ansell. A canary to be caught.'

Sam was becoming a little alarmed, and he hoped that Alfred's choice of clothes would be less overstated than his metaphors. 'We mustn't overdo it, Mr Taylor,' he remarked carefully.

'Overdo, Mr Ansell? No, Sir. No indeed. Not overdo. And not underdo, either. Just plain old do. Let's begin.' He clapped his hands. 'Joseph!' he shouted. 'Bring me the white silk dress shirt Number Four. Let's see…' Alfred studied Sam's neck. He had no need for a tape measure. '…That's a size fifteen and a half neck,' he called. Moments later, a young boy scurried out with a beautifully wrapped dress shirt for Sam to try on.

What followed was quite remarkable. Whilst

working, Alfred was a changed man. Gone was the effusive, ponderous pumpkin. Instead, he was transformed into an artistic master of his trade who was in command of every stitch of the clothes that he chose for Sam. The metaphors were temporarily banished, and he dressed his customer with barely a comment except for the instructions he shouted to his young apprentice. Thirty minutes later, the master of his trade stood back and studied Sam.

'There's always a girl, Mr Ansell, and if you can't steal her heart wearing this then I truly am a pumpkin. Have a look.' He gestured towards the mirror.

Sam looked at his reflection and nodded his approval. The tailor had fitted him out perfectly to match his tall, dark features and slim physique. He was dressed in a white silk shirt with ruffles and a matching white neck cloth. His knee length drop-front breeches were made of a mid-blue linen with silver buckles, and his stockings were also of white silk and led to some flat shoes made of black patent leather. Over this, Mr Taylor had selected a bright canary yellow waistcoat, and finally a dark blue double-breasted tailcoat. It was a transformation marred only by the angry line of stitches on Sam's forehead, and even those might be regarded as a badge of honour rather than an uncouth blemish. Overall, Sam was delighted with the outcome, and he knew he would fit in very nicely at the ball.

'To catch a canary, we need a canary,' Alfred murmured at Sam's side. 'This is my best waistcoat, Mr Ansell, 'It is made of an extremely rare Chinese silk which I obtained from your father, and I must say it suits you very well indeed.'

Mrs Taylor had arrived behind the counter and

agreed with her husband. 'Oh, Mr Ansell. You do look handsome. That will do very nicely, I'm sure.'

Alfred looked satisfied, but he had some finishing touches. He clapped his hands again. 'Joseph! The accessories, please! Size seven and a half hat.' The lad appeared moments later and offered Sam a top hat, ebony cane and white leather gloves for dancing.

Sam was very pleased, but suddenly he thought of the cost. 'Er, Mr Taylor,' he began, but Alfred had read his mind and interrupted him.

'Naturally, there will be no charge for any of this, Mr Ansell.' He declared briskly. 'I will have everything boxed up and delivered to the infirmary for you. It should arrive on Thursday, and you can return the items to us after the ball.'

Sam was about to object, but Alfred grew uncharacteristically serious. 'Please, Mr Ansell,' he said softly. 'Let us thank you in our own way. This is the least that we can do.'

It was a kind gesture, and Sam knew that to insist would be impolite, so he chose not to pursue the matter. Instead, he dressed in his own clothes, thanked them both for their kindness, and left the shop after promising to report back on the outcome of his romantic endeavours.

Chapter 7

The Ball

Alfred Taylor was as good as his word, and on the Thursday of the following week, Sam received a message that there had been a delivery for him. The porter was wide-eyed as he told Sam that everything was stacked up outside his door, and when Sam saw the large consignment of goods, he understood the reason for the man's astonishment. There were boxes of fine tailoring and expensive accessories, and they implied a luxury that was far beyond the means of a house surgeon.

As Sam checked the clothes to make sure everything had arrived, he wished his friend was there. The place seemed a little empty without Will's humour and his healthy disregard for authority. He once again ate alone and retired early after asking the porter to book him a carriage to take him to High Cross Manor on Saturday.

Eventually, it was time to leave. Sam decided that it would be impolite to arrive in his evening clothes, and so he carried his precious eveningwear in a large leather bag which his father had given to him when he had left home to work at the infirmary. Sam used his Sunday best for travelling but singled out the cane and hat. As he walked past the porter's desk, he felt like quite the gentlemen. It lifted his mood, and he made a theatrical swagger and twirled his cane at two giggling nurses as he made his way to the waiting carriage.

The Kirtland's country house was more than an hour away from Oxford by carriage. It was an elegant Tudor manor set at the end of a long tree-lined drive. The road took visitors past a man-made lake set in beautiful estate parkland that was grazed by a herd of red deer. There was no need to ring the bell because as soon as Sam started to climb the steps, the large oak door opened, and a servant wearing white gloves looked out at the visitor and quickly appraised the gash on Sam's forehead.

'Mr Ansell?' he asked. Sam nodded. 'Welcome to High Cross Manor, Sir. Please come in, your bags will be brought up.' The man gestured for Sam to enter and stood to one side to allow him to pass.

Inside, the house was as grand as Sam had imagined. The door opened into an impressive entrance hall lined with oak panels and gilt framed family portraits. An impressive staircase lay to his front with a gallery on the first landing that allowed the curious to observe the hallway below. To his right, there was a spacious dining room with a large table covered in starched linen. The staff were starting to put out the food, and Sam could see that the guests would be well fed that evening. To his left was a sitting room ready for those with tired feet and the need for quiet conversation and a brandy. Beyond the stairs, two double doors had been opened to reveal a sizeable hall beyond. Sam could see a small orchestra was already setting up their instruments. It was an impressive ballroom, and Sam suddenly felt a little out of place and apprehensive.

The footman appeared at his side. 'Please follow me, Sir,' he said impassively and led Sam up the stairs. The manor was built on four levels with the family's bedrooms on the first floor, guests on the second, and servants at the top. Sam's room was at the end of the corridor on the second floor.

'Here we are, Sir,' the footman gestured. 'Your bags will be brought up directly. The Ball starts at seven o'clock, and there will be a receiving line as you enter the ballroom.' The man looked along the corridor a little furtively and reached into his pocket to withdraw an envelope bearing Sam's name.

'I was asked to give you this, Sir. In secret,' he added disapprovingly. Sam took the envelope and joined whatever household conspiracy was at hand by slipping it into his coat rather than opening it in front of the servant. The footman was clearly uncomfortable with his role in the unspoken plot, and Sam thought it best to spare him any further embarrassment. The awkward situation was rescued by the arrival of Sam's bag, carried by a youth who was panting from the weight of Sam's finery. He started to unpack the contents, but Sam told him it was unnecessary. The two servants looked surprised but left Sam alone to complete the task himself.

As soon as their footsteps faded along the corridor, San removed the letter. There was a faint smell of perfume about it which was familiar, and even before he had opened the envelope, he knew it must be from Anne. No wonder the footman had been uncomfortable. It was most irregular for a single woman to send unsolicited mail to an unmarried man. Especially as she was the daughter of a nobleman. Sam was excited by her boldness and walked to the window to read her words.

My Dear Mr Ansell

I do hope you won't find this note to be in any way improper, but I hold unconventional views on such matters and feel quite capable of looking after my own reputation without being bound by today's social norms. I did so want to tell you how glad I am that you have accepted my father's invitation to stay as a houseguest, and how much I am looking forward to having at least two dances with you this evening. Perhaps we might even dance a Waltz if you are familiar with it? At the ball, we will find it difficult to converse in a way that is unconstrained by the presence of my chaperone for the evening. I should also warn you that my mother is somewhat set against your presence which she seems to regard as some kind of threat to her daughter's honour. I tell you this because she may have rather a sharp tongue when you are introduced, and I wanted to tell you that from my perspective, you are most welcome in this household.

Yours affectionately

Miss Anne Kirtland.

Sam let the hand holding the letter fall to his

side. He had been taught the Waltz by his aunt who had learned it whilst visiting her cousin in Austria. Sam knew that the dance had once received a scandalous reception in England owing to the closeness of the dancing partners and because it involved only two people. His aunt had told him that those who had opposed the dance had once used it as a way of expressing anti-German sentiments and a safe way to criticize the old king, George III. Sam knew that even twenty years later, there were still some parents who forbade their daughters to dance the Walz and enjoy such intimacy with young men. For Sam, however, that was precisely the objective, and he was flattered that Anne had reserved it for him. He tried not to think of what Anne's mother might make of it and busied himself with his preparations.

***

Sam was on time, but the evening got off to a slightly difficult start at the receiving line. 'Your card, Sir?' The footman held out a silver tray.

Sam shook his head and lied. 'Er, I seem to have mislaid them, I'm afraid.' The footman raised a disbelieving eyebrow, but after Sam had whispered his details, the man announced him anyway.

'Mr Samuel J Ansell Esquire,' he bellowed. Ahead of Sam, guests were queuing to complete the formalities of the Kirtlands' receiving line. Towards the end, Sam could see Lord Kirtland standing next to a slim, middle-aged woman with a pointed face and a sharp jaw that Sam imagined could convey effortless displeasure when it was felt necessary. When the footman called out Sam's name, Lady Kirtland glanced at him, and Sam got a foretaste of the contempt that was waiting for him at the end of the receiving line. The queue moved slowly along, and he exchanged pleasantries with various aunts, uncles and cousins, but with mounting dread. As he got closer, he saw Anne arrive from within the room and take up a place between her mother and father. Finally, he arrived at Lady Kirtland. Anne saw him coming and managed to give him a reassuring smile without her mother noticing. Sam was about to introduce himself when Anne intervened and did it for him.

'Mother, this is Mr Samuel Ansell, the House Surgeon at the Radcliffe Infirmary. He's the brave gentleman who saved me from serious hurt last week. As you can see, he suffered a nasty injury on my account.' It was a splendid effort to take the wind from her mother's sails, but Lady Kirtland's jaw was set forward, nonetheless.

Sam bowed. 'Good evening, Lady Kirtland, and you too, Miss Kirtland. I would like to thank you for your kind invitation to the Ball, and for honouring me as a house guest.' Anne curtseyed, but Lady Kirtland looked Sam straight in the eye.

'Well, your invitation was from my husband, Mr Ansell,' she said to remove any doubt that it had anything to do with her. 'He has an eclectic mix of acquaintances which I sometimes find a little, shall we say, unusual. Now then,' she added, pretending to search her memory. 'Do tell me, where is your family seat? I have been told, but it seems to have slipped my mind.'

Sam knew it was pointless to try and hide his lack of breeding, and in any case, he doubted there was anything he could do or say that would garner Lady

Kirtland's approval.

'My father is a cloth merchant. He sources fine material and threads from all over the world. His premises are by the canal, and my family home is nearby in central Oxford.'

Lady Kirtland nodded and wrinkled her nose as though Sam had brought the smell of the waterway with him. It took a skilful practitioner to humiliate someone whilst maintaining a veneer of good manners, and Lady Kirtland was a master of the art.

She looked past Sam and dismissed him with a vague and disinterested 'Oh! How very interesting. Well, Mr Ansell we must keep the line moving along. I shall watch out for you later,' she added meaningfully to make sure he understood that there would be no opportunity to steal the family's precious jewels: either alive or inanimate.

At her side, Anne was flush with anger at Sam's treatment, but as Lady Kirtland flashed a brilliant smile at a high court judge waiting behind Sam, Anne took advantage of her mother's momentary distraction.

'I'm sorry about that. You look like a pirate with your wounded head and your splendid clothes,' she giggled quietly. 'Did you get my note?'

Sam nodded and smiled; he was pleased that Anne approved of his clothes, but he did not dare to speak in case he was overheard. Beside him, Lady Kirtland was already winding up her conversation with the judge, and Anne had just enough time for some final whispered instructions.

'Come and find me for the second dance after the interval. My brother will be with me, but he knows what to do.'

Sam was conscious that Lady Kirtland was

glaring at him for holding up the line, so he bowed awkwardly to Anne and moved along to meet her father. Lord Kirtland shook his hand, welcomed him warmly, and told him they would speak later.

'I like that waistcoat, Samuel,' he added as Sam moved off. 'You must tell me the name of your tailor.'

The evening seemed to pass slowly as Sam counted down the dances until his moment with Anne. The food was excellent, and he made pleasant conversation with Oxfordshire's finest to pass the time. His stitched forehead marked him out for popular attention, and he was surprised that so many of the other guests had already heard of the incident outside the infirmary and wanted to ask him about it.

Eventually, the orchestra stopped playing, signalling the onset of an intermission. Sam was being careful to drink only modestly, and he was about to find a small glass of port when he saw Lord Kirtland talking to four men at the side of the ballroom. Sam was surprised to see that Sir George Roach was part of the group, and that the Duke of Marlborough was standing next to him. Lord Kirtland caught Sam's eye and waved him over.

'Gentlemen, can I introduce this young man, Mr Samuel Ansell who is the House Surgeon at the Radcliffe Infirmary. I owe him a great deal as he undoubtedly saved my daughter's life last week by acting with great bravery and without regard for his own safety when our carriage ran away. You can see he bears the marks of his gallantry.'

The Duke of Marlborough had witnessed the accident from the steps of the infirmary and agreed.

'Yes, Mr Ansell, that was a brave thing that you did. I swear I thought you would be dragged under the wheels. I'd be honoured if you'd take my hand, Sir.'

Sam blushed and bowed to the Duke who shook his hand warmly and then gestured to the other three men.

'This is Lord George Kenyon, Baron of Gredington, and this is Lord Charles Vane, the Marquess of Londonderry. I think you will know Sir George Roach from the infirmary.'

Sam bowed. 'I'm honoured to meet you, gentlemen. Sir George,' he added, nodding at the Treasurer who was staring at him thoughtfully.

Lord Vane studied him intently. Sam noticed he had several fingers missing on his left hand, and he seemed to move with an instinctive precision that hinted at military service. His eyes seemed to bore into Sam's soul, and it felt like he was searching for something profoundly personal.

'Yes, Mr Ansell, we were just discussing politics and investments. Do you own any shares in the Oxford Canal Company?'

Sam was immediately cautious. Out of the corner of his eye he thought he saw a movement. He could not be certain, but he thought Sir George might have shaken his head at the peer as though warning him not to pursue the matter.

'I do not, Sir, but I believe that there was once a scandal after the shares suffered badly following an announcement of a competing venture. But that must be thirty years ago, and I have no knowledge of how the Company has fared since.'

Lord Vane nodded, 'There was indeed a problem, and it was a long time ago. Some of us think that the shares are still a good investment. If you are looking for a reliable income, they certainly pay an excellent dividend.'

Beside Vane, Lord Kenyon had been silent. He was much shorter than his noble colleague and had a thin face and narrow eyes that seemed to speak of a devious streak. Sam could easily imagine the man to be at the centre of any parliamentary intrigue, and his intuition was soon proved to be correct when Kenyon decided it was time to move the conversation on to politics.

'Well, Mr Ansell, if not finance, how about politics? Do you have any views on Ireland and the Catholics?'

Sam thought politics was even worse territory for a discussion, especially at a ball. He could see the orchestra starting to return to their seats at the other end of the ballroom. The Waltz would follow soon.

'I apologize if I seem ignorant, Lord Kenyon, but Irish politics is not something that I am familiar with. For the past four years, I have dedicated my time to my professional studies, and even though I have earned my fellowship at the Royal College, I still enjoy conducting my own scientific research. I'm afraid that politics has passed me by, though I'm aware that there is a heated debate over Ireland at parliament.'

Lord Kenyon looked disappointed but nodded his understanding. However, standing next to Kenyon, the Duke of Marlborough was studying Sam intently as though gauging Sam's opinion. For a moment, Sam thought he might interject, but the Duke held back and looked away when Sam met his eyes. Sam sensed that there were some deeply held convictions within the group, and he was relieved that he had managed to avoid stating his own views in case he offended anyone.

At Sam's side, Lord Kirtland had also recognized that the conversation needed moving on to something more mundane. He pointed at Sam's chest.

'I say, Mr Ansell, that waistcoat of yours really is splendid. Where did you get it?' Sam told them and, after a brief talk on the merits of Chinese silk, he informed the group that he was booked for a dance and asked them to excuse him. He was relieved to leave the discussion, but it had raised several questions in his mind, and he was particularly troubled by the presence of Sir George Roach and the Duke of Marlborough together at a discussion about Oxford Canal Company shares.

The question of who was involved was becoming important but frustratingly elusive. However, it would have to wait, he decided, because Sam could see Anne Kirtland standing next to her brother on the other side of the dance floor. She looked across the room at him and smiled as he approached.

Anne's brother, Thomas, was about the same age as Sam and was clearly very close to his sister. Anne introduced them to each other, and Thomas shook his hand.

'Good evening, Mr Ansell. I understand that you are the House Surgeon at the Radcliffe Infirmary?'

'Yes, I was appointed earlier this year. And you, Sir?' Sam enquired.

'Please call me Thomas. I work in London for the Duchess of Kent. I'm one of the senior aides in her household. But I'm forgetting my manners, Mr Ansell. I must thank you for acting so bravely to save my sister. Also, Anne tells me that our mother was a little rude to you earlier, and I'd like to apologize for that. She gets very protective of Anne who, in any case, is more than capable of looking after herself.' He looked over at the orchestra. 'I think your dance is about to start so I shall busy myself.'

Sam bowed and thanked him before offering a gloved hand to Anne as the music began. The next four minutes really were perfect, as Sam held Anne close and whirled her around the dance floor. They must have made an attractive couple as those standing around the edge stopped talking and stood silently to watch the well-dressed gentleman and his attractive partner as they progressed around the room. Unfortunately, one of those spectators was Lady Kirtland who scowled her disapproval when Sam briefly met her eyes. However, Sam barely noticed. All he could sense was Anne's warm proximity and her perfume.

'You dance well, Samuel,' she told him, using his first name for the first time. 'When the music stops make for those doors at the end of the ballroom. They lead out onto the veranda, and I need some air.' There was enough time to complete one more circuit before the music ended and Sam was forced reluctantly to release his partner.

'This way,' she said and led him through the crowd surrounding the dance floor. To one side, Sam saw Thomas Kirtland, and for a moment Sam was worried that Anne's chaperone might reclaim his ward. However, Thomas just winked at him slyly and continued his conversation. It was an extraordinary conspiracy cooked up by brother and sister.

'Through here,' she whispered and took his hand to lead him through a gap in the heavy curtains towards a dimly-lit veranda beyond. Outside, the air was still, and it smelled of the sweet hay that had just been cut in the neighbouring fields. Anne gestured to a seat in the shadows, and they sat together shoulders almost touching and heads leaning in.

'Anne,' Sam whispered urgently. 'What if someone comes and finds us alone together?' He was acutely aware of her closeness. More so even than during their recent dance.

'I don't care,' she replied firmly. 'My honour is mine to preserve and mine alone. I hold quite modern views on such matters which I hope you will approve of one day,' she added, raising a shared future with Sam as a possibility. Sam was impressed by her independence, but he was concerned by his status as a house guest and wanted to avoid any suggestion that he was abusing his position. Anne saw his concern and, as Sam would come to recognize as being Anne's way, she addressed him directly.

'Please listen, my dear Sam. I hope you don't think it too forward of me to tell you how much I enjoy our talks at the infirmary. I feel that we have much in common, but I also sense that we have developed growing feelings for each other.' She took his hand, and suddenly looked a little vulnerable as she considered the possibility that her feelings might not be reciprocated. 'Tell me, Samuel Ansell. Tell me you feel the same way.' Sam was at once astonished and delighted. He took her hand and pressed it to his lips.

'Dearest Anne, of course I feel the same way. I never thought for a moment that…well…that someone like you could form an attraction to a lowly house surgeon.'

'That's my mother talking, Sam. All that matters to me is that a man is good and caring. That he will respect me as an equal, not treat me as a chattel.'

Sam looked into her eyes. 'I could never do that, Anne.' Their heads leaned in further, and finally their lips met. Their feelings had been developing over many months. What had started as occasional discussions on science and philosophy had gradually developed into something much more personal. It was about mutual respect and love. It had not been a sudden transformation; their attachment had taken hold gradually, but that precious moment on the veranda marked a moment of sudden clarity and realization for both of them. It was intensely moving, but disappointingly short-lived. Behind them, the curtains rustled, and Thomas Kirtland's voice called out softly into the darkness.

'Anne, where are you? Mother is looking for you. Quickly!'

The spell was broken, and her brother's intervention seemed to highlight Sam's impossible position. He knew he loved Anne, but he could not see how he could ever gain her parent's approval. He was elated by their brief moment of intimacy, but also a little angry that he was powerless to overcome the realities of his birth and the customary rules of the British aristocracy.

Anne sensed his melancholy and squeezed his hand. 'We will talk soon. At the infirmary, perhaps, but soon.' And then she was gone. Sam waited for a few minutes and then retraced his steps to the ballroom. Lady Kirtland was waiting nearby. She was brimming with suspicion and thrust out her jaw as she glared at him.

'Have you been somewhere, Mr Ansell?' she demanded.

'No, Madam,' Sam replied. 'I was just taking the night air.' And then he had an impetuous idea. Perhaps it was the elation Sam was feeling following his encounter with Anne, or maybe it was the port that he had consumed. Whatever the reason, he just could not resist tweaking the lioness's tail.

'I say, Lady Kirtland, I haven't seen you dancing with anyone this evening. I would be honoured if you would have the next one with me.'

Lady Kirtland was taken aback, and for once was speechless. Nobody had ever played her at her own game. The sheer arrogance of it.

'Erm, I apologize Mr Ansell but… my hip you see. I'm no longer quite so able to... I'm sorry, but no.'

Sam smiled, 'I'm sorely disappointed, Madam, but I understand your predicament. Perhaps I should see you professionally to see if there is anything that can be done?' He laughed as she turned pale at the idea. 'Or perhaps not,' he continued. 'As for the dance, maybe another time then.' He touched his forelock and left Lady Kirtland open-mouthed with shock. He had made an enemy, but he was too elated to care. Not long after, Sam retired and fell quickly into bed where he slept soundly until his dreams were curtailed unexpectedly early the following morning.

***

It was six o'clock when an urgent hammering roused Sam. He stumbled out of bed, bleary-eyed, and was still wearing his night gown when he opened the door to find the housekeeper standing there. She was panting from the exertion of running up the stairs and looked at Sam anxiously.

'Pardon me, Mr Ansell. Lord Kirtland asked me to fetch you, Sir. There's been an accident. It's Lord Vane. He's fallen from a horse.' Sam told her that he would be along directly and quickly dressed. It was easy to find the patient because all he had to do was follow the noise.

Lord Vane was sitting on a chair in the sitting room, groaning loudly as a footman tried to help him remove his tailcoat and boots. He was surrounded by Lord Kirtland, Anne's brother, Thomas, and some of the other house guests who had risen early for a morning gallop across the estate. It was clear that Vane was in a great deal of pain, and his right arm was dangling uselessly by his side. Sam hoped that he was not going to be faced with another compound fracture and amputation, but he was encouraged to see that there was no blood on the man's clothes.

'I need to examine you, Lord Vane,' Sam told him once the coat had been removed. The man nodded through gritted teeth and muttered his approval. Sam gently felt up his arm and found the head of the man's right humerus was bulging out at the front of his shoulder joint.

'Fortunately, there is no fracture,' Sam told him. 'But I'm afraid you've dislocated your shoulder, My Lord. It is a relatively easy matter to fix, but the reduction of a dislocated joint is an extremely painful procedure. Without it, however, your arm is useless. Would you like me to perform the task? Are you willing to let me try?'

Lord Vane nodded. 'Please,' he said, 'but get a bloody move on, man!'

Sam looked over at Lord Kirtland. 'My Lord, may we clear the room, please? And we should give

Lord Vane half a pint of brandy. I fear he is going to need it.' Lord Kirtland nodded and gave the necessary instruction. Soon, there was only Lord Vane, Sam and the footman remaining in the room.

'Here, drink this, Sir,' Sam told the peer who drank the brandy without pausing for breath.

Somewhat fortified, Vane looked at Sam who could tell from Vane's face that military determination had joined the fight against the excruciating pain in the man's shoulder. Vane was resolved and issued his orders directly.

'Whatever I may say in the next minutes, you do your work, Mr Ansell. Do not waver or be deterred. Just put it back in place. For my part, I will try not to alarm the house with my noise. Go ahead, Sir. Do your worst.'

Lord Vane was certainly brave, and he remained silent as Sam and the footman laid him on his back on the floor. Sam knelt beside him and took the peer's hand and slowly brought it across the man's chest as though it was in a sling. He then gradually moved the hand outwards away from the patient's body. Beads of sweat formed on Vane's upper lip and his breathing became rapid. In most cases, this simple manipulation would have been sufficient to reseat the joint, but Lord Vane's humerus was resolute in its refusal to return to its proper place. Sam realized that he would have to perform the second part of the manoeuvre, and he knew it would hurt the man greatly.

He looked down at Lord Vane. 'I'm sorry, Sir, this will be the worst of it.' And with that Sam raised the man's elbow. The pain was immediate, and Sam thought Lord Vane might call out or even lapse into unconsciousness, but, incredibly, he remained silent such that when the joint did relocate, all three men heard it do so with a dull clunk. The relief was immediate.

'By God, Sir. You've done it!' Lord Vane announced. 'Thank you indeed.' He looked up at the footman. 'Perhaps another half pint of brandy if I may?' Once the footman had left the room, Sam helped Vane to his feet. He was a tall man with an intimidating presence, and Sam was shocked when he realized that far from wanting to thank him, Vane wanted to use the opportunity presented by an empty room to threaten him. When it came, it was without any vestige of subtlety.

'Thank you, Mr Ansell. You are an accomplished doctor, but that's where you should limit your expertise.' He lowered his voice and glared menacingly at Sam. When he continued, his voice was venomous and unequivocable. 'You've been interfering in matters that are not your business, Ansell. Matters of far greater importance than you know. If you value your job and the safety of those you love, you should concentrate on your medicine and stop interfering with things that don't concern you.' He glared at Sam but allowed his features to soften as footsteps approached and the door opened. It was an anxious Lord Kirtland accompanied by the footman who was carrying the remainder of the brandy bottle. Sam was confused by Lord Vane's threats, but he managed to act normally. He asked for some linen and put Vane's arm in a sling. He then helped the peer into a leather armchair and warned him to treat his shoulder carefully for a month until the damaged ligaments had tightened up again.

The sudden change in tone felt surreal, but

there was still some residual tension in the air which Lord Kirtland sensed but attributed to the drama of the injury and the quantity of brandy used in its treatment.

'Well done, Samuel,' he told the surgeon. 'That's twice you've been on hand to help us out. Thank you indeed.' Sam nodded and glanced at Vane who glowered at him with dark eyes that reinforced his previous threats.

Later, as he packed his things away, Sam reflected on his visit. It had certainly been an eventful 24 hours, and he was looking forward to telling Will about it when he returned to the infirmary. His bag was brought down to the waiting carriage, and he found Lord Kirtland reading a paper in the sitting room. He looked up at Sam and winked before pointing at the leather armchair in the corner. It was occupied by the sizeable form of Lord Vane who was snoring loudly whilst sleeping off the effects of a pint of Lord Kirtland's finest brandy. Sam forced a smile and thanked Lord Kirtland for his hospitality. He was fairly certain that Anne's father was not party to Vane's behaviour, and he was relieved that his loyalties would not be divided. There was no sign at all of Anne or her mother. But that was probably just as well, he reflected, as the coach set off down the long drive.

Chapter 8

A Burglary

That Sunday evening, Sam was delighted when Will reappeared from his suspension. As usual, they ate together, and this time they were joined by the Matron. Sam regaled them with a description of the ball at High Cross Manor, but he left out any mention of Anne, his intriguing conversation with Lord Kirtland's group of peers, and Lord Vane's warning. It would be a further two weeks before Matron's next bible reading, and so the two men were able to make their excuses as soon as the meal had ended.

'Well?' Will demanded when they got back to Sam's room. 'I can't believe that you've been hobnobbing with the nation's nobility. Is there anything else to tell? Anything that the Matron couldn't hear that would interest your good friend?'

Sam laughed. Will was fishing for scandalous gossip. 'Well, there is actually,' Sam began, 'but not what you might think. You see, I have formed a romantic attachment.' He then went on to describe the events with Anne, but he left out the details of the stolen kiss on the veranda. 'She really is a most extraordinary woman, Will. Some might say she is too forward, but I see her independence as modern and rather liberating.'

Will nodded. 'I'm very pleased for you both, Sam, but you must be careful as you are entering the world of our nation's aristocracy, and they have firm views on who is admitted into the club. It sounds like Lady Kirtland is not to be trifled with, and although your account was very funny, I think it was unwise to challenge her if you hope to secure her daughter's hand. Perhaps charm her next time?'

They were wise words from his friend, but they were sobering too, and Sam fell silent as he considered the difficulties he would face if he tried to put his attachment with Anne on a more formal footing. Will noticed his friend's face drop and tried to lighten the mood.

'Erm, I don't suppose she has a sister for a poor, lonely apothecary?'

Sam's worry lines disappeared. 'I'm afraid not, Will, but fear not, we will find someone soon. Matron, perhaps?' Will threw a piece of paper at him which Sam caught and returned. They both laughed, and then Sam moved on to more serious matters.

'There is something else. I think we've become embroiled in something far more serious than we thought. This financial scandal is only the half of it.'

Will's face darkened. He was still angry at being blamed and then punished for raising a legitimate concern with the treasurer.

'How so?' he asked.

Sam described the exchange with the group of Lord Kirtland's friends, and then Lord Vane's threats the following morning.

Will was incredulous. 'So, you put the man's arm back into place and then he threatened you? Who are these people?'

'Well, that's the issue isn't it. We don't know what this is really about, and we don't know who is involved. It may be completely innocent but why was George Roach there? And the Duke of Marlborough too? They were all discussing the Oxford Canal Company shares, which confirms that this business is not confined to the infirmary.'

Will nodded. 'Yes, I agree that Sir George Roach is an unlikely guest of the Kirtlands. He may be a knight but he's no aristocrat, and his presence there looks a bit suspicious coming so soon after our intervention. But the Duke of Marlborough? He doesn't strike me as a likely fraudster, and neither does Lord Kirtland. It's not as though either of them needs the money, and yet they were both present. And the other two men, Lords Vane and Kenyon. What is their part in all this? I must admit that I'd never heard of either of them until you mentioned their names. It's a mystery, but it's one we want to solve, don't we?'

Sam had already made up his mind. 'Yes, we cannot let this rest now. Besides, it seems they are already on to us so it's no use trying to back out of it.' Sam looked at his friend who nodded his agreement.

'So, what next?' Will asked, polishing his glasses.

Well, on the way back to the infirmary, I had an idea. We need to establish who is getting the money.

Originally, I wondered whether it was going into Whiting's pocket, but I'm now certain he's just facilitating the theft for someone else, maybe George Roach, although he too might be just another link in a longer chain. If Whiting is diverting infirmary funds, then it's possible there's some kind of record of the fraudulent transactions hidden in his office. George Roach shares the office with Whiting and has a desk there for his work as a governor and treasurer. I propose that we search their room to see what turns up. But we'll have to be careful as the office is right by the porter's desk in the entrance hall.'

Will was excited by the prospect of a burglary. At last, they were acting positively. 'That's an excellent idea, Sam. I do happen to know that the porter, James Moss, sleeps in a room at the back of reception. Overnight, the desk is manned by a lad called Jacob Littleworth whose job is to keep the oil lamps replenished and to wake Moss if a visitor arrives.'

Will seemed to be remarkably well-informed on the overnight arrangements for manning the infirmary reception, and Sam was about to ask how he knew of such things when Will read his mind.

'It was… erm… a romantic matter, and no, I'm not going to tell you,' he added, as Sam raised an eyebrow at his friend who was suddenly anxious to move the conversation along.

Will cleared his throat. 'Anyway,' he continued quickly, 'Littleworth will top up all the oil lamps at around three o'clock. We could wait until he leaves the desk and then get the key to Whiting's office and search it while the lad is absent. We will probably have about twenty minutes. If he catches us, I know from experience that he is not immune to pecuniary persuasion and a shilling will buy his silence.'

His friend finished, and Sam laughed at the idea of Will creeping around the infirmary and bribing the staff. They continued talking about the plan and decided they would break into the secretary's office that same night.

***

Hospitals are never totally quiet, and even at three o'clock in the morning the silence is broken by the distant murmur of human suffering and broken dreams. However, for Sam and Will, the early hours were perfect for mounting a burglary because the only people moving about at that time of night were Jacob Littleworth at the desk, and a single night nurse who patrolled the wards in case anyone needed attention.

From their vantage point under the stairs, they watched Littleworth collect a vessel containing the lamp oil and set off on his rounds. Shortly after, Nurse Messenger checked the ground floor wards and climbed the stairs to the first floor. As they listened to her footsteps recede, the foyer was left empty and silent except for the tremulous snoring of James Moss coming from behind a closed door at the back of the reception area. Sam nodded, and the two men crept across the tiled floor. Will pointed at a rack behind the desk, and it took Sam only seconds to lift the keys to Whiting's office which was located just to the side of the reception area. When he unlocked the door, Sam winced as the hinges squeaked a brief protest at their intrusion, and the two men froze. A few yards away, the porter's nasal chorus continued uninterrupted, and after a brief pause, they continued inside. Will closed the door behind them and lit a candle.

'We must be quick,' he whispered.

Sam nodded. 'I'll do Whiting's desk, you do Roach's. Then we'll look in there.' He pointed to a large cupboard containing the infirmary files. Ten minutes later, the desks had failed to yield anything of interest, and after finding a key in Whiting's top drawer, they opened the cupboard.

'I'll start at the top, you do the bottom, 'Sam whispered. It was a difficult task as the cupboard was packed full, and Whiting did not seem to have a filing system that was easy to follow. However, after a further ten minutes, Will stood up triumphantly.

'Here! I think I've found it.' He was brandishing a small brown ledger which he laid on the desk. It was marked, 'Canal Investments', and it contained only a few papers. Will brought the candle closer, and Sam started to flip through it as they both read.

The first few pages displayed a record of dividend payments, and there were several letters pasted in bearing the address of Mayhew and Mayhew where John Crosley had worked. One letter confirmed that the infirmary was still sitting on huge paper losses even though it was thirty years since the share price had crashed. Then, further on, there was a copy of a letter addressed to Colonel William B Fairman at an address in Oxford. It said little other than to refer to a payment made to Fairman by the secretary for unspecified services rendered to the infirmary.

Sam frowned. 'Look! It's for exactly the same sum as the amount that went missing: sixty-eight pounds.' He looked at the earlier pages and found several similar transactions all paid to the same individual. Further forward, there was a draft balance sheet. The missing sums were shown as a deduction, but each transaction was referred to only as an 'Equalization.' Neither man was familiar with accounting procedures, but something was clearly wrong. Someone was diverting the infirmary's investment income from the Oxford Canal Company to an individual called Colonel Fairman. Sam scribbled the man's business address down on a piece of paper and was about to return the book to the cupboard when he noticed some initials at the side of the entry on the balance sheet.

'Look, he said pointing at the abbreviated signature, "GWR". George W Roach. So, he is involved. I thought he must be. But we need to hurry, Will. We've been here too long, and Littleworth will be back soon.'

But Sam was wrong. Littleworth was already back, and he had noticed a dim light coming from underneath the poorly fitted door to the secretary's office. Moss was always grumpy if he was roused before six o'clock, and so Littleworth had decided to investigate for himself. However, Will was already waiting for him, and as the lad opened the door, Will grabbed him and put a hand over the boy's mouth to prevent him from calling out.

Sam looked at the terrified boy and whispered, 'Hush now, Jacob. You know us well, I think. It's Doctors Ansell and Perks. It's very important that you remain quiet, do you understand?' The boy nodded and Will removed his hand.

'What are you doing here, Mr Ansell,' the boy whispered a little nervously, but flattered that the doctor had remembered his name.

Will had an answer prepared and interjected. 'Well, it's a bit of a secret, really, Jacob,' he said. 'But if we tell you, can you promise to keep it? Perhaps, if I give you this shilling it will help you to remember to keep quiet.' The boy looked at the coin and nodded.

Will then went on to tell the lad that somebody had been stealing from the petty cash box, and that suspicion had fallen on those working closest to the secretary's office. In other words, Littleworth and James Moss. He told the startled boy that they did not really think he was the guilty party, but if he talked about it and alerted the actual thief then suspicion was likely to fall on him. Will warned him that the punishment would be severe, and that prison and transportation were the minimum he could expect. It was a shameless invention, of course, but it had the necessary effect on the terrified boy who scuttled off behind the reception desk as the two men locked Whiting's office and returned to Sam's room. Littleworth would keep silent. Sam was certain of it.

Chapter 9

The Letterbox

The day after Sam and Will broke into the secretary's office was a Monday, and both men were busy at work. Dawn had been about to break by the time they had eventually taken to their beds, and Sam was feeling quite fatigued. Before retiring, they had discussed the ledger and the possible reasons for the unusual payments. However, after half an hour they were no clearer. The answer seemed to lie with the man called Colonel Fairman, and they had agreed that Sam would try to find out more by following the trail of money to the Colonel's mailing address.

Sam decided to make that visit on the following day during his Tuesday afternoon off, but in the meantime, he had patients to see and treat. Most of Sam's cases were routine, but there was one occurrence of note, and that concerned an incident that contravened the infirmary's strict rules on patient behaviour. Sam had seen the funny side of the episode and was looking forward to sharing the story with Will later that evening. It was amusing because it highlighted that for many individuals, the impact of illness and injury can sometimes be as much a matter of the mind as a physical phenomenon. It just depended on what precisely was driving the patient forward. For Charles Houndrew, that driving force was something that is as old as the hills and with a propensity to cause trouble whenever it arises: human desire. It all began when Sam went to treat a patient and discovered that Charles Houndrew was missing from his bed on North Attic Ward. Sam was surprised, as the man had been barely able to walk when he was admitted to the infirmary with a nasty ulcer on his leg. Sam was planning to debride the sore during his next theatre list that Wednesday morning, but as he looked at the empty bed, he could see it had been made ready for the next patient. An explanation arrived with Nurse Wallace.

'Good morning, Mr Ansell,' she breathed into his ear. 'Are you looking for Mr Houndrew?'

'I am, Nurse Wallace; he can't possibly have died, has he? I didn't see anyone lying in the Dead Room when I passed by it earlier?'

Nurse Wallace smiled at him. 'Oh no, Sir. Mr Houndrew is alive and a bit too well for his own good. He has been discharged for lewd behaviour.' She lowered her voice. 'He went all the way to Litchfield Ladies Ward and was discovered sitting on a patient's bed. They were talking quite normally, but Mr Houndrew…erm…well, he had his hand up her night dress.'

Sam was incredulous. 'Surely, he could barely walk there with an ulcer as bad as his. And what about his leg? It still needs treating?'

'Well, Sir, you know how determined some men can be in these matters,' she whispered. 'It was Mr Whiting who ordered his removal, but he has allowed Mr Houndrew to remain on the books as an outpatient.'

Sam nodded. The infirmary regulations were continually updated by the Board and were enforced rigorously. The rules for patients were particularly strict and covered all aspects of misbehaviour including drinking, gambling, bad language, lewdness, and smoking. He was not surprised that Houndrew had been evicted as lewd behaviour was one of the most serious offences, and Sam was certain the governors would uphold the secretary's decision when they discussed the matter at the next weekly board meeting.

'Well, perhaps there is a lesson for us all, Nurse Wallace,' he suggested philosophically. 'Justice is swift in this infirmary so we must stay on the right side of the rules and immerse ourselves in our work.' It sounded overly pious, but Sam liked Catherine Wallace, and she sometimes trod a precarious path of over-familiarity that would attract no mercy from Matron if she was overheard. The infirmary would be a dour place without Wallace's sense of humour, so a friendly warning seemed appropriate. He smiled to reassure her that he meant well, and he could tell that she had understood.

It was episodes like this that made the work in the infirmary so interesting. There was always some kind of drama to enjoy. Later, Will laughed loudly as the two men imagined Houndrew in his nightdress hobbling down the stairs looking for the ladies' ward. Patient expulsions were a regular occurrence, but there was usually a comical side to them, and they broke up the daily routine and brightened up the grim surroundings of the infirmary.

***

On the day following Houndrew's eviction, Sam missed lunch and set off into central Oxford. The weather had turned hot, and he left the infirmary by the front entrance to avoid the unpleasantness of the burial ground. He had been hoping that he might receive a note from Anne, but he had heard nothing since the ball at High Cross Manor. That meant that he had little to distract him as he crossed the road by the Royal Oak. The public house stood out from the many other inns in Oxford because it was owned by the infirmary and let out to a tenant landlord. Sam thought it was peculiar that an institution that imposed such strict moral codes on its staff and patients could quite happily profit from a drinking establishment. He knew it was the haunt of some of the staff, and he occasionally went into it when he was out with Will. However, it was usually at his friend's insistence, otherwise Sam rarely went there.

As he walked down St Giles' Street, Sam thought about Colonel Fairman. Whiting's letters had been sent to an address in a backyard off Fish Street in central Oxford. It was a strange place for a Colonel to frequent as the area was a little disreputable, and Sam was glad that he had set off early to ensure that he entered the back streets in broad daylight. As he approached the area, there was a strong aroma of animal dung and human waste floating on the air. It was a foul gas that seemed to poison his every breath, and Sam wished he had a scarf to tie around his face. Even the rats seemed to be running in one direction only, and that was away from the smell and in the opposite direction to Sam's.

A few minutes later, he was in the correct part of Fish Street and searching for Number 6B. He was eventually forced to ask for directions from an old woman who was outside her front door scrubbing the step. She looked up at Sam and pointed to a narrow passageway that led to the rear of the street properties.

'Down there, Mister. We don't often get your kind around here, she added. 'Except for that soldier gentleman, I suppose.' Sam must have displayed too much interest because the information dried up when he started to ask her about the man. Eventually, he reached into his pocket and took out a shilling which he flipped and caught.

'Madam,' he said, 'I'm sure if you think hard enough you will remember more about this soldier. What say you?'

She cackled. 'Calling me, "madam" might have been enough, Sir, but I'll take your coin as well if you swap that shilling for half a crown.' Sam groaned inwardly. He knew little of backstreet etiquette and bribery, and it looked like it was going to be an expensive afternoon.

He told the woman that he would pay once she had answered his questions. She nodded and told Sam that the soldier came to the house twice a week, on Mondays and Fridays. He was always dressed in uniform and made no attempt to conceal the two pistols in his belt. He would go straight to Number 6B in the backyard and was there for less than a minute before he retraced his steps. The house was occupied by a widow who had emigrated from Ireland along with her husband who had been in the army too. He had been discharged after being wounded at Waterloo, and he had eventually found work as a labourer on the canals before he was killed in an accident. The old woman fell silent as she reached the limits of her knowledge about her neighbour. She paused, trying to think of something more that would justify the increase in price she had demanded from Sam. There was not much to add, and rather lamely, she finished by saying that the widow was a devout churchgoer.

'Do you know what happens while he's at her address?' Sam asked her.

'Well, I'm not certain, but he once walked out of the passage holding an envelope, and he hadn't been carrying one when he went in.'

Sam had heard enough. It sounded like Colonel Fairman was using Number 6B as a mailing address. The widow was probably being paid off, and it seemed possible that her late husband had served under the Colonel's command at some point.

Sam decided to visit the widow. He knew it was unlikely that she would know what this was all about, but she might know a little, and it seemed worth a try especially as her house was so close. He left the old woman scrubbing her step and promised he would pay her when he had been to Number 6B. He went through the passageway she had indicated and carefully dodged around some unpleasant looking debris lying on the dirt floor. The passage was only a few yards long and opened out into a yard. A single brick privy stood at one end and serviced several ramshackle dwellings.

The stench from the overflowing cesspit was overpowering, and he started to rush, desperate to escape the cloying atmosphere. He noticed one of the doors had a faded 6B painted on it, and as he approached it he thought he saw the curtains twitch in an upstairs window. He hammered on the door several times, but the occupant remained concealed, and Sam soon realized she was not going to speak to him. He gave up after a few attempts and returned to the old woman who was still working on her step. She looked up at him.

'I don't suppose she answered you, but I'm certain she's there.' she said dropping the brush into her bucket. For a moment, Sam wondered if it was all a story made up to extract his money, but he decided that the old woman's account was too detailed to be a fabrication. He glanced down at her and tossed a coin.

'I may have need of you again especially if you remain silent about my visit today,' he promised. 'And I shall know if you break your promise,' he added.

The woman nodded her head vigorously. 'Bless you, Sir. It is hard enough to get by these days, and if my silence gets me more of your coin then you shall have it.'

Sam thanked her and took his leave. He was disappointed that he had learned nothing particularly new about the canal fraud, only how the payments were being made. He glanced at his pocket watch. He had planned to visit the John Radcliffe Library that afternoon to see if he could discover anything about the two peers he had met at the ball, Lords Kenyon and Vane. There was still time before it closed, and it was on his way back to the infirmary.

He set off along Fish Street at a good pace, but

at the junction with the High Street he stopped abruptly to look in the window of a jewellery shop on the corner. He was considering buying a locket for Anne to seal their relationship, and the shop had a fine selection of the proprietor's work on display. However, the locket was temporarily forgotten when Sam became aware that he was being followed.

The man was about fifty yards behind him, and he had been caught out by Sam's sudden halt. He looked around unsure of what to do and then decided to try and mirror Sam by pretending to look in a shop window. That might have worked in a busy street, except there were no shops in that part of Fish Street, and so the man turned and instead faced the front door of an unoccupied house that was semi derelict. As the man pretended to find great interest in a disused door, Sam's pulse quickened. If his pursuer worked for Whiting and Roach, then Sam's days at the infirmary might be numbered. He looked carefully at the man. He was wearing a crumpled suit and no hat which made his balding head gleam in the afternoon sunlight. His glasses looked a bit unusual and seemed to have a particularly thick frame rather than the wire ones which were the fashion of the day. Sam had seen enough, and he turned quickly into the High Street and then almost immediately into a passageway where he hid in the shadows. The man following him appeared, looking flustered and began searching up and down the road. Eventually, he gave up and went off along the High Street towards the castle. Sam remained hidden for a further five minutes and then left the shadows and walked in the opposite direction towards the library.

***

By the time Sam reached the John Radcliffe Library, his disquiet had grown. He had been followed once before to Mrs Crosley's house, and now he was being followed again. But who was responsible? Perhaps it was Roach again? Maybe the boy, Littleworth, had confided in the porter who had reported the burglary up the chain. By visiting the widow's house, Sam had drawn attention to his interest in Colonel Fairman's affairs and defied Lord Vane's threats. He suddenly felt very exposed and wished he had some kind of lever that would ensure his safety and preserve his job. He considered Crosley's notebook. It did not provide definitive proof of embezzlement, and he wished that they had taken the file from Whiting's office. Together, the two items might have provided sufficient evidence of a fraud to secure their jobs. Instead, Whiting and Roach could forestall any investigation by destroying the ledger and any incriminating documents. It would then be all too easy for Roach to invent some contrived reasons for having the two doctors dismissed. He sighed. It was going to be a difficult few days to find out if he was compromised. In the meantime, he told himself, he should stick to the plan that he had agreed with Will and that required access to a particular reference book.

The library was an unusual building. It was round with a spectacular dome and had opened to great architectural acclaim in 1749. The great philanthropist, John Radcliffe had paid for the work through a large sum that he left to his trustees. The same trust founded the Radcliffe Infirmary and continued to provide financial assistance as the institution grew.

Inside, Sam marvelled at the portraits that hung in the library, and the sheer number of shelves housing books, journals and other hidden literary treasures. One of those books was called Burke's Peerage which the librarian eventually located for Sam after experiencing some difficulty with the index system. Sam sat at a reading table and studied the leather-bound book in front of him. Burke's Peerage had been established in 1826 by John Burke who still edited the annual publication. It provided an authoritative genealogical record of historic families which included the two peers who Sam had met at Lord Kirtland's ball. He decided to start with Lord Vane.

Vane was an Anglo-Irish nobleman who had been a soldier and then politician. Sam could see that he had been born Charles William Stewart, but he had changed his name to Vane, the family name of his second wife. He had served during the Irish Rebellion of 1798 and under Wellington during the Napoleonic and Peninsular Wars. After leaving the army, he served in diplomatic posts in Berlin and Austria and was eventually summoned to the House of Lords. While serving in Vienna he was ennobled as Baron Stewart of Stewart's Court in Ballylawn in County Donegal. He had also been awarded honorary degrees by both Cambridge and Oxford Universities and had been admitted to the Privy Council. When he married his second wife in 1819, it was on condition that he adopted her family name, Vane. Three years later Vane's elder brother committed suicide, and he became the 3rd Marquess of Londonderry. The following year he was appointed Earl Vane and Viscount Seaham in the County Palatine of Durham.

Sam finished the final entry and felt a little

dispirited. It looked like a distinguished career, and there was nothing here to explain how Lord Vane could have got mixed up with a petty fraud or provide a reason for the man's threatening behaviour

He thumbed through the book to find Lord Kenyon. The man's record was less impressive but nonetheless distinguished. George Kenyon had been born in 1776 and succeeded as the 2nd Baron Kenyon of Gredington, of County Flintshire in Wales. He had been educated at Christ Church College, Oxford and was called to the bar in 1811. He had five children, and his wife had died in 1815. During his time in parliament, he had written several pamphlets on Irish politics which had been controversial at the time.

Sam looked at his notes. There was no link to canals that he could see. But then he remembered the conversation at the ball and suddenly he saw it. This did not concern canals at all.

Chapter 10

The Man From the Journal

'Ireland?' Will exclaimed that evening after listening to Sam's account. 'Why Ireland?' Sam was still worrying about his pursuer, but as he sat with his friend that evening, he could not help feeling a little smug about his discovery.

'Well, we should consider the facts. The key suspects all have some link to Ireland. George Roach is Irish and was present at the ball even though we remarked that he seemed an unlikely guest of the Kirtlands. Then there's Lord Vane whose family seat is in Ireland and who has extensive interests there. Next is Lord Kenyon who has written political pamphlets about Ireland and even asked me about my views at the ball. Even the widow providing this Colonel Fairman with a mailing address is an Irish immigrant.'

'But what about Lord Kirtland and the Duke of Marlborough? They were present too,' Will protested.

'Well, we don't know for certain that either of them is involved. I don't think Lord Kirtland is part of it although I'm biased of course, but I'm still suspicious of the Duke of Marlborough. He looked at me very intently when Roach asked me about my views on Ireland. It was almost as though he was assessing me in some way.'

Will suddenly looked concerned. 'What about this man who followed you? Are we compromised? These are important people, Sam, and given that Crosley may have been murdered, might we be in danger too?'

Sam shrugged. 'I just don't know. I keep expecting to be told to attend the chairman's office, but until then, I think we should continue, regardless. Neither of us is a political animal, but I can't help wondering if Irish politics is behind all of this.'

Will nodded. 'Is there anyone we could ask?'

Sam laughed. 'I know just the man. He's a reporter for the Oxford Journal. I've met him a couple of times when I've given evidence at coroner's inquests. Henry Lipscomb would sell his soul for a pint of best ale, but I think he is well informed on parliamentary matters. Also, if I can persuade him to keep his counsel on our enquiries then he might prove to be useful, especially if someone acts against us.'

Will laughed. 'Well, you know what reporters are like. I think this almost guarantees that we make headline news, but it might be worth a try.'

Sam knew his friend's scepticism was justified. A reporter was unlikely to agree to stay silent for long especially if there was a good story at hand. However, Lipscomb just needed to be persuaded to stay silent for long enough to allow Sam and Will to unravel the conspiracy. And Sam was increasingly certain that they were indeed dealing with a conspiracy although the objective was still unclear.

***

The following morning Sam rose early and went to the reception desk where he promised to give Jacob Littleworth a sixpence to deliver a message to Henry Lipscomb at the Journal. Moss was yet to rise, and Sam swore Littleworth to secrecy. He told him that the note concerned the fictional investigation that Will had used to scare the lad previously, and Sam was reassured by Littleworth's frightened face when he reminded him of the implications of any indiscretion. He told him to wait for Lipscomb's reply and to bring it to him at lunchtime.

While Sam waited for Lipscomb's response, he worked through a list of minor surgical cases in the operating room. He had just finished the final operation and was putting on his jacket, when a nurse came to the door and told him he was needed at the reception.

The man who had come to fetch him was standing next to the reception desk. He was breathing heavily; his face was dirty with soot, and he smelled of woodsmoke. He looked at Sam and seemed reluctant to speak.

'What is it?' Sam asked him.

'Sir, my name is Whitworth. I work for your father. I'm afraid I have some bad news for you. There's been a fire at the warehouse.'

Sam's pulse quickened. 'And my father?' he

asked, fearing the answer.

'He is alive, Sir, but he has breathed in a lot of smoke, and he's in bed at the house.'

Sam nodded. 'Thank you for informing me, and for helping to fight the fire. Are you well, Mr Whitworth? You look as though you've been in the thick of it.'

The man nodded. 'I am well enough, Sir, but it has been a long night. Your father's premises are badly damaged and quite a lot of stock is either destroyed or badly damaged by smoke.'

Sam nodded and gave the man half a crown for his trouble. 'Please tell my family that I will attend directly.' The man tipped his cap and left the infirmary. Sam found Whiting and explained why he would be absent for a few hours. The secretary expressed his regrets, but his reaction felt insincere, and Sam noted that Whiting did not seem particularly surprised by Sam's news.

With his absence agreed, Sam marched into central Oxford, and when he arrived at his family's house, he rushed past a startled Mrs Seddon and went straight up the stairs to his father's room. The local apothecary was just leaving. Sam knew him a little, and they exchanged nods.

'He is in some discomfort,' the man said, 'but I believe he will live.' Sam thanked the man and went into the room to find his father bent over a spittoon coughing uncontrollably.

'Oh, Papa,' he said, 'you didn't try to take on the fire by yourself, did you? His father shook his head but was unable to explain without precipitating a renewed bout of spluttering. Sam told him not to speak, and they conversed for ten minutes through a system of questions answered by nods and shakes. As far as Sam could discern, the fire had occurred during the night after the household had retired. Help had arrived quickly, and the fire was eventually extinguished before the building was totally destroyed. Sam was especially relieved to learn that his father's insurance was up to date, so despite a great deal of disruption, his father would not be financially ruined. After a few minutes, Sam told his father to rest and promised that he would look in on him soon. His father nodded, and Sam left the house to inspect the damage for himself.

The warehouse was about a quarter destroyed, and when Sam arrived, there was already an army of carpenters and masons making a start on repairs. Sam spotted Mr Anderson, his father's foreman who was directing the staff and making sure the surviving stocks of cloth were made secure. He saw Sam and nodded.

'A bad day, Master Ansell, he observed dryly. 'Thank goodness your father kept his fire insurance subscriptions up to date.' He pointed up to a point high up on the building and just below the eves. Sam squinted and could just make out a plaque in the form of a sun-face with a reference number cast into the metal. It was the plaque that told the insurance company's private fire service that the owner of the building was insured. It was a blessing indeed.

'What happened, Mr Anderson?' Sam asked.

The foreman pointed to a barge moored alongside the charred building. 'Fortunately, it was noticed quite quickly,' he said. 'That barge arrived yesterday evening and was waiting overnight to be unloaded this morning. The bargee spotted the fire and raised the alarm. It was lucky that he saw it so soon otherwise the whole lot would have gone up.' He paused, looked around, and lowered his voice. 'Master Ansell, he told me that he heard voices and saw two men running up the towpath just before he saw the flames. You don't think this could be arson?' he whispered. Sam's blood ran cold as he remembered Vane's threats. He shrugged at the foreman, but he knew it was too much of a coincidence for the fire to be anything else but deliberate. It wasn't just Sam and Will who were now at risk, he thought. It was those around them too.

***

Back at the Infirmary, a chastened Sam went to find Will, but as he went past reception, he was intercepted by Moss who handed him two envelopes. One was plain and the other bore the elaborate wax seal of the Duke of Marlborough. It was addressed to Sam in flowing handwriting, and Moss told him that it had been delivered by one of the Duke's servants. Sam thanked the porter and went up to his room to read them in private.

When he broke the Duke's seal he discovered that he was invited to a shooting party at Blenheim Palace, two weeks' later. Sam knew nothing about shooting, but he recognized that the invitation was either a real honour or an invitation for something far worse. He was unsure whether the Duke of Marlborough was part of the conspiracy, but Sam did know that a shooting party offered the perfect opportunity for someone to stage an accident. Coming on the heels of the warehouse fire, this no longer seemed such a far-fetched concern.

He turned to the plain envelope and was pleased to find it was from Lipscomb. He had written to say that he was pleased to hear from Sam, and he was intrigued to hear what he had to say. He agreed with Sam's suggestion that they should meet at the Royal Oak at eight pm that evening.

Sam burned the letter and went downstairs for the start of the Wednesday evening ward round with his mentor Charles Wingfield. Despite the worrying events at his father's property, Sam forced himself to concentrate, and as usual, he learned much during the following two hours. Wingfield always taught politely, he never spoke down to Sam, and he corrected him respectfully when Sam answered incorrectly or without precision. This was entirely different to Mr Cleobury who turned on any shortfall in knowledge and would happily humiliate a dresser or trainee surgeon in front of the staff. His manner towards Sam had improved since Sam had gained his fellowship of the Royal College, but Sam still preferred the company of Wingfield and learned more from him than his belligerent counterpart. Wingfield should be known as The Gentleman Surgeon, he told himself, privately.

One idea often germinates another. Sam knew nothing about shooting and needed some advice before he went to Blenheim Palace. If Wingfield was a gentleman, he reasoned, then perhaps he might also enjoy field sports and be able to provide some helpful advice. Sam picked his moment to find out.

'Mr Wingfield. Sir, could you spare a moment?' he asked as they completed the evening's rounds.

'What is it, Samuel?'

'Well, I have received this.' He handed over the invitation to his mentor.

'Goodness me, Samuel,' he exclaimed, 'this is quite an honour. You are socializing in high circles these days. But what's the problem here?'

'Well, Sir, I don't own a gun, I don't know how to shoot, and I know nothing about shooting etiquette or even what to wear!' Aside from that, I'm delighted, of course.'

Wingfield laughed. 'Well, I don't suppose you will want to look out of place if Miss Kirtland happens to be present. And I can't imagine for a moment that she will be absent when she hears that you are to be a guest.'

Sam reddened. 'I…erm… I'm not sure if she'll be there or not. How...'

Wingfield's large frame was shaking with laughter. 'Well, it's quite obvious. You only have to watch the two of you together.' By now, even Sam was laughing, but his face fell when he remembered Lady Kirtland.

'I'm not sure her mother approves of me. She was very sharp at the ball.'

''Look Sam, you're a charming fellow, with a bright future, and I think that with time you'll be able to bring her round. Be patient and all will be well. Certainly, her father thinks highly of you.'

So, they had discussed him at some point, Sam realized. He nodded at Wingfield. 'I like Lord Kirtland; he doesn't seem to worry about my background.'

'Well, we'd better make sure it stays that way. We need to make sure that you fit in at the Duke's shooting party, and I need to teach you enough about the sport to prevent you from accidentally killing something that hasn't got feathers. Come to my house next Tuesday afternoon, and we will see what can be done. I shall send a carriage for you.'

Sam was once again indebted to Wingfield who had read the situation well and without asking Sam any embarrassing questions either. He felt greatly reassured, and decided he would write a short note to Anne to make sure that she would know of his invitation to Blenheim Palace and still have time to get one for herself. He then turned his mind to his meeting with the journalist, Henry Lipscomb.

As usual, Will was on duty that evening, so Sam only had a brief moment to tell his friend about the fire. Will was furious initially, but as the severity of the incident dawned on him, he became reflective.

'We must talk about this, Sam,' he said. 'It is getting very serious now. Perhaps when you get back from meeting Lipscomb?'

Sam nodded. With Will on duty, he had to go to the meeting alone. He was a little concerned about being available for emergency surgical admissions, but his friend reassured him that he would send a runner across to the Royal Oak if Sam was required at short notice. He knew that Will was disappointed to be left behind, but Sam promised to update him when he returned. He decided to evade the porter's scrutiny and left the infirmary through a door at the rear.

As Sam walked around the side of the building, he hoped there would be nobody familiar amongst the drinkers inside the Royal Oak. It was popular amongst the staff, but Sam knew most of them went drinking on Friday evenings after they had been paid. His assessment proved to be correct, and he found Henry Lipscomb waiting for him in the back room, away from the loud revelry of the front parlour. Lipscomb stood up, shook his hand, and let Sam order them both a pint of ale. He was a small, wiry individual, dressed in a worn brown suit that needed some urgent tailoring. He looked tired as though he had spent too long meeting newspaper deadlines and dealing with demanding editors.

'It's been a while, Mr Ansell. I think we last met at the inquest of that chap who accidentally shot himself climbing over a gate near the turnpike road.'

Sam remembered his invitation to Blenheim Palace and made a mental note not to climb over any fences when he attended the shooting party later that month.

'Yes, I remember it,' Sam replied politely. 'I gave you a little bit of background on the medical findings, I recall.'

The reporter nodded. 'That's it. Well, let's get straight to it. Your note didn't say what this is all about, but I'm hoping you have a story for me.'

'I do,' Sam replied. 'And I also need some information from you. However, before I tell you what this is about, I need your word that you won't publish anything until we have completed our investigation. My colleague and I believe we may have uncovered some kind of conspiracy involving several important and well-known persons, but we need time to find out exactly what is going on and precisely who is involved.'

Sam stopped to take a mouthful of ale. He leaned forward and lowered his voice. 'We think it's a serious matter. Indeed, we believe that one man may have been murdered for asking too many questions about it. I have been threatened and followed by a stranger on at least two occasions, and last night there was a suspicious fire at my father's warehouse. I'm certain it's all connected. If you break your promise and print an incomplete story, then we will lose our jobs, and you may be placing all of us, including you, in danger.'

Sam paused to allow the gravity of his account to sink in and then added, 'in return for your discretion, we will give you exclusive access to the facts once it is over.'

Lipscombe stroked his beard. It was always difficult to decide when to publish this kind of story. Too early, and you missed much of the interesting material that might emerge as a story matured. Too late, and there was a risk that a promising news story broke elsewhere, and your own draft article became just another paper mirage on the editor's spike. This one sounded like it was worth a bit of patience, and he had no doubt that Sam was being sincere.

'Very well, Mr Ansell, I will sit on this but at least give me a taste of it otherwise I won't know what to tell you.'

Sam knew it was a reasonable request and told Lipscomb about the Oxford Canal shares, the money being diverted from the infirmary, and the likely link to Irish politics. While Sam spoke, the reporter sat impassively. To the casual observer, he might have seemed tired and slightly vacant, but Sam could tell that he was recording everything he heard. Lipscomb took no notes, but with an encyclopaedic mind like his, he had no need for pencil and notebook. Eventually, Sam finished his account, and Lipscomb's mind stopped recording and began to deliver the stored facts.

'There is a great deal to tell,' he started, 'and I'm not sure if it will help you to uncover the mystery, but I'll start by asking you whether you've heard of the Orange Order?'

'Well, yes, I have,' Sam replied, taking out his notebook. It's an organization that represents protestant interests in Ireland, named after King William of Orange, who defeated the Catholic King, James II at the end of the last century. I think it's quite controversial.'

'Yes. When it comes to Irish politics there is very little middle ground, and in Ireland it usually splits along religious lines. Over the last thirty-five years, there has been much violence instigated by both sides but perhaps more commonly by Protestant supporters. The Orange Order is particularly demonstrative, and they hold marches each year to commemorate William of Orange's victory over James II, and to celebrate the battles that he fought along the way. You may have heard of the Battle of the Boyne, for example.'

'Yes, I have.'

'Well, their opponents regard this marching as very provocative, and it has led to a surge in Irish republicanism. More recently, the British Government has tried to encourage a political accommodation to bring the two sides together.'

Lipscomb paused to check that Sam was following him. 'In 1823, there was a ban on Unlawful Oaths. This included the Orange Order which was forced to dissolve and reform under a new constitution. In 1825, the same thing happened again following the Unlawful Associations Bill. To the supporters of the Order, these Acts seemed vindictive and one-sided, a perception that was sharpened when Parliament passed the Catholic Emancipation Bill. This legislation allowed Catholics to take seats as MPs and to fill other posts and influential appointments that had previously been denied to them. In my opinion,

Catholic emancipation was long overdue, but it has been extremely controversial, and it has resulted in an even more extreme Orange Order. Not only that, but it has split the opinion of the entire British establishment including institutions like the legal system, Parliament and the Church.'

'So, what about our conspiracy? How does that fit into what you have described?' Sam asked, as he tried to reconcile a minor financial fraud at the Radcliffe Infirmary with events of strategic importance taking place far from Oxford.

'Well, this is where it gets interesting,' Lipscomb replied after he had drunk half a pint of beer and wiped his beard again. He pointed at the empty glass. 'But perhaps we should first have another drink to keep us on our toes. Your round again, I think, Mr Ansell.'

Sam did not argue and went to the bar to order two pints of ale, The front parlour was busier now, and it was much rowdier. In the corner, there was a group of young men with a woman who looked old enough to be their mother. She was heavily made up and dressed quite provocatively with a low-cut dress that emphasized her ample bosom. The young men were pawing at her, but she looked unconcerned and seemed to be actively encouraging them. Sam knew that the highest bidder would retire with the woman later. Or perhaps the top two bidders, he laughed to himself. It was then that he noticed that one of the men was William Little, the gardener, and Sam turned his back quickly to avoid being recognized. The landlord returned with two pints of ale, and Sam was relieved when he was able to retreat to the rear room unobserved.

'Here we are, Mr Lipscomb. More lubrication for your voice.'

'Thank you, Mr Ansell.' He took a large gulp while he gathered his thoughts. 'Now, we talked about the Orange Order. Let's turn to your group of peers. Lord Vane, first. You already know a lot about his official biographical information from Burke's Peerage including his family links to Ireland. But it's his unofficial record that is interesting, although I can't yet see how it links to your conspiracy.'

Sam had brought a notebook and scribbled as Lipscomb continued.

'You know that Vane was a soldier, but what Burke doesn't reveal is that he was a ruthless one who attracted quite a reputation for brutality during the Irish Rebellion of 1798. It is true that he fought bravely during the Napoleonic Wars, but the idea that he resigned from the army due to ill health is a myth. I have it on good authority that Wellington dismissed him from his staff.' Lipscomb took a sip of ale as Sam waited patiently. The reporter was not a man to be rushed, and he blew his nose on a soiled handkerchief and drank more beer before starting again.

'Now, Vane's time spent in Vienna as an ambassador was colourful too. He was well known for promiscuous behaviour and heavy drinking, and he openly visited prostitutes, attracting the name, Lord Pumpernickel after a character in a popular play of the time. Finally, he is an extremely rich man. His marriage to his second wife brought him extensive lands in the Durham area that are rich in coal, and it has allowed him to refurbish the family home in Ireland. He has written some books if you need more about his views.'

'That's very interesting,' Sam said, 'Lord Vane

threatened me about continuing our investigation, and it wouldn't surprise me if he had a hand in arranging last night's fire. I'm certain he's a key member of the conspiracy. However, none of this helps us to identify what they are up to.'

'That's true,' Lipscomb replied 'but I think it is guilt by association at this stage. Let's quickly talk about the others. Lord Kenyon is more easily identified with the Orange Order because he is the deputy Grand Master of the organization. In fact, if this is about Ireland then it is unusual that they're meeting in Oxford because the senior Orange Order officials normally meet at Kenyon's house in London. He has held staunch anti-Catholic views over many years, and he has written several pamphlets on the subject. He was certainly against Catholic emancipation and played a leading role in the political campaign against it.'

'Ah, yes. I remember,' Sam said. 'Didn't Wellington resign as Prime Minister over the Bill only to be asked by the King to form a new government shortly afterwards?'

'That's right. The King initially told the officers of his household to vote against the legislation, and when Wellington heard about it, he tended his resignation. There was an attempt by the Duke of Cumberland to form a new government that was opposed to the Bill, but his attempt failed when it became apparent that most MPs in the Commons actually supported Catholic emancipation. In the end, the King recalled Wellington, and the Bill was passed. Incidentally, the Grand Master of the Orange Order is the Duke of Cumberland, but he is not active beyond Parliament and is more of a useful figurehead for the Order in my opinion.'

'And what about Marlborough and Kirtland? And this mysterious Colonel Fairman?'

Lipscomb smiled at Sam. He had once chased stories with similar enthusiasm. These days he let them come to him.

'I have little to say about the Fifth Duke of Marlborough's politics although he is a Whig, and they tend to take a more liberal view of Irish matters. However, the Fifth Duke's son and heir to the title, known as the Marquess of Blandford, is certainly active in parliament and he is very anti-Catholic. Whilst the current duke's views are a little unclear, you must have heard about his financial difficulties?' Sam shook his head.

'Well, despite the grandeur of Blenheim Palace, the Duke is in quite a bit of financial distress. For many years, he chose to live at the family home, near Reading. However, he ran up some hefty debts by collecting some extraordinarily expensive antique books, and eventually those debts were called in. His collections were seized along with the rest of his estates, and he moved back into Blenheim Palace where he lives off a small annuity granted to the first Duke by Queen Anne. So, you see, Mr Ansell, for some within our aristocracy, ennoblement does not necessarily mean wealth. If your conspiracy involves money, then the Duke of Marlborough would certainly have a motive.'

Sam's pencil finished scratching. 'And Lord Kirtland?'

'I don't think Kirtland is involved.' He holds quite moderate views and, as a Whig, he voted for Catholic emancipation. I would be astonished if he was mixed up with an Irish plot of some kind.'

Sam thought of Anne and was relieved that her father seemed to be an innocent party. He had one last question to ask. 'Finally, there's this Colonel Fairman. Have you ever heard of him?'

Lipscomb's brow became lined as the great brain rummaged for a particular memory. 'His name sounds familiar, but I can't quite place him. I have some notes back at the office. I can check them for you.'

Sam leaned back. Lipscomb had provided him with some useful background information, but he was no closer to understanding what the mystery was about.

'I don't understand why this is happening in Oxford?' he asked eventually.

'Well, there is one thing that all three peers have in common and that is they all attended Christ Church College at the University,' Lipscomb replied. And then he seemed to have an idea. 'Actually, I can think of another connection, but it's a bit tenuous. Have you heard of the Oxford Movement?' Sam shook his head.

'Well, it's another religious matter. There are some elements in the higher echelons of the Church of England, and particularly at Oxford University, that want to restore to the English Church certain liturgical and devotional customs that look very similar to Roman Catholic practices. It has become quite controversial because at the parish level, the English Church is influenced more by protestant evangelism and John Wesley. The Government has been involved and made matters worse by reforming the structures and financial arrangements of the Church of Ireland. This has fuelled Protestant suspicion here and deepened the schism within the Church of England. I can't quite see the connection to your enquiries, but there are certainly firm views about the movement within Oxford's religious and academic institutions.'

Sam nodded and looked at his pocket watch. It was time to leave.

'Well, you've been very helpful, Mr Lipscomb. 'We may not know what exactly the conspiracy is about, but at least I know a little more about some of the characters and the politics involved in it. I must return to the infirmary now, but I promise to stay in touch and keep you informed. I have an invitation to a shoot at Blenheim Palace in ten days, and I may learn some more there.'

Henry Lipscombe rose too and shook Sam's hand. 'Please call me Henry, and Sam, please be careful. I have a nose for trouble, and this one has the stink of political corruption about it. Act cautiously and don't draw attention to yourself by being too direct. I am certain that you have received this invitation for a particular purpose. Make sure you don't place yourself in danger, or worse, become implicated in a plot. I shall wait for your news, and if I discover anything about Colonel Fairman, I will let you know.'

The two men shook hands and made for the door. As they left, Sam could see that the drunken group of young men and the woman had already departed, leaving Sam to speculate on whether the gardener was the eventual winner of the woman's attentions.

Chapter 11

The Chairman

The Duke of Marlborough's shoot was not scheduled to take place for another ten days, but there was plenty to occupy Sam at work. He told Will about his discussion with Lipscomb, and they had agreed to do nothing further until Sam had been to Blenheim Palace. In the meantime, Sam worried about the man who had followed him into the Oxford slums, and he wondered whether he worked for Roach. After two days, he had heard nothing from the infirmary management, and he was beginning to imagine that his pursuer had been on an alternative mission on behalf of someone else, or even on business entirely unconnected to him. He was ever more confident when, on the Friday morning, Absolom Whiting tracked him down and told him that The Reverend Thomas wanted to see him immediately. Sam's heart sank. The chairman always did the dismissals. The weekly board meeting had taken place on the previous day, and Sam knew that if he was going to lose his job, then it would have been discussed and agreed at that gathering. As he followed Whiting up the stairs to the chairman's office, he wondered whether the secretary knew of his impending dismissal but was slightly reassured that Whiting displayed none of his usual smugness. Instead, he seemed quite distracted and climbed the stairs slowly as though carrying a heavy load. It offered Sam a morsel of hope that became a feast of relief after he knocked on the door to the chairman's office. The Reverand Thomas opened it and surprised Sam by shaking his hand.

'Come in, Sam and take a seat.' He gestured to the armchair where Roach had sat on the previous occasion. So, it was not to be dismissal after all.

'I wanted to have a brief word with you,' Thomas started. 'I have been very pleased with your work since your appointment as House Surgeon, and I hope that one day you will apply to be considered as a consultant to this great institution. I know that you are always keen to introduce new treatments and procedures. However, I'm afraid that, from now on, you will have to provide the secretary with a list of any special equipment or treatments needed for patients, and that list will need financial approval from the weekly board meeting. I want you to know that I share your ambitions for medical progress, but our financial situation has become so perilous that you may not get everything you request. You will be aware that we are funded by subscriptions and charitable donations?'

Sam nodded. 'Yes, Sir. I have seen the annual accounts.'

'Have you, indeed? Excellent, excellent. Well,

you'll know that we are barely solvent, and that we must try to save every penny.' He paused and was uncharacteristically uncertain of how to frame his next words. There was a long silence, and Sam saw that the man was close to tears.

'Is everything alright, Sir?' Sam asked with genuine concern.

'Yes. I mean no, it is not alright. I want to share something with you in great confidence. I am doing so because I perceive you to be a man of conscience, honesty and high moral standards. After all, it is not often that men of your age attend bible readings.'

Sam's conscience almost detonated, but he lacked the heart to tell the man that he only attended them out of politeness to Matron, so he smiled encouragement instead.

The chairman seemed to draw strength from Sam's unspoken reassurance and continued. 'Well, it is indeed hard times for the infirmary, but since you were last in this office, I've developed a terrible suspicion that a portion of our funds is being diverted for some other purpose.' He paused again, uncomfortable that he harboured such unpleasant doubts. 'It is a disgraceful thing to imagine that someone would defraud a charitable enterprise like ours, but I just can't help it. To be honest, I don't really understand accounting procedures, and neither do I know who to trust on the board. The reason I am disclosing this to you is that I do feel that I can trust you. You have a good head on your shoulders, and you have business in all areas of the infirmary and are therefore likely to observe something if it was going awry. I mean, have you? Have you noticed anything untoward?'

It was a dreadful choice to face. If this was a

genuine plea for help, then of course Sam would support the chairman. The Reverend Thomas could be an irritating nitpicker, but his heart seemed to be in the right place. On the other hand, what if he was involved with the conspiracy? Certainly, he had given Will no quarter during the laudanum incident. Lipscomb had explained the theological divisions within the church, and Sam doubted that the Reverend Thomas would ever have supported the Oxford Movement. His moral code seemed to echo with Wesleyan principles, and Sam could easily imagine him supporting Orange Order objectives if not their methods. He decided to play it safe until he could be certain that this was no trap.

'I haven't noticed anything amiss, Sir,' he lied. 'But I was unaware that there is a problem, and so I haven't really been looking for one. Like you, I find this most distressing, and I shall certainly be more alert as I go about my business.'

The chairman looked pleased and stood up. 'Thank you, Sam. I appreciate your support and loyalty. A financial scandal would ruin the reputation of the infirmary if it became widespread knowledge, so please be discreet and speak only to me if you discover anything suspicious.' He glanced at the door as though there was someone listening behind it and then stuck out a hand which Sam shook before leaving to return to work.

Later, Sam told Will about the conversation. 'I think he was genuinely upset, Will. I don't think he's in on the fraud.'

'Well, that may be so, but we can't take a risk on it. I think we should keep quiet about what we know and only share it with him once we're certain of his position or if we suddenly need his help.'

Sam agreed that there was no urgent reason to share their knowledge, and he was pleased to observe that his friend had started to exercise a little uncharacteristic caution.

Chapter 12

Preparations

With his position at the infirmary seemingly secure, at least in the short-term, Sam was counting down the days until the shooting party. He visited his father who was recovering well, and Sam was pleased to note that the repairs to the damaged warehouse were proceeding without any hitches.

With little of immediate concern, he increasingly thought about Anne. He missed her and was a little disappointed that he had heard nothing from her since the ball. One evening, a ward round had finished early, and he had rushed out to the jewellery shop on the corner of the High Street. He arrived there just as the proprietor was about to close and spent twenty minutes looking through various lockets trying to find one that he could afford. He had intended to get one containing his portrait, but that would have involved sitting for an artist, and it was far beyond the financial reach of a house surgeon. Instead, Sam had come away with an enamel of a countryside scene set in gold. It had still cost him nearly a pound which had made him wince, but when he thought of the locket dangling from Anne's neck, it felt worth it. Now all he needed was an opportunity to give it to her, and he did not have to wait long.

The day after his visit to the shop, Sam had just climbed the stairs to the first floor when he heard Anne's voice drifting up from the foyer below. He glanced over the banister on the landing and saw her standing with her father at the porter's desk. As he listened, it became apparent that Lord Kirtland had business with the chairman, and Anne was intending to visit some patients while her father was engaged. Sam realized that this was a perfect opportunity to deliver his gift and steal a few moments alone with her. He dodged into one of the wards and pretended to be busy until he saw Lord Kirtland pass by on his way to the chairman's office. Once the man had disappeared, he went down to the ground floor and intercepted Anne as she was leaving the ladies' ward at the southern end of the building. She was startled and then delighted when he appeared in front of her.

'Sam! I was hoping you'd be here.' She lowered her voice. 'Where can we go?'

'Go?' a voice interrupted from behind her as Will appeared from the ward. 'That sounds like misbehaviour to me.' Anne flushed in embarrassment.

'It's alright, Anne,' Sam reassured her. 'This disreputable character is my very good friend, William Perks. He has an unfortunate habit of turning up when he's least wanted,' he laughed.

Will made a theatrical bow. 'I'm very pleased to

make your acquaintance, Madam. I have been wondering why my friend has been so preoccupied, and now that I've seen you, I'm no longer surprised in the very least.'

Anne blushed again, but then shook Will's hand solemnly. 'I am pleased to meet you, Doctor Perks, but I have already heard enough about you. Your reputation proceeds you.' She gave him a stern look, and Will turned red and thought he'd overstepped the mark. However, when she saw his discomfort, she smiled and then burst into fits of laughter. Will realized she was joking at his expense and laughed too when he realized he had been outfoxed.

He turned to Sam. 'My word, she is a feisty one, Samuel, I will wear armour next time.' Then he remembered how the conversation had started and excused himself by claiming he was needed urgently at another ward. As he walked away along the corridor, he pointed to a doorway. 'I'm led to believe that there might be a disused storeroom behind that door. Try in there!' They laughed and followed his advice.

Inside it was dark and Sam opened the drawn curtains to let a crack of light enter the room. The beam fell on Anne's face, and she looked lovely.

'I do like your friend,' she said. 'Will has a wonderful sense of humour.'

'Yes, I'm very fond of him,' Sam replied. 'He's a bit like an older brother.'

Anne looked at him and took his hand. 'I'm so sorry that you haven't heard from me. My mother has been watching me so closely since the ball, and I haven't been able to send you a note. She is so awful sometimes, and I don't know why she has taken against you.'

Sam understood the reason full well, but he did not want to spoil the moment. Instead, he smiled down at her face. 'I am optimistic, Anne. I'm sure I can find a way to win her approval but, in the meantime, we should keep our attachment a secret.' He took the box containing the locket from his pocket and opened it for her to see. 'Here, I have a gift for you. I was unable to afford a portrait, but perhaps this plainer version will be more discreet and survive your mother's scrutiny. It may not bear my face, but you will understand its significance.'

'Oh, Sam, it's beautiful, thank you. I shall never take it off.'

'Here, turn around, I'll help you with it.' Anne turned, and Sam placed the locket around her neck and fastened the clasp. As he did, his fingers brushed against the nape of her neck, and he sensed that her breathing had suddenly increased. She turned and kissed him on the lips. He sensed her desire and felt his own kindle from spark to flame.

'Dear, Sam,' she said, breaking contact. 'I know I am in love with you, but will we ever be together? Properly, I mean.'

'I am sure of it, but only if you are willing to wait for me,' he replied. 'I need time to win your mother's approval.'

'Of course I'll wait, Sam,' she answered, kissing him again. 'But there is something I want to discuss with you, and we haven't much time.' Sam smiled at her ability to change romance into business in a single instant. It was typical of her strong character and the independence which he admired so much.

'What is it?' he asked.

'Well, it's my father. I am rather worried about

him. He has always been a moderate man with liberal views. He is a Whig, you know. However, he has recently been keeping company with some men that I don't particularly like. I think you met some of them at the ball. Lords Kenyon and Vane?'

Sam nodded. This was going to complicate matters he told himself.

'Yes, I was introduced to them. The Duke of Marlborough was there too, along with Sir George Roach. Why? What have you discovered?' he asked her.

'Well, nothing in particular, but I overheard part of a conversation between Lord Kenyon and Lord Vane. It was something to do with Ireland, and it sounded much like a political plot. They were discussing my father. I couldn't hear the details, but I'm worried that they intend to involve him in something that he may later regret. Did you hear anything at the ball that might shed light on what this is all about?'

Sam shook his head. He hated deceiving her, but Anne was headstrong, and he did not want her to get involved and place herself in danger. The less she knew about this, the better.

'I heard nothing specific that would help,' he ventured. 'But I did feel that there was a common purpose when I was invited into their conversation. Would you like me to probe a little to find out?'

'Please do, Sam. It's probably nothing, but it would set my mind at rest.'

'Well, there is another social event coming up that might provide me with an opportunity to make further enquiries. I think I sent you a note explaining that The Duke of Marlborough is holding a shooting party at Blenheim Palace next weekend, and that I have an invitation to stay overnight. Will you be attending too?'

She laughed. 'Yes, I received your note. Blenheim Palace is a spectacular setting for a secret assignation! My father mentioned that he might attend so I will try to come along as well. Actually, I'm rather a good shot so perhaps they'll let me shoot too. Or perhaps I'll load for you.'

Sam laughed. 'I'm not sure that I want you watching my pathetic efforts. I've never even fired a gun before. Mr Wingfield is going to give me some instruction before the event so that I don't embarrass myself.'

She hugged him. 'I'm sure you'll do well, Sam Ansell. But I must be on my way, or I'll be missed.' Sam nodded and his heart sank. They had been together for such a short time, and already it was time for her to leave. He wished they did not have to hide their attachment, but he knew it had to be so. He opened the door a crack and let her out into the corridor after checking that it was clear.

***

A few days before the shoot, Wingfield arrived in his carriage to collect Sam from the infirmary. It was Sam's afternoon off, and he was surprised that they were using a carriage as Wingfield's house was within walking distance.

'We are going to Holywell Common,' his mentor explained. 'If you are going to be a shooting guest of a duke then we need to make sure you are prepared, and that means that you have at least fired a gun once in your life. I thought it best to go to an open space in case your aim is a little wayward. We don't need to create our own patients,' he laughed.

Sam got into the carriage, and his mentor pointed at two boxes. 'I have brought everything that we need.' As the carriage made its way to the common, Wingfield explained what Sam would encounter at Blenheim Palace.

'You will stand with the other shooters in a wide line abreast, with your loader standing behind you. Once you've fired your gun, you can pass it back to him and exchange it for another gun that he will have reloaded for you. I will teach you how to load the weapons as it's important that you know how the gun works, even though it's likely that it will be done for you.'

Sam nodded. He knew his mentor would be as thorough at teaching weaponry as he was at surgery.

Wingfield continued. 'Now, a line of men, known as beaters, will drive the birds through some woods or scrub and onto the line of guns. It's essential that you don't fire too low, or you may shoot one of the beaters walking towards you, and there is no social faux pas worse than that. Make sure the bird is flying high before you fire. It's very important.'

Sam leaned forward to reassure Wingfield that he was listening.

'Now, about the birds. You must ensure that they are yours to shoot. Never shoot a crossing bird. If you shoot one and it lands closer to your neighbour than to you, it will be considered very bad form and seen as ungentlemanly conduct. You will be judged as much by the birds you leave as the ones you kill. Wait until you are certain. The ideal bird is one that is flying directly towards you at height. If in doubt, don't shoot. Now, the only other things to remember are to make sure you congratulate your neighbour if he takes a good shot and do tip your loader with ten shillings at the end of the session. Finally, never point the gun at anyone even if it's unloaded. Keep the barrels pointing down at the ground. These shooting parties used to last three days, but I think the Duke of Marlborough has recently been forced to tighten his belt, so I understand it will be for one day only.'

Sam nodded. 'Yes, I believe it is for one afternoon and one morning session with an overnight stay between.'

At that, the carriage lurched to a halt, and the driver announced they had arrived at Holywell Common. For the next hour, Wingfield taught Sam about the construction of the guns, how they worked and how to load them.

He opened the first box. 'This pair of guns is made by James Purdey, and they are extremely high quality. I am lending them to you because they will never let you down if they are loaded correctly. We have both seen what can happen if a shotgun bursts.'

Sam remembered a recent case and knew exactly what Wingfield was referring to. The patient had survived but had been badly disfigured.

'So, here's how to load one.' He took out a measure that looked a little like a tobacco pipe and showed it to Sam. The measure had an adjustable base so that the volume of the bowl could be changed to suit requirements.

'I have adjusted it for you. It's for measuring your powder and shot. It's important that you use the correct quantities or the gun will burst. First, we add the black powder.' He reached for a powder horn hanging around his neck and poured some until the measure was full.

'We add this down the barrel. Then we insert a wad and tamp it down with this ramrod.' He withdrew the rod from its stowage between the barrels.

'Next, we add an equal measure of shot. Finally, we add another wad and tamp it all down. The gun is reasonably safe now until you add a percussion cap.' He showed Sam the small metal cup-shaped charges and how to fix them onto the nipple under the hammers.

'When the hammer falls onto one of these caps, it detonates, and a flame is transmitted down a tunnel into the main charge which ignites to propel the shot.' He handed Sam the other gun of the pair. 'Right, now show me you've been listening and then we'll talk about shooting.'

Sam went through the loading procedure on both barrels of the second gun exactly as he'd been shown. He fitted percussion caps and let the hammers down gently to rest on the caps.

'Good,' Wingfield said. 'When the gun is handed to you, it should be like that. When you've received it, and it's pointing in a safe direction, you may raise the hammers fully and apply this safety catch here.' He pointed to a small lever on the side of the gun. When you're ready to fire, slide this back and squeeze the first trigger to fire the first barrel. If you miss, just squeeze the second trigger and the second barrel will fire. Apply the safety catch and return the empty weapon to your loader. One last thing: never drop a loaded and cocked gun onto its stock. The safety catches are very good, but they are not infallible. Right then, you seem to have grasped all of that, let's discuss how to hit something.'

They moved away from the carriage so as not to scare the horses, and for the next half hour, Sam learned all about how to aim, when to shoot, and how to judge the lead angle. There were no fowl to shoot at, so it was all theoretical which Sam thought was probably just as well. When they had finished, Wingfield allowed him to discharge both guns so that he knew what to expect. The noise was tremendous, and the kick into his shoulder was ferocious.

Wingfield saw him rubbing his shoulder 'Sorry about that, Samuel, I forgot to tell you to hold the stock very firmly into your shoulder otherwise the recoil hurts.'

An hour later Sam was back in his room with the guns cleaned and stored in their boxes, and the percussion caps and powder secured separately in a metal container. He was as ready for the shoot as he ever would be.

Chapter 13

The Nameless Man

The object of an infirmary is to save life, but occasionally there is a need to understand death too. The governors of the Radcliffe Infirmary had always opposed the use of dead patients for anatomical dissection by medical students, and the matter had been a source of friction between the infirmary management and the university colleges. Whilst dissection was prohibited on moral grounds, the Board did consider it was important to establish why a patient had died, and so postmortem examinations were considered routine especially if there was to be a coroner's inquest. These occurred infrequently, but the day after Sam's shooting lesson, a case came into the infirmary that would require post-mortem work in the Dead Room followed by an inquest shortly after. It was a strange case because the man had no name.

Earlier that evening, Sam had been showing

Will the guns he had borrowed from Wingfield when there was a knock at the door. It was the porter who told the two doctors that an emergency case had been brought in. They rushed down and faced the dreadful spectacle of a middle-aged man with much of his lower face blown away. He looked slightly familiar to Sam, but with such a terrible disfigurement, it would have been difficult even for the victim's mother to identify him.

'Gunshot wound?' Will asked.

Sam looked at the damage. 'I would say so. And a large-calibre ball by the look of it.'

'But do we admit him?' Will asked. Sam knew what lay behind his friend's question. The infirmary rules stated that an accident victim should be admitted only if they had a realistic chance of survival. Where that was not the case, the patient could be treated for pain but then given into the care of friends or relatives to manage their passing.

'I doubt he will survive for long' Sam whispered in case the man could hear them. 'Does anyone know who he is?'

A nurse had been present when the patient arrived, and she shook her head. 'He was brought in by a farmer who was on his way home in a cart. He was found like this at the side of the road.'

'Well, we can't discharge him in this condition so he'll have to be formally admitted,' Will declared. 'The secretary will complain, but it's my decision to make as the House Apothecary.' He looked at Sam and winked. "A surgical case, Mr Ansell, but I will assist you if you wish.'

Sam feigned a glare at his friend. He knew why they were being slightly light-hearted about the situation. When faced with an injury and suffering like this there often nothing else to do but introduce a little graveyard humour. It kept them detached from their patients and allowed objectivity to inform their medical decisions.

The two men worked on the unconscious man for nearly two hours before he eventually died. They took him up to the operating room where Sam attempted to use a flap of skin and tissue from the side of the man's neck and shoulder to fashion some kind of protection for the missing part of the man's lower face. The blood had stopped oozing from the wound, but it was all too much for their patient, and the man expired before Sam had finished stitching around the flap.

'That was a fine effort, Sam. I have never seen anyone attempt surgery like that before,' Will remarked afterwards with a great deal of admiration.

'Well, I hope I won't be criticized for exceeding my capabilities, but by the time Wingfield or Cleobury could have been called, he would have died anyway. It was me or nothing.'

'You did your best for him, but we'll need to inform the coroner because it looks like foul play. I'll send a runner to fetch Whiting to make the arrangements.'

'Yes, while you do that, I'll get him moved into the Dead Room for the post-mortem examination. I'll also get the nurse to bring up his effects for the coroner to see.'

While Will was away, Sam and the porter managed to move the man onto one of the tables in the Dead Room and cover him with a shroud. The nurse appeared with a small box of effects and left it by the dead man's feet. Sam looked inside and picked up some spectacles. As he studied them, he became aware that his friend had returned and was standing in the doorway. Sam looked up at the apothecary.

'I know this man,' he whispered. 'He's the one who followed me the other day.'

***

Sam awoke the following morning feeling tired and distracted. He tried to busy himself on the wards, but he found it difficult to concentrate as he mulled over the previous evening's events. As soon as Sam had seen the unusual spectacles, he was certain that they belonged to the man who had followed him on Fish Street. But who was he? Who had killed him and why? He had discussed it with Will after they had finished work, but neither of them had been able to come up with a plausible explanation. The old woman had told Sam that the mysterious Colonel Fairman was habitually armed, and the two doctors wondered whether he might have been responsible. There was no evidence, however, although both men agreed that it was an idea worth pursuing. In the end, Sam had agreed to return to Fish Street to see whether the old woman could provide anything new. He planned to go in the afternoon and was relieved to note that it was not a day on which Fairman habitually collected his mail. Sam thought of the dead man lying under a shroud in the Dead Room. The last thing he wanted was an unplanned encounter with the Colonel in the quiet backstreets of Oxford.

While Sam was worrying about the afternoon's activities, relief came in the form of Mr Cleobury who had been asked to conduct the post-mortem examination of the nameless man. Sam played no part in the procedure as he had been operating on the patient when the man had expired. However, he asked the consultant if he could observe his work as it was the one area of Sam's medical training that Wingfield had skipped over lightly. Mr Cleobury agreed, and Sam realized that he intended to capitalize on the exercise when the Consultant's dresser joined Sam as a fellow pupil under instruction. Sam did not ask the chap how much he was paying to be Cleobury's apprentice, but he thought it would probably be extremely costly.

The autopsy started at eleven o' clock and was finished within an hour. As he began, Mr Cleobury raised the sheet to reveal the man's head and glanced at Sam when he saw the facial surgery from the night before. For a moment, the consultant looked as though he was about to unleash a barrage of his customary criticism, and Sam braced himself. However, Cleobury seemed to change his mind, and he addressed them both in measured terms as he began his examination.

'Gentlemen, the first thing you should record is any disfigurement caused by medical treatment such as this surgical work here.' He pointed to Sam's efforts from the previous night but made no comment. He then pulled the shroud off the victim completely. The man's body was naked, pale and stiff, and it made for a pitiful sight.

'Once that is complete, you can start looking for any non-medical damage. Look for anything that bruises or breaks the skin no matter how small. Record everything and decide at the end whether it's relevant. Gunshot injuries, and most stab wounds, are easy to see but some trauma is not.' He rolled the man towards him onto his side and peered over to inspect the man's back.

'Check the front and the back of the body because many wounds will not pierce both sides of a victim. Pay particular attention to areas covered with hair although that is not going to be a problem for this gentleman.' He pointed at the man's bald head and then walked to a trolley and picked up a scalpel and a saw.

'Right, we must examine inside the head. We are looking for any damage or bleeding in the brain which can't be seen when the head is examined from the outside.'

Cleobury showed the two men how to use a scalpel and a saw to cut through the skull and then remove the brain, which he placed on some scales. He weighed it and then sliced through it in several places but found no sign of damage. He recorded his findings and then replaced the brain and sewed the skin back over the top of the patient's skull. He then moved on to inspect the man's lower face. He undid Sam's careful stitchwork and revealed the damage caused by the ball.

'There is extensive damage here which I would assess as being caused by a large calibre pistol or rifle. The ball passed through the lower jaw from just below the right ear and emerged from the mouth. It is possible the man was running away and was looking back when the shot was fired.' He turned to his notebook and scribbled furiously.

When Cleobury had finished writing, he looked up at the two observers. 'Finally, we should examine all the major organs. We start by entering the chest cavity from the front by cutting through the cartilage where the ribs meet the sternum.' He demonstrated the incision and invited them closer as he lifted the man's ribcage and then identified and removed all the major organs before weighing them. 'As you can see, they are all normal,' he announced, eventually.

He replaced the organs inside the cavity and then stitched up the front of the man's torso.

'Make sure everything is returned and try to make the stitching as neat as possible. Some relatives insist on viewing the body, and the coroner is certain to look at the inquest.'

Cleobury began washing his hands in a bowl of water. 'We seem to be done here. The cause of death is obvious, and aside from the gunshot wound to this man's face, there is nothing else of a suspicious nature. Now, have either of you any questions? No? Very well, that's it. You may go, but please might I have a word with you, Sam?'

Sam made ready and consoled himself with the thought that his admonishment was to be in private. However, once the dresser had left the room, Mr Cleobury looked at Sam with a degree of respect that was new.

'The work you did on this man's face last night was really first class,' he said to Sam's astonishment. 'But it was never going to work. Putrefaction would have slowly finished him off within two weeks so his death from shock was a blessing really. I believe that a day will eventually arrive where such reconstructive surgery will become possible, but it is not today, Sam. Our resources are constrained, and I do think it would have been better to apply dressings and let nature take its course, though I completely understand that you were trying your best for him. You have a bright future, Sam, but pace yourself a little as it's a long road ahead of you. Wingfield has taught you well.' He paused, but there was nothing else. 'We should find some lunch,' he added, reaching for his coat.

***

The remainder of that day was slow to pass, and it was after four o' clock before Sam was able to leave the infirmary. Nobody had come forward to identify the man, and the inquest had been arranged for the following day.

As he turned into Fish Street, Sam looked around carefully but was unable to detect anybody following him. He made his way down the road towards the side street where the old woman lived. It was easy to find again; he just needed to follow the neighbourhood stink which had become far worse in the hot July sunshine. Eventually, he arrived at her door. He knew it was the correct address because it was the only one with a clean doorstep. He knocked, and a moment later she appeared looking anxious and fearful.

'Oh, it's you,' she whispered, peering down the street to see if Sam had been followed. 'Please go away, Sir. I cannot talk to you.' She tried to close the door, but Sam wedged it open with his foot.

'Wait, Madam. I mean you no harm. I just have a couple of questions to ask. I will pay you well and then leave you alone. Shall we say another half-crown?'

At Sam's mention of money, the old woman stopped trying to crush his foot and looked behind him again. 'Well, not out here,' she said. 'It's no longer safe for either of us.'

Sam entered the doorway. The house was

barely furnished, but it was spotlessly clean. The hallway was tiny and just big enough for the two of them to stand. He felt uncomfortable by her proximity, but she seemed unconcerned and made no effort to invite him further inside.

'What is it that you want?' she asked.

'Well, will you tell me what has happened to make you so afraid? Have you been threatened since I was last here?'

'Well, it's that soldier man with the guns. He's been here asking questions like you.'

'Have you seen anyone else?' She looked at him slyly, but Sam was tired with her games. 'There is no more money, Madam, just half a crown. Please tell me what has happened since we first spoke.'

She seemed to realize that Sam had reached the limit of his monetary enticements and sighed. 'Very well, Sir. About half an hour after you last called, another man appeared and started to ask questions about you. It seemed to me as though he had been following you.'

'Can you describe him?' Sam interjected.

'Yes, he was losing his hair, and he wore a most peculiar pair of spectacles.'

Sam nodded. 'Go on.'

'He already knew about the soldier and was more interested in your visits. He asked me about your purpose, so I told him about our conversation concerning the soldier man and his regular visits to the widow in the backyard.' She gestured with her hand towards the rear of the house. 'That was all we said.'

'Where did he go after your conversation?'

'Well, I saw him go into the backyard so he must have spoken with the woman at Number 6B. He wasn't there very long, and I saw him walking off up Fish Street.'

'And what happened next? What about the soldier?'

'Well, he arrived yesterday morning, He went to Number 6B and then appeared here and threatened me with violence for directing the bald man to the widow's house. He told me that if anyone else came around asking questions about him, then I should let him know.'

Sam tried to ask the next question as casually as possible. 'And did the soldier mention me or just the bald man?'

'Well, he didn't mention you directly, but he seemed to know that it wasn't just the bald man with the glasses that had been there. The widow probably told him about you. I promise you I didn't volunteer anything more than I've told you. I don't like being threatened by armed men, but I do like gentlemen calling me, "madam" and I do like receiving your coin, so I kept my promise to you.'

Sam smiled at her. He liked this toothless old lady. 'Well, Madam, you've been very helpful, but I don't want to endanger you further so I will take my leave. That soldier is a dangerous man, so be careful who you speak to and make sure you don't cross him. This is for your trouble and for your continued silence.' He gave her half a crown and then added a shilling. She curtseyed awkwardly in the cramped space of her hallway and cackled toothlessly when she almost fell on him. Sam opened the door slightly and confirmed the street was empty. Ten minutes later, he was in the safety of the High Street.

As he returned to the infirmary, Sam thought

about what he had learned. The balding man had indeed been following him, but if he was not part of the conspiracy, who was he working for? Sam's shadow had paid with his life after questioning the widow about Fairman. Sam had attempted to do the same, and although the widow had hidden inside, if she had seen enough of Sam's face to be able to provide Fairburn with a description, then he might now be in considerable danger too.

The shooting party was approaching rapidly, and Sam was quite certain that it would provide an excellent opportunity to discover more. However, was it safe to attend? Sam considered the question carefully and decided that he was already compromised. Furthermore, it seemed inconceivable that the Duke of Marlborough would allow murder to occur on his estate. His reputation was just too great. No, if Sam was going to be dealt with, then it would happen in the backstreets of Oxford, not in public at Blenheim Palace. Besides, he knew Anne would be there too, and that seemed like an opportunity not to be missed.

Chapter 14

The Afternoon Shoot

The local nobility had always regarded the Duke of Marlborough's shoot as an important social event, but the party's shortened duration attracted some raised eyebrows amongst those that gathered at Blenheim Palace to enjoy their host's hospitality. The Duke's financial difficulties were a popular topic for whispered gossip, but for those who had become bored by such old news, there was always the man's marital difficulties to dissect. The Duke had married Lady Susan Stewart in 1791, but his financial difficulties had proved too much for her, and she now resided permanently in London. The Duke was unabashed and had started a relationship with a local woman called Matilda Glover. She was installed at the Palace as his companion and had produced several illegitimate children. Nobody was quite sure of the exact number, but it was said to be as many as six. The extent of the

Duke's illicit brood made a popular subject for idle speculation by visitors, and the Duke's guests that day were no exception. However, amongst those enjoying his generosity, there were also some present with an altogether more malign purpose.

Wingfield had kindly given Sam the use of his carriage, and the journey to Blenheim had taken nearly two hours. He knew he was getting close to his destination as scrubland gave way to neat estate parkland ringed by iron railings containing brooding cattle and ruminating sheep. Closer still, there were herds of deer, and the woodland floor became alive with colourful pheasants, pecking at the ground, but ever alert for threats. Sam knew that danger would soon come calling on the birds in the form of beaters and armed men, and he wondered if a similar existential danger lurked waiting for him. As he drew closer to the palace, he began to question his decision to attend and whether he was making a costly mistake.

The palace stood majestically at the end of a long drive, and the arrival arrangements had been well organized. As soon as the coach pulled up, Sam was met by three servants. One greeted him and showed him to his room deep within the palace; his bag followed on, carried by another; and the guns went with a third to the armoury where they were to be checked and taken to the shoot for him. He was told that lunch would be eaten outside.

The Duke might have been tightening his belt financially, but there was no sign of it in the splendid buffet that he served to his guests that day. It was a feast, and it was laid out in the Temple of Diana, a large folly that was a short walk from the rear of the Palace. As Sam approached, he saw several familiar faces who were already eating in small groups. He immediately noticed Anne who was looking radiant and standing with her father talking to a man that was unfamiliar. Sam was relieved that there was no sign of Lady Kirtland, and he was delighted when Anne saw him and smiled. She was wearing his locket around her neck, but she looked slightly strained, and her smile was a little forced. He went over and greeted them both. Lord Kirtland smiled and introduced him to the stranger.

'Hello, Samuel, I'm very glad to see you are here.' He turned and addressed the man at his side. 'Judge, this gentleman is Samuel Ansell; he's the brave chap I was telling you about who saved my daughter's life.' He looked at Sam. 'Samuel, may I introduce you to His Lordship Justice Hector Brontley KC. He is a High Court Judge who is visiting Oxford for the next quarterly assizes.'

The Judge studied Sam closely, and for a moment, Sam pitied those who might fall under the man's stare. It was a look that the Judge might adopt on those occasions when he placed the black cap on his head and delivered the awful judgement of the law. It was deliberate, practiced, and intimidating.

'Mr Ansell,' he said in a gravelly voice. 'I have heard all about this act of bravery. It is a pleasure to meet you.' He put out a hand. Sam bowed and shook the man's hand. His grip was firm and conveyed the unspoken message that this was a man who was not to be trifled with. The Judge's name seemed familiar, but Sam could not remember why.

'Are you a regular shooter, Lord Brontley?' Sam asked when his hand was released.

'I am not, Sir. I am here on other business, but

the Duke kindly invited me to take lunch with the shooting party. I have meetings to attend this evening,' he added cryptically.

Sam nodded, and there was an awkward silence before the situation was rescued by a familiar face. It was Lord Vane. His arm was no longer in Sam's sling, but he held it stiffly as he walked over to them.

'Good afternoon, Lord Brontley, I see you've met Mr Ansell.' He nodded a greeting to Lord Kirtland and Anne. 'Mr Ansell is a fine surgeon; he fixed me up in a jiffy when I popped my shoulder. However, I'm afraid it's still a bit too sore to shoot so I'll be missing out on the sport on this occasion.' He looked meaningfully at Sam as an unspoken message was transmitted between them. Vane wanted Sam to have no doubts that he was still on the hook.

The Judge was impassive. 'Brave and talented, Mr Ansell. Useful for all manner of endeavours, eh Vane?' he said meaningfully to Lord Vane who nodded his understanding but offered no explanation. Sam did not understand the cryptic exchange, but he knew it could only be something bad. Next to Sam, Vane was ready to feed Sam's doubts.

'Did you bring a man to load for you, Mr Ansell?' he asked pleasantly.

Sam reddened and shook his head. 'I'm afraid not, Lord Vane, The porter at the infirmary was required for his duties so I have… I have no man with me.'

Lord Vane smiled at Sam's lie. He knew the truth. 'I thought you might not, but I have my valet with me, and he could load for you if you like. I'm sure he won't mind. It's the least I can do to repay you,' he asserted reasonably.

The idea that Vane's man would be responsible for loading his guns filled Sam with dread. Wingfield had explained that it only took a little too much powder to burst a breech with disastrous consequences for the firer. If Vane wanted to orchestrate an accident then this was surely it. But how could he refuse the offer? By his own admission, Sam had nobody to load for him. Vane's offer would seem generous to those listening. It had been made in public, and Sam would seem inexplicably churlish to turn it down. He had no choice but to accept. Vane nodded and looked very pleased with himself. Meanwhile, Judge Brontley seemed to have grown tired with the small talk.

'Miss Kirtland, Mr Ansell, would you please excuse us for a moment; there is a confidential matter that I need to discuss with Lord Kirtland and Lord Vane before the shooting begins. It's parliamentary business of a constitutional nature,' he added as though that would excuse his bad manners. However, Sam did not mind being excluded because it left him alone with Anne.

'Certainly, Lord Brontley,' Sam replied. 'I shall walk with Miss Kirtland,' he said, guiding her away from the group.

Once they were out of earshot, the reason for her forced smile became apparent. 'Do you see what I mean about my father? It's all about clandestine meetings and intrigue at the moment. Who was that Judge and what business has he with my father? Look!' she said, nodding towards the far side of the gathering. 'Now they've been joined by the Duke of Marlborough and Lord Kenyon.'

Sam glanced across at the group of men. They were all leaning in to avoid being overheard, but they quickly restored a normal spacing when the Duke's companion, Miss Glover, walked over to them and intruded on their discussion. It did look highly suspicious.

Sam looked at Anne. 'Yes, I agree it's very strange behaviour. Are you staying the night here?'

'No, father has business in Oxford early tomorrow, so we will be leaving after this afternoon's shooting.'

Sam was unable to hide his disappointment. 'That's a pity. I was hoping we might steal away somewhere to spend some time together.' He laughed and gestured towards the palace. 'I'm sure there must be lots of disused storerooms in this building!'

She smiled but was still worried. 'What do you think is going on, Sam?' she asked.

'I don't know, but I'm staying here tonight, and I could try to find out a bit more. That Judge mentioned some business this evening. Perhaps that has something to do with it.'

Sam was about to say more, but he was interrupted by the Duke Of Marlborough who rang a small bell for silence and addressed his guests.

'My lords, ladies and gentlemen. Welcome to Blenheim Palace and thank you for attending today. In a moment, my head gamekeeper will address the men on shooting matters, but in the meantime, Miss Glover will now escort the ladies up to the palace for games, reading and music. Please enjoy your afternoon with us.'

As the ladies began to gather, Anne looked up at Sam. 'I'm sorry, Sam, I must go. I will try to come to the infirmary next week so keep a look out for me.' Sam wanted to take her hand but was forced to bow instead. As she walked away, Sam became aware of a servant waiting patiently beside him.

'Mr Ansell? I'm William Gasser, Lord Vane's valet. I'm here to load for you, Sir.'

Sam turned to look at the man. He searched the man's face carefully. He had an open and honest appearance, but Sam detected a whiff of apprehension about him. Was it just that the man was loading for a stranger or had he received more malign instructions? Sam could not be sure either way, and the lack of certainty preyed on his mind and stimulated the darkest corners of his imagination. He was in an impossible situation, and he knew he would probably spend most of the time that afternoon watching Gasser load his guns than searching for game birds. He sighed.

'Mr Gasser. Yes, thank you for helping me.' He lowered his voice. 'This is my first shoot, so if you have any advice when we're out in the field please let me know.'

The valet was unused to being addressed so informally but nodded and was about to say more when the Duke's gamekeeper interrupted them to give his briefing for the afternoon drive. Sam listened carefully as the man told the guests where they would shoot and reminded them of some of the safety aspects. Much of it was just as Wingfield had taught him. The gamekeeper finished with a stern reminder.

'And, gentlemen, please can we ensure that there are no low birds taken today. We don't want any accidents. If you'd like to follow me, your guns have been placed on the line ready for you.'

The men followed the gamekeeper down a path and into a field with woods beyond. As they made their way, Sam noticed that Gasser walked with a limp and seemed to be in considerable discomfort. The man's lower leg did not look quite right, and Sam wondered if he had a prosthetic foot. He knew that Lord Vane had been a soldier with active service and wondered if his valet had been one too.

'Gasser,' he said, 'do you mind if I ask about your leg? Is it giving you some trouble? I might be able to help you.'

'I don't think you'll be able to help me, Mr Ansell. You see, I have an artificial foot from my army days. I served with Lord Vane. I was his batman during the Napoleonic Wars. In fact, I was wounded, had my foot amputated, and was discharged from the army; yet His Lordship kept me on as his valet, even so.'

'Yes, I wondered if you had lost part of your leg. Is it giving you problems?'

'It certainly is, Sir, and it's gradually getting worse. I'm worried that I may not be able to work for much longer. Lord Vane has indicated that his patience will only last for so long before I have to go elsewhere.'

Despite his concern over the safety of his guns that afternoon, Sam felt sorry for the man and decided that he could help. 'I'm a surgeon at the Radcliffe Infirmary, Gasser,' he explained. 'Would you like me to have a look for you? It might be that I can get you a new prosthetic that is more comfortable, but I need to examine you first.'

The valet looked grateful. 'That's very kind of you, Sir. When should I attend the infirmary?'

'Well, there's no point in delaying. Why don't I take a look today after we've finished here,' he replied as they arrived at the bottom of the slope. The valet nodded, and the two men surveyed the site of the afternoon's game drive.

The line stretched for about 200 yards with a shooter positioned every 20 yards or so. The edge of the woods lay to the front, and Sam could hear the occasional call from the birds which lurked, unseen on the woodland floor. Gasser led Sam to a position near to one end, and Sam was relieved to see Wingfield's valuable guns propped up on a stand waiting for him.

The valet set about loading the first weapon using the adjustable scoop that Wingfield had demonstrated to Sam.

'Do you mind, Gasser?' Sam asked and inspected the scoop to check that it was set for the correct volume of powder for Wingfield's Purdeys.

'You can never be too careful,' he explained, anxious not to hurt the man's feelings.

The valet looked at him and very carefully and deliberately said, 'You need have no fear, Sir. I would never allow myself to overcharge a gun, no matter the circumstances.' It was a strange thing to say, but Sam understood that the servant was trying to reassure him of his intentions. He didn't press the man to explain why he felt it necessary to provide that reassurance, but Sam accepted it at face value. When Gasser handed him the first gun, hammers down and loaded, Sam received it without any doubts concerning the weapon's safety. It was one less thing to worry about, which was just as well because the loading procedures were only the start of Sam's troubles.

As he waited for the start of the afternoon drive, Sam felt a little nervous, but it was only moments later that the Gamekeeper blew a loud whistle, and the shooting commenced. Sam cocked the hammers and waited for a target. From within the wood, he could hear makeshift drums and shouting as an unseen line of hired men and boys made their way into the wood from the other side. It did not take long before the first bird emerged, and there was a loud retort from Sam's right as Lord Kenyon brought it down with a single shot. Sam remembered to congratulate his neighbour but was interrupted by Gasser.

'This one's yours, Sir.'

Sam looked ahead as a brightly coloured cock pheasant flew up out of the wood directly in front of him.

He fired, missed, fired and missed again. He cursed as he handed the empty gun back to Gasser who remained impassive as he handed Sam the other loaded weapon. From his left, Sam's neighbour offered his commiserations and tried to provide Sam with a feeble excuse about there being a tricky wind. Unfortunately, there is only a finite number of excuses that can be made before the shooter's lack of skill is left as the only inescapable conclusion. Sam's neighbour did his best to spare Sam's blushes, but after Sam had missed five consecutive birds, the man fell silent and pretended not to notice when Sam missed the sixth. It was a humiliation that Sam felt sure had been noticed by everyone present and especially by his two neighbours. However, just when all credibility seemed lost, Sam was rescued by Gasser.

'If I may say, sir?' He lowered his voice. 'I don't wish to be impertinent, but might I suggest you try two things: keep both eyes open and look between the two barrels as you point the weapon just ahead of the bird.'

The effect was transformational, and Sam's next bird fell to a single shot. He felt much relieved and bagged another before the whistle blew to signal the end of the session. He handed the spent gun to his loader and smiled.

'Thank you, Gasser, that was excellent advice. You saved the day.'

'It's a pleasure, Sir, and very nice shooting at the end, if I may say so.'

Sam remembered Gasser's foot. He thought it would be better to avoid drawing attention to Gasser's impairment, and the armoury sounded like it might be in a suitably discreet part of the palace.

'I haven't forgotten your foot,' he told the valet. 'I'll come with you now, and we'll find a room suitable for my examination. Don't worry, we'll make sure it's out of sight of any gossipers.'

Gasser nodded gratefully and gathered up the guns. As they started back up the hill towards the palace, Lord Kenyon joined them looking very pleased with himself. It soon became apparent that he had been hatching a joke at Sam's expense and was itching to share it.

'Struggling there a bit, Ansell.'

Sam was unsure whether it was a question or an observation. 'Hello, Lord Kenyon. Yes, I was a bit rusty at the start,' he said, trying to conceal the true extent of his ineptitude.

Lord Kenyon started to laugh, and eventually his joke burst forth. 'Well, I thought you were out for a duck until those last two birds,' he spluttered between guffaws of mirth. Sam could tell that Kenyon had been planning to wield his ambiguous cricketing analogy for most of the afternoon, and his irritation rose. It was a calculated effort to belittle him, to put him in his place. However, Sam did not want the peer to see that he had succeeded in getting under his skin, so he smiled politely and waited for Lord Kenyon's moment of great hilarity to subside.

Eventually, Kenyon's laughter dried up, and his face suddenly became serious. He looked behind to see whether Gasser could overhear their exchange, but the valet had fallen behind a little and seemed to be concentrating on his load. Lord Kenyon lowered his voice. His warning was delivered less dramatically than Lord Vane's, but it was still menacing.

'Look Ansell, you've been warned several times to keep your nose out of other people's business, but here you are again. Don't you care about the welfare of the people around you like your father, Anne Kirtland, or Dr Perks? By the way, how is your father? I understand there was a nasty fire at his business premises the other night. They do say that you can't be too careful. But perhaps you're not being careful enough. Go back to your hospital and stick to your own business. There's nothing for you here. You're out of your depth.'

Before Sam had a chance to reply, the two men reached the end of the path, and Kenyon stalked off with a curt nod. He had given his warning, and there was nothing further to add. Sam turned to Gasser who had caught up, and they went to find somewhere where Sam could examine the man's limb. The threats were becoming serious, and Sam still had a dinner and another shoot to endure before he could escape back to the relative safety of the infirmary. He thought of Anne's concerns about her father and his promise to find out what was going on. The dinner seemed like a good place to make some gentle enquiries and there was safety in numbers. However, it would be a nervous few hours, and he hoped his bedroom door could be locked from the inside.

Chapter 15

The Duke's Dinner

Dinner at Blenheim Palace. The very words made Sam realize just how far he had strayed from the familiar warmth of his family home down by the Oxford Canal. He felt like a stranger at the Duke's table, and he decided he preferred the humdrum of infirmary life to the pretence that he was leading that weekend. As he surveyed the fine table with its pressed linen, silver plate and wigged footmen, he could not resist making a comparison with the awful conditions of those living in the backyards just off Fish Street. Sam was no radical, but he nonetheless found it astonishing that anyone could think that the Duke was in any way financially impoverished. He glanced at the other end of the table and could see the man dressed in his best finery sitting between Lords Kenyon and Vane. The three men were deep in conversation, and Sam would have paid handsomely to hear what they were saying.

As he reflected on his position at the Duke's table, Sam took comfort from the knowledge that he had improved the quality of life for at least one individual that he had met during his visit to the palace. He had examined Gasser's amputated leg in a small storeroom next to the armoury. The long-term healing process had caused the stump to shrink such that it no longer fitted properly inside the cup of Gasser's prosthetic foot. The sloppy fit was causing the chafing and pain that were impairing the man's mobility although the root cause of the problem was the choice of surgical procedure. While Sam was examining the leg, the manservant explained that his amputation had been performed in the field after he had been wounded at the Battle of Waterloo. Sam thought that the military surgeon had probably been rushed and had made a bad job of the operation. Modern techniques would have suggested that the leg be removed from just below the knee whereas Gasser's limb had been removed just above the ankle. This was the underlying cause of the man's problems which Sam was unable to fix without further risky surgery. However, a new prosthetic would certainly help to keep the man working, and he had instructed Gasser to make an appointment to see him at the infirmary. He had yet to decide how to persuade the chairman to fund the man's new artificial limb.

As Sam considered Gasser's foot, he became aware that the man sitting to his left was addressing him. His name was Canon James Marshall, and he was the special advisor to the Bishop of Oxford. He was a lanky individual with a long nose that reminded Sam of a plague mask. His interest in the proceedings did not take long to establish.

'It's Mr Ansell, isn't it?'

'It is, Canon.' Sam held out a hand which the cleric took gingerly as though he was shaking the hand of the devil.

'And did you enjoy your sport this afternoon?'

'I did, Sir,' Sam lied. 'The weather was perfect, and the grounds are beautifully landscaped.'

The Canon studied Sam thoughtfully, much like the Judge had done earlier in the day. Was he being assessed?

'You look like a well-informed gentleman,' Marshall said changing the subject. 'What are your views on the Oxford Movement, Mr Ansell?' Sam was instantly alert and realized that this was a test of opinion that he needed to pass. He remembered what Lipscomb had told him about the matter being contentious and decided that the majority of those at the table would probably hold anti-Catholic views. He decided to herd with the majority of those sat around him.

'Well, Canon. It is more than two hundred and fifty years since King Henry VIII established the English Church, and it has become deeply rooted in English traditions. I'm no expert in ecclesiastical customs, but it seems to me that the Oxford Movement is an attempt to take us back into the Roman Catholic Church and to a time when religious violence and hatred were commonplace. I believe it might even hold implications for our Royal Family and our unwritten constitution.'

Sam was unsure about the accuracy of the constitutional implications, but the Canon's face told Sam that he had succeeded in convincing the cleric that his convictions were deeply held and lay on the correct side.

'Exactly, Mr Ansell. Exactly.' The cleric leaned forward conspiratorially. 'Most of those present this evening share your views. I know there are some that believe you are opposed to our protestant project, but I think that might be a mistaken opinion. Anyway, Sir, your religious views seem sound enough to me, although I have a particular interest in such matters, of course.' he laughed. The Canon was about to say more when their host stood up and brought the dinner to a close with a short speech and a toast to the King. As the ladies made their way to their sitting room, Sam left the cleric and went to the drawing room where he was intercepted by the Duke of Marlborough.

'One moment, Samuel, I'm glad I caught you. In fact, I've been wanting to have a word with you all day. In a moment, a few of us will be having a business meeting in the library. It should last no more than half an hour. I'm afraid that you are not invited, but I wanted to reassure you that it is nothing personal. It's just that our business is confidential. It shouldn't take us very long to conclude matters, and then we'll be out for port and billiards. I do hope you'll wait for us.' Sam nodded and was about to ask about the meeting when a man wearing a red army uniform appeared at the Duke's side. He had missed the shoot and the dinner, and he apologized to his host in a thick Irish accent. It was Colonel W B Fairman.

I'm sorry, Your Grace, my carriage shed a wheel, and it has taken several hours to have it repaired and complete my journey.'

The Duke waved his apology away. 'That's alright, Colonel. Let me introduce you to Mr Ansell, House Surgeon at the Radcliffe Infirmary. Samuel, this is Colonel William Fairman.'

The hairs on the back of Sam's neck stood up as he looked at the Colonel and remembered the shocking gunshot wound on the face of the nameless man. He could easily imagine Fairman behind the trigger. The Colonel was aged about forty and had a vicious scar down one side of his face. His stare was cold and unforgiving, and he oozed evil intent as he studied Sam's face. It felt like Fairman was searching him for signs of guilt or perhaps some vulnerability that might be exploited. It was extremely unsettling, and Sam had to force himself to appear relaxed. Fairman's presence was unexpected, and the fact that he was a guest of the Duke was worrying. What was he doing at Blenheim Palace? Sam tried hard to conceal his discomfort and stuck out a hand. The Colonel took it, but his expression suggested that he had found enough in Sam's face to judge him as an imposter.

'Good evening, Mr Ansell. I have heard a great deal about you recently,' he said without explanation.

Sam tried to remain calm. 'Well, you have the better of me, Sir,' he said, trying to sound casual. Had the Canon already briefed the others on Sam's political beliefs?

'I have heard that you are brave and hold firm views on certain political and religious matters,' Fairman continued, 'but we will see about that,' he added, leaving ample space for doubt. Sam felt as though he was trapped in the coils of a giant serpent as Fairman heaped innuendo onto implication. He was clearly trying to intimidate Sam, and he was succeeding. The Duke shifted uncomfortably.

'Well now, Colonel, we must go to our meeting. We will be along to see Mr Ansell later.' He turned to Sam. 'We won't be long, Samuel.'

Sam watched them leave, and he was soon the only occupant remaining in the drawing room. He had no intention of waiting; he felt excluded and wanted to find out what was going on and then leave as quickly as possible. He waited a few minutes, and then crept along the long corridor to see if he could hear what was being said. He was in luck. The library was served by two sets of glazed double doors, but only the pair at the front had been closed to the corridor. The rear ones had been left ajar, and Sam could hear the discussion.

The Duke was standing at the front with the others facing him in two rows of seats. Sam was disturbed to discover that they were arguing about him.

'I think Ansell is to be trusted,' the Duke said. 'In fact, I think he's just the man for the job. Canon Marshall pressed him this evening, and he seems to have opinions that chime with ours.' Sam could just see the back of the cleric's head nodding in agreement.

'Well, I disagree, Your Grace.' Fairman stood up to emphasize his point. 'I've heard that someone's been snooping around the infirmary asking questions that might embarrass us: questions about the canal shares. I don't trust him at all.'

There was an indistinct mixture of grumbling and support from the audience. Sam thought it sounded like opinion was split roughly half and half.

'Well, see here,' said the Duke, 'Roach has been watching the situation at the infirmary and has seen nothing about Ansell to concern us. It's the man Perks that we need to worry about. All we want from Ansell is his help to raise more funds. We don't need to involve him in anything beyond that.'

This time, the murmurs sounded more

agreeable to the Duke's opinion. However, Fairman was having none of it.

'Listen,' he insisted. 'My sources tell me Ansell has been to our mailing address and started asking questions. I don't know for certain how he managed to find that address but it's possible he's been searching around in the infirmary files. And that Crosley man. Where's his notebook? Has Ansell got it? That book could cause us a lot of damage if we don't find it.' This time, it was obvious from the angry murmurs that opinion had swung firmly behind the Colonel. The Duke reluctantly allowed a vote which was won handsomely by those supporting Sam's exclusion. Sam was officially *persona non grata*. But at least he knew it.

Someone else then spoke, but it was too quiet for Sam to hear what was said. He was about to lean further towards the door when a hand was placed on his shoulder. He almost called out in shock, but when he turned it was Gasser standing behind him with a finger to his lips.

'I think that if you want to know what's going on in there, you need to come with me where we can talk. It's much safer, Mr Ansell,' he whispered. 'Follow me, Sir.'

Sam followed the valet as he limped along the corridor to a dark part of the Palace where the oil lamps were left unlit, and the rooms were cold and unused. He led Sam into a small reception room where Sam could make out that some of the furniture was covered in dust sheets. Gasser removed two small chairs from a stack and put them close together. He gestured to Sam and sat opposite him. Sam looked at his pocket watch.

'We have ten minutes,' he whispered. 'We must

be quick.' William Gasser nodded and gave Sam an astonishing description of what he had witnessed.

'You have been very kind to me today which is the reason that I am trusting you with my account. You were correct to check the guns this afternoon. I had been instructed to charge them with a quantity of powder that I thought might easily have caused a breech to burst. Lord Vane has always treated me very well, and there are many other senior officers who would have abandoned me after I lost my lower leg. Without Lord Vane's support, I might well have ended up in the workhouse along with many other of my wounded comrades. But I draw the line at murder especially of someone who wanted to help me. And what I am about to tell you has split my loyalty between His Lordship and my Sovereign.'

'Sovereign?' Sam repeated. 'Is this to do with His Majesty the King?'

Gasser shook his head. 'Not yet,' he replied, 'but it is to do with the Royal Family and Princess Victoria. Please let me explain.' Sam leaned back to let the man finish.

'About six weeks ago, Lord Vane started an extended visit to Lord Kirtland's manor house, and I was asked to accompany him. While I was there, several other guests arrived, many of them here tonight. In fact, this is the fourth time they have all met. Previously, it has always been at Lord Kirtland's.'

Sam leaned forward. 'Go on,' he whispered.

The valet listened for any noises coming from the corridor and when it remained silent, he continued.

'On the second occasion, they were in Lord Kirtland's drawing room, and I listened in like you were doing this evening. They were talking about

Princess Victoria in disparaging terms saying that she was too young to be Queen, and that she was biased towards the Whigs in Parliament and a supporter of Catholics in Ireland. They were suggesting that when the King passes away a regent should be appointed to rule until the Princess is aged 25. Some of them even suggested that she might not be allowed to take over at all. That was when I decided I had to put country before my master even though I owe him much. It just sounded like treason to me.'

'And did you hear who they wanted to install as Regent?' Sam asked.

'Yes, it was that Duke…Ah yes, the Duke of Cumberland. Ernest Augustus or some German name like that. Someone told me that he is the Princess's Uncle.'

Sam remembered that Lipscomb had told him that the Duke of Cumberland was the Grand Master of the Orange Order and suddenly it all made sense.

'That's correct,' Sam told him. 'The Duke of Cumberland is the oldest of the King's surviving brothers. If Victoria has no children, then he would be next in line for the throne after her.'

Sam frowned as he considered Gasser's account. This was now a political conspiracy that was only likely to succeed if it was oiled with plenty of money. Sam knew that political campaigns were expensive which explained why the conspirators were expending so much effort on fund-raising. However, the plot had constitutional implications, and it was far more serious than Will and Sam had first thought. Sam recognized that it needed bringing to the attention of the authorities, but it was unclear who they could trust. The tentacles of the conspiracy seemed to extend deep into the local establishment, and seemed to have attracted the support of many with great power and influence. Sam had already met a high court judge, a senior cleric, several peers and a senior army officer. He knew there was also an academic from Christ Church College involved. He had not yet been introduced to the man, but he was present, and Sam had overheard him talking to the Canon earlier that evening when they had gathered for pre-dinner drinks. Sam looked up at Gasser. The valet had taken a big risk by revealing his knowledge.

'Mr Gasser, you mustn't talk to anyone else about this. There are some very senior people behind this plot who would have much to lose if it became common knowledge. A patient of mine became involved and was murdered for asking too many questions.'

The valet nodded. 'Yes, it's always the way in such matters. Nobody of any importance would notice if a valet suddenly disappeared.'

Sam wanted to return to the library, but he had a final question. 'William, did you hear how they planned to install a regent or when?' The valet looked at him and shook his head.

'No, Sir. It was not mentioned at that meeting. I got the impression that the main effort at that time was to raise funds for the plot, but they did not say how the money would be spent. Before you go, Sir, I have one more thing to add, although I'm not sure what it means.' The valet paused while he searched his memory for the precise details of what followed.

'Later that same evening, I was asked to help the staff clear up after the meeting had finished and the guests had departed. I went to recover some glasses from the drawing room and found Lord Kenyon talking with my master, Lord Vane. They didn't see me at first, but before I was noticed, I heard Lord Kenyon say something about Lord Kirtland. I think his precise words were: "Kirtland will do as he's told, and if it all goes wrong then we have at least positioned him to take the blame." They both laughed but then became aware of my presence and changed the subject.'

When Gasser mentioned Lord Kirtland, Sam looked up. He did not understand the role of Anne's father in the conspiracy, and it was dividing his loyalties. His spirits had sagged when Gasser revealed that Kirtland was hosting regular meetings at his home because it suggested that he played a central role in the scheme. However, this latest revelation seemed to suggest that Kirtland was considered expendable and was being manipulated. Sam's optimism rallied as he considered the possibility that Anne's father was acting under duress or blackmail rather than from a misguided political conviction. Sam remembered Anne's concern, and he knew that one day he would have to decide how much to tell her. However, that decision would have to wait. Sam put out his hand. He had much to thank Gasser for.

'Thank you for sharing this information with me. Your decision to confide in me must have been a difficult one to make. I will decide who to share it with, but I will keep your involvement a secret. Will you be loading for me in the morning?' Gasser shook his hand and nodded. 'Good, if I think of anything else I will ask you about it tomorrow. In the meantime, I'll see if I can discover a bit more.'

Gasser led him back to the library and then disappeared into the bowels of the palace. Sam was surprised that the man knew where to go as he was a visitor too. However, Sam knew he had to concentrate. His visit to Blenheim Palace might be the last time he was able to get any information especially as it seemed that he was no longer trusted. He resumed listening at his spot outside the rear doors of the library, and it became evident that the discussion had moved on to the subject of money. A man stood up from the front row and introduced himself as Professor Dinsmore.

'Thank you, gentlemen, we have continued to raise substantial amounts of cash for our campaign, and we feel there is the need for only one further investment meeting before we achieve our target.' There was a rumble of approval from the floor.

Dinsmore paused until silence returned. 'As you know, one of our most lucrative channels is from our investment introduction company where we get paid by companies for introducing investors to them. Now, we intend to hold one more of these meetings. It will be at Christ Church College again, on 31st July at 8pm. The visiting company is the Great Western Railway Company who are trying to raise new capital to finance a branch line into Oxford. Remember, the more capital that is promised for the railway, the more we raise for our own cause, so please bring along anyone who you think might be persuaded to invest.'

Sam felt that the meeting was drawing to a close. Now that a popular vote had determined that his presence at the shooting party was officially unwelcome, Sam felt intimidated and not at all inclined to socialize. The nature of the conspiracy was now clear except for the timing, and there was no need to put his own safety further at risk. He retired to his room without telling anyone and then spent the next eight hours wide awake as he listened for an assailant that, in the end, never arrived.

Chapter 16

A Winged Bird

The following morning, Sam rose early for the final shooting session although his heart was no longer in it. His discovery of the plot - and the likely involvement of the Duke of Marlborough - had tarnished his view of the surroundings, and even the buildings seemed less palatial despite being bathed by a golden sunrise under another cloudless sky. However, Sam knew that he had to keep up appearances, and he had no choice but to attend the morning shoot, even though he would have preferred the faded familiarity of the infirmary. He ate a hearty breakfast and made his way down to the Temple where he found Gasser waiting for him.

The valet nodded, and they exchanged formal greetings as befitting their stations. The casual observer would have seen nothing to suggest that the two men were anything other than houseguest and manservant.

Sam was determined to keep Gasser's secret, and neither man risked an unguarded comment nor spoke of the previous evening's discussion.

Shortly after Sam arrived, the Duke appeared. He nodded at Sam carefully, but as the two men exchanged terse greetings, Sam struggled to hide his anger, and he wondered if his face had betrayed his true thoughts. He considered trying to make amends, but it was too late as the Duke was followed by his gamekeeper who started his brief.

It did not take him long. The morning shoot was to take place in a different field bounded by similar woods. The gamekeeper made the same safety points and finished by reminding everyone not to shoot birds that were low or crossing. Fifteen minutes later, Sam was standing by Wingfield's pair of Purdey shotguns surveying the rest of the line. To his left, he could see Professor Dinsmore, but to his right there was a gap in the line where someone was absent. However, just as the shoot was about to begin, Fairman appeared with one of the Duke's footmen. He made no attempt to apologize for his late arrival, and he just scowled at Sam as the footman hurried to load the Colonel's two guns.

'Don't forget to watch out for crossing birds, Ansell,' he shouted. It sounded like an implied threat, but it became an explicit one ten minutes later when the beaters disturbed a hen pheasant that had been feeding right on the edge of the wood in front of the line.

The drive had nearly finished, and the beaters were just becoming visible as they approached the edge of the wood. Sam would not have won any prizes for his shooting, but he had downed a respectable number of birds and was not embarrassed. Next to him, he was aware that Colonel Fairman had scarcely needed to use his second barrel, and he was clearly an expert shot. The evidence of his skill was apparent from the substantial pile of dead birds to his front which made what followed even more suspicious.

The gamekeeper was just about to raise his whistle to call time on the drive when the hen pheasant made a bid for freedom. However, the bird had insufficient space to climb, and Sam decided there was no safe shot and lowered his gun. The startled pheasant saw the line of men and jinked towards the Professor who also declined the shot. However, to Sam's right Fairman was undeterred. When he fired, the first shot went across Sam's front and winged the bird, preventing it from climbing any further. Beyond the injured pheasant, a frightened shout came from inside the woods as one of the beaters took to the safety of the ground after Fairman's shot passed close by and peppered the tree next to him.

If the incident had ended there, it might have all been resolved amicably by a simple apology, but Fairman fired at the low-flying pheasant again. This time, the shot flew by Sam, who had turned slightly to his left to follow the flight of the bird. He felt a tugging at the material of his coat and a vicious stinging sensation in his upper arm as the extremities of the spread passed through his coat and into his shoulder. If Fairman had fired even a foot further to the left, then Sam would have taken a full load of shot into his back. As it was, Sam thought he had probably been pierced by two or three pieces of shot in the top of his right arm. They would need to be removed, but his coat had reduced the speed of the projectiles, limiting the depth that they had penetrated his flesh to around an inch which felt deep enough. Beyond Sam, the beater was safe, but only because he had wisely remained face down after Fairman's first shot so that the contents of the second barrel passed safely over his head. The bird fell to the ground just as the Gamekeeper saw what had occurred and blew the emergency stop signal of three long blasts on his whistle.

He ran past Fairman with a quick 'Make your gun safe, Sir' and rushed to where Sam was nursing his arm and talking to Gasser.

'Are you alright, Mr Ansell?' the Gamekeeper asked anxiously.

Sam nodded, as his wound started to ache. 'Better than the bird,' he said, pointing to where the pheasant had fallen midway between Sam and the Professor.

The gamekeeper was speechless. 'Was that shot fired by Mr Fairman?' he asked in astonishment.

'Colonel to you,' came Fairman's voice as he walked over to inspect his handiwork. 'Sorry, Ansell, I was trying to apply the safety catch when the second barrel fired of its own accord.' He looked meaningfully at the footman who had been loading for him. 'Perhaps the Duke's man needs some extra instruction.'

It was a cowardly slur on an easy target who was unable to answer back. The Gamekeeper was incandescent, and when he seemed about to explode, Sam interjected to defuze the situation.

'I accept your apology, Colonel Fairman,' he said, holding Gasser's clean handkerchief to his arm. 'I'm sure it wasn't intentional,' he added, making sure that his intonation left sufficient space for a good measure of doubt to cloud the thoughts of those within earshot.

Fairman was about to say more but decided against it when the Duke of Marlborough rushed over. The Duke looked genuinely concerned for Sam, and, for a moment Sam forgot his anger. He reassured his host that there was no need to call for a surgeon and told him that he would seek treatment back at the infirmary. The other shooters were to have one final drive in a field further along the estate, but Sam offered his apologies, thanked the Duke for his hospitality, and took his leave. He just wanted to get away.

As he trudged back up the hill, Sam became aware of heavy breathing and footsteps behind him. It was Gasser who had managed to catch up despite his limp. The valet checked that nobody else was around.

'That shot was deliberate, Sir, I was watching him after you lowered your gun.'

Sam agreed. 'Yes, I know. Fairman is far too talented to make a basic mistake like that. I think it was a warning, and it is one that we must both heed.'

The valet nodded, and when they were back at the palace, he tied his handkerchief around Sam's wounded arm. By the time Sam had packed and made his way to the waiting carriage, Gasser had cleaned the guns and was waiting with them by the horses.

Sam thanked him for his help at the shoot and tried to give him a tip which the valet politely declined. Sam understood, and as he climbed into the carriage, he turned to Gasser and said, 'Come to see me at the infirmary when you can get away and I'll fix that foot for you.' The valet smiled and nodded.

'I will, Sir, and thank you again.'

As Sam's carriage set off down the long driveway, he could not help feeling a little fortunate that he was leaving Blenheim Palace with only a superficial injury to his upper arm. However, it was a price that he was content to pay. Fairman might have been trying to intimidate him with his wayward shot, but the Colonel had no idea that it was too late, and that Sam knew exactly what the group was planning. He just needed to discuss it with Will and then decide how to expose them all.

Chapter 17

The Inquest

By the time Sam had returned to the infirmary, his wound had left a dark stain on his clothes. The porter, James Moss, brought up his bag and the wooden case containing Wingfield's guns. When he opened Sam's door, he was shocked to find the House Surgeon seated shirtless on a chair with the Apothecary attending to Sam's bloodied shoulder by digging into it with a pair of surgical tweezers. Will looked up as he came in.

'Ah, Moss, you've come just at the right moment. Bring me that tin on the desk, would you?' Moss picked up the tin and became a little pale once he got a clear view of Will's excavations. Sam sensed the man's discomfort.

'It's alright, Moss. There was a shooting accident that has left me slightly punctured.' Sam grimaced as Will probed a little deeper. 'Make sure you get everything out, Will, especially if there's any cloth in there from my clothes. It may not be a deep wound, but it will suppurate if you leave anything behind.' His friend nodded and described what he was doing.

'There are three entry wounds, and each is about an inch deep. Here comes the first.' He pulled out the tweezers from a hole in Sam's deltoid muscle and dropped a piece of bloodied shot into the tin that Moss was holding. He repeated the procedure twice more and was pleased to rescue a small piece of cloth from the final entry wound. By that time, a bead of sweat had formed on Sam's upper lip, and he asked Moss to fetch a glass of brandy. While the porter was away, Will washed the shoulder and applied a bandage. Eventually they were sitting in armchairs, sipping drinks, and Sam was able to recount everything that had happened during the previous two days.

When he had finished, Will shook his head in disbelief. 'Well, that is quite some story, Sam. I never imagined that this plot would extend right up to the royal family. But this gives us a real problem: who do we tell? We can hardly go knocking on the door of Windsor Castle without some proof.'

'I don't think there are many people we can trust at the moment. However, we do need to get someone into that investment meeting, and I wondered if Wingfield might help us. We need to find out when this plot is going to happen and identify the main ringleaders. The conspirators are definitely onto the two of us, but Wingfield might not attract the same scrutiny. He could attend as a potential investor, but scout around and listen to what is being said. If you agree, I'll approach Wingfield, but I'll have to explain everything to him unless you can think of a different approach. The investment meeting is not for another month, so we don't need to rush.'

Will shook his head. 'No, there's no other way of persuading him. Wingfield will have to be told, but I'm sure he can be trusted.'

'Good, I'll approach him soon. In the meantime, I think it's important that for the moment the two of us remain publicly distanced from each other,' Sam told him.

Will nodded. 'I agree, Sam, but I've been thinking about this, and I believe there's something else worth trying.'

Sam leaned forward to hear his friend's suggestion. 'Go on,' he said. 'What is it?'

'I think we should visit Christ Church College before the meeting and take a look. It sounds like most of these people are foot soldiers, chosen for their undoubted influence and strong religious beliefs, but unaware of the actual purpose of the conspiracy. I wouldn't be at all surprised if most of them truly believe they are fund-raising for Protestant charities and have no idea that they're taking part in a constitutional plot. If I'm right, then the scheme is being orchestrated by a small group of people, and it's those individuals that we need to identify before we tip off the authorities.'

Will paused to take a sip of sherry. After wetting his lips, the apothecary continued.

'From what you said, it sounds like their plan is just about ready for execution except for a bit of fund raising. If so, I think it's quite likely they will hold one final coordination meeting to check that there are no last-minute problems and to confirm they've got everything in place for their political campaign. I would expect attendance at that meeting to be restricted to the inner circle and to be held in private. Now, I might end up being hopelessly wrong on this, but I do feel that there's at least a fair chance of this happening under the cover of the investment meeting on 31st July. Having Wingfield inside the main meeting is useful, but I don't think it's sufficient. We need to listen in on what the inner core has to say privately in the margins.'

Sam nodded 'Yes that's key, but how do we do this?'

Will smiled. 'Well, the porter at Christ Church was a patient of mine, and I think he could be persuaded to grant us access to the venue beforehand. If we're really lucky, he might even remember what happened at previous meetings there. On the night of 31st, we need to get one or both of us into a hiding position where we can hear what's being said. However, that will only be possible if we have already identified where to hide. I admit the timing of this is a bit of a guess, but I can't see how else to proceed. In any case, it would be worth a visit to the college to see the lie of the land. At the very least, we could check on escape routes while we're there,' he added, acknowledging the risk they would face.

Sam nodded approvingly. A prior visit would improve their chances of success and minimize the risk of discovery. In the worst case, they might decide a secret infiltration was impossible and decide to back out altogether. In that eventuality, they could always report their findings to the authorities even though the facts were incomplete.

Sam knew it would take Will a few days to make the arrangements, and in the meantime, the clinical work was unceasing. However, on that particular Monday the infirmary's work routine was interrupted by the coroner's inquest into the death of the unnamed man.

***

The Coroner for the Central Oxford area was Mr George Cecil Esquire. At that time, coroners were paid by the case and worked within defined areas. Their courts were held in places such as inns, public houses and village halls; in fact, anywhere close to the place of death where the court could view the body of the deceased. The venue also needed to be large enough to accommodate the coroner, his clerk and twelve jurors. At the Radcliffe Infirmary, coroner's courts always took place in the conference room.

In the event, the case of the nameless man was over very quickly. The jury had been selected from people in the local area who were of sound mind and good character. The twelve chosen individuals were sworn in and viewed the dead man's body lying in the Dead Room. It was obvious that the victim had been shot in the lower part of his face, and this was confirmed in evidence provided by Mr Cleobury. Sam was also required to attend as a witness because the patient had expired on the operating table whilst under his care. He described the dilemma he faced when he first saw the extent of the man's dreadful injuries, and he explained how he had decided to operate even though there was the slimmest chance of success. The coroner and several of the jurors nodded sympathetically, and Sam was relieved when Mr Cecil summed up and praised the efforts made by the infirmary staff to treat the man. At the end of the

Coroner's summary, the jury retired but returned to give their verdict only five minutes later. An unknown man had been unlawfully killed by a person or persons unknown. Mr Cecil agreed with the jury and ordered an investigation into the matter, before releasing the body for burial and adjourning the court. As Sam left the room with the others, he felt a nudge in his side. He looked over and saw that Henry Lipscomb had been present at the hearing and wanted to speak with him. Sam was cautious.

'Not here, Henry. It's not safe. Meet me outside in the burial ground. It's at the end of the gardens, at the back of the infirmary. There's a gate on Walton Street.' The reporter nodded, and ten minutes later they were able to speak freely. As they stood near the unnamed man's freshly dug grave, there was the usual smell of decay hanging in the air, and both men were keen to exchange their knowledge as quickly as possible. Neither of them wanted to inhale the foul air just for the sake of small talk.

Sam started to describe the events of the weekend at Blenheim Palace. When he told Lipscomb about Fairman shooting at him, the reporter's eyes widened.

'I've remembered why I know his name. Fairman is the Deputy Secretary of the Orange Order. He is a highly committed loyalist, and I'm not surprised that he shot at you. He has previously been implicated of fomenting violence against Catholics in Northern Ireland.'

Sam rubbed his sore shoulder and said, 'that's not the half of it, Henry. Wait until I tell you what they're planning.' He then spent five minutes describing the plan to install a regent. The reporter was shocked by the detail that Sam had uncovered.

'There have been rumours about this for several months,' he said after Sam had finished. 'The public likes the Princess, but there are many within parliament and our institutions that don't want her to accede and believe that a regent should rule for her until she is older. I had no idea that the Orange Order was involved, but now it makes sense. If the Duke of Cumberland became Regent, then the Order would have positioned their Grand Master right at the very top. Can I write about this yet?'

Sam shook his head. 'I don't think that's a good idea, Henry. We don't yet know how the regency will be put in place, and we need more proof. We have a plan to obtain it, though.'

Sam described the investors' meeting and how they planned to infiltrate it. He told Lipscomb that, as soon as they had secured the necessary proof, they would send a message to him so that he could release the story. The reporter agreed and promised Sam that he would not break the news until after he had heard from them. They shook hands and Sam returned to the infirmary.

***

That afternoon, the surgical ward round was led by Mr Wingfield, and Sam thought it was a good opportunity to arrange to speak with him privately. Once their work was complete, Sam told Wingfield that he would fetch the man's shotguns and bring them to his carriage. When he returned, Wingfield was sitting on the rear seats. Sam placed the Purdeys on the front seat and thanked his mentor for their use. Wingfield then asked him how the weekend had gone.

'Actually, Mr Wingfield, there is a matter of grave importance that I wish to share with you, but I think it is best done somewhere more private.' Sam looked up at the roof towards the driver.

Wingfield understood. 'Well, Samuel, I am intrigued. Perhaps if you attend my house on your afternoon off tomorrow, we could take tea, and you can tell me all about your mystery.'

'I am indebted to you, Sir,' Sam replied as he climbed down the steps. 'I shall be there at two o'clock if that is convenient?'

The Consultant nodded and waved at Sam as the carriage set off on its journey home.

Chapter 18

Death in Service

On the day that Sam was to take tea with Charles Wingfield, it became apparent that William Gasser's life of military and domestic service had been brought to an abrupt end. He never managed to get his new foot; in fact, he never even got as far as the infirmary steps before he was silenced. Sam was certain it was murder, but the law in Oxford was corrupt and said otherwise.

Sam had been negotiating with Absolom Whiting on behalf of a female patient who needed the services of the Rubber Nurse. The patient was recovering from a nasty fracture and dislocation of her elbow and Sam felt her recovery could be speeded up by specialist treatment. The Rubber Nurse was specially trained with an expertise in limb massage. Her services were quite expensive although in many cases, her treatments speeded up a patient's recovery, freeing up their bed for somebody else. Sam was certain that it was money well spent, but he had to persuade Whiting to recommend his proposal to the Board to secure the necessary funds. Since Sam had attended the shoot, Whiting had become even less helpful than normal, but Sam eventually persuaded him to support up to three patient sessions with the Rubber Nurse when the matter was discussed at the next weekly board.

As Sam left the secretary's office, James Moss waved at him from the desk. 'Mr Ansell, Sir. There's a man from Lord Kirtland's house. He wants to speak with you urgently. I sent him around to the back of the infirmary and told him to wait by the Donkey Boy. He…er…he looked a bit grubby, and there was a nasty aroma about him,' he added by way of explanation. Sam nodded his thanks to Moss and left by the back door. Part of him hoped that the man might be carrying a secret note from Anne, though the porter's description of his visitor made the man sound like an unlikely Cupid. Sam arrived at the well and found him talking with Jack Rance about the relative merits of donkeys and ponies for powering water pumps. When Sam came up to them, the man stopped talking and took off his hat.

'Mr Ansell, Sir. I must speak with you on a matter of some urgency. I am Lord Kirtland's groom, John Sheffield.' Sam was conscious that anyone looking out of a window on the rear aspect of the infirmary would be able to see him talking with this man, and he decided that their conversation should take place in private. He gave Sheffield directions to Walton Street but made him go there from the front entrance of the infirmary. Sam went by his usual route through the burial ground and out onto Walton Street, opposite the University Press building where he hugged the wall to remain out of sight of any prying eyes behind him. A few minutes later, Sheffield arrived. He was hot and blowing steam from his exertions. Sam waited for the man to catch his breath and then asked what he wanted. Sheffield looked around. His face was creased with fear, and he had trouble maintaining eye contact with Sam. He was clearly frightened of something.

'Well, Sir', he began nervously. 'Do you know a man called William Gasser?'

Sam's spirits sagged as he sensed what was coming. 'I do,' he replied. 'Is he well? I was expecting to see him as a patient.'

'I'm afraid he's not alright, Sir. He was found dead last night at the side of the road near to the Eagle and Child Public House on St Giles'. Everyone is saying that he met with an accident, but I'm not so sure.' Sam waved a hand to stop him. The man was distressed and was getting ahead of himself.

'Now stay calm, John. Let's start at the beginning. William Gasser is Lord Vane's valet so what was he doing at Lord Kirtland's house?'

'Well, Sir, Lord Vane's nearest house is in London, and he had arranged to stay with my master once the shooting party had finished at Blenheim Palace. William told me that you were there as well, and that he had loaded your guns for you.' That was a true statement, Sam noted as his confidence in Sheffield grew.

'And why did he confide in you?' Sam asked gently.

The groom looked upset. 'Well, Lord Vane has stayed with the Kirtlands on several occasions recently, and William and I had become good friends. We went out drinking together and would often go looking for village girls to court. It's always easier when there's two of you.' Sam smiled as he compared the man's romantic ventures with his own complicated situation.

'Now, John, what exactly did William tell you?'

'He told me about the shooting weekend, and that he had become aware of a plot involving some of their Lordships. He didn't say what it was, but he told me that if anything bad happened to him then I should come and tell you.'

'And do you know what he was doing in St Giles'?'

'I don't, Mr Ansell. I have no idea, and I have nothing else to tell you. Perhaps he was coming to see you?'

'Perhaps,' Sam replied as a more pressing thought came into his mind. 'Does anyone else know you've come here today?'

The man shook his head. 'No, Sir, it is my afternoon off, and I sneaked out and managed to get a lift in a farmer's cart.' He paused. 'I'm sorry, I probably don't smell very good. It was full of horse dung.'

Sam laughed. 'Don't let that worry you, John. You have done your friend's bidding, and nobody can find fault with such loyalty. But listen.' Sam lowered his voice. 'What are they saying about William's supposed accident?'

'Well, the coroner's inquest is tomorrow at the Eagle and Child Public House. I heard Lord Vane talking to the master and telling him that he would provide his own doctor to perform an examination of William's body. He told Lord Kirtland that the doctor would ensure that the jury would find the correct verdict, and that he knew a judge who would help the coroner to arrive at the right decision. Lord Kirtland seemed quite angry, but then I had to move away before I was discovered. It all sounded a bit strange to me, Sir.'

Sam nodded and silently agreed. 'Listen, John. You've done your bit and now you need to let me take over. Please don't tell anyone about any of this. It has become very dangerous. Two men have lost their lives so far, and we don't want a third. Here.' He gave the man a half crown. 'Get yourself a coach home. It's a long way to High Cross Manor on foot. And John, try to have a bit of a wash first or the coachman won't let you get onboard.'

They both laughed, and John Sheffield set off to find a horse trough, leaving Sam to reflect on the life of William Gasser and the seemingly casual way that it had ended. His anger grew.

***

Will was adamant after Sam had described his conversation with Sheffield.

'This must be investigated,' he growled. 'Good men are losing their lives, property has been destroyed, and threats issued like confetti. It has to be stopped.' Sam was angry too. William Gasser had suffered a nasty personal injury whilst on active service for his country, and he had proved to be a loyal servant and subject. More recently, he had stepped up to help as Sam's loader, and without his advice Sam's humiliation at the shoot would have been complete. He owed it to Gasser to get the man justice.

'I want to examine the body,' Sam said. 'From

what Sheffield told me, it sounds as though they intend to deceive the coroner with false medical evidence. And why is a judge assisting? Is he assisting or is he making sure that the inquest delivers the correct verdict? And we both know the verdict will be left open. There is no likelihood whatsoever that the conspirators will allow the coroner to find that Gasser's death was unlawful.' He sighed. 'Why does everything official eventually become so corrupt?' he asked rhetorically.

'Money and power, Sam,' his friend replied.

Both doctors fell silent as they turned over the problem in their minds. Eventually, Sam looked up.

'There is one question we haven't addressed,' he said. 'How did the conspirators find out that Gasser knew about the regency plot? Who told them? Did someone hear him telling me about it or perhaps he confided in someone else that we know nothing about? Could it even be Sheffield? In any event, someone has informed the conspirators of Gasser's involvement, and someone, probably Fairman, seems to have silenced him. We must tread very carefully, or we could be next.'

Will's face filled with doubt and misgivings. 'Perhaps we have reached the sensible limit of our involvement in this, Sam? We are but two doctors against a group of powerful men who seem to have limitless resources and influence. Perhaps it's too much.'

Sam thought about the risk. If they gave up their investigation, they would still have to tell somebody in authority, but who? The meeting at Blenheim Palace had been full of those in positions of power, each brought in for their particular expertise and influence. He suspected that High Court Judge, Lord Brontley, would be the one to supervise the coroner. It was a good example of how far the group could reach into local institutions to manipulate decisions for their own ends. Such people could deal with two unknown house doctors as easily as swatting a couple of troublesome flies. Balanced against this was the cynical misappropriation of charitable funds and the seemingly casual use of violence. Both doctors were determined to get justice for Crosley and Gasser who were just two ordinary men who became involved through no fault of their own. The thought of the two innocent victims bolstered Sam's resolve.

'No, Will, we are committed now. We must reveal the full extent of this. If nothing else, we owe it to the two men who have died.'

Will nodded. 'Very well. How should we proceed?'

Sam thought carefully. 'Until we can decide who we can trust, I think we should keep trying to discover everything that we can and record our findings in a portfolio of evidence. I also think it's important that we confirm Gasser was actually murdered. We only have Sheffield's word on it, and I would like to see for myself. I think that we should go to the Eagle and Child tonight and see whether we can find Gasser's body and inspect it for ourselves. We may have to break in though, so we would be placing ourselves outside the law.'

Will nodded. Now that they had decided to proceed, he was keen to get a move on. This sounded like a good idea, albeit a hazardous one.

'We are becoming expert burglars,' he observed wryly.

'Yes, but think of the penalty if we get caught,' Sam replied. 'It would mean transportation to the colonies, or maybe even the noose, so we must be careful.' Will nodded and looked uncharacteristically grim as they agreed to meet again after Sam had returned from Wingfield's house.

***

Two hours later, Charles Wingfield sat quietly in his drawing room as Sam told him everything that had happened since the amputation of John Crosley's leg. When Sam had finished his account, Wingfield took a sip of tea and buttered one of the scones that his wife had served to them before retiring to her reading room. Eventually he spoke.

'You are a brave man, Samuel. These are powerful people. Have you considered the personal risk you are taking here? Even if you keep your life, you could still lose your professional reputation if things go badly.'

'I am determined, Sir,' Sam replied, 'But will you help us?'

'Naturally, I will. You want me to attend this meeting as a potential investor in a railway company?'

'That's all we want,' Sam reassured him.' We will do the rest while you are there pondering your investment and listening in on the conversations around you.'

'Well, it already sounds like a fool's venture,' Wingfield laughed. 'But I can pretend to be a fool!' He laughed again and then suddenly became more serious.

'Er, Samuel, we are both peaceful men, but I wonder if you ought to arm yourself from now on.

This Fairman character sounds to be entirely ruthless, and I would sleep better at night if I knew that you were able to defend yourself when you are away from the infirmary. I have a pair of duelling pistols that would be ideal.'

Sam thought for a moment and then accepted Wingfield's offer. It seemed an anathema for a doctor to arm themself, but by deciding to pursue the conspiracy, Sam knew he was already working outside the usual boundaries of his profession. He thought of the nameless man with his wounded face and knew that his mentor was right to be concerned.

An hour later, Mrs Wingfield arrived with more tea and scones to find the two men discussing loading and unloading techniques whilst waving two pistols around. If she was perturbed, she did not show it. She was used to her husband's eccentricities and left the trolley for the two men to deal with. If they could unload a gun, she reasoned, they could unload a tea trolley.

Chapter 19

Corruption

The sun is a reluctant sleeper in early July, and Sam and Will had to wait until two o'clock in the morning before it was dark enough to break into the Eagle and Child Public House. Will had brought some tools that they had discovered in a drawer in Matron's office. Sam carried nothing except the two loaded pistols which he had put under his belt at the back where they were concealed by his coat tails. They paid Littleworth a customary shilling for his silence and set off to the public house which was little more than a brisk ten-minute walk from the infirmary.

There was nobody around at that time of night, and the heavy drinkers had either gone home or were sleeping it off in the filth of the backyard passageways. There was always a risk that they would run into a constable, but Sam felt they could explain away their presence on the street. They were, after all, returning home from dinner with the esteemed Charles Wingfield or some such fiction as seemed appropriate for the circumstances of the moment.

The police in Oxford were a piecemeal organization which reflected the different competing civic interests. In 1829 the University had formed a private force called the Oxford University Police known by the students as the Bullers or Bulldogs. These constables carried warrant cards and were responsible for nighttime patrolling of the university and areas of Oxford within 4 miles of any university building. From 1835, the city authorities had created another force of Constables under the control of the Watch Committee, and they policed the city by day. There was a general lack of accountability, and both forces were quite corrupt. They usually refused to cooperate with each other and were largely ineffective. On that night, the university constables were conspicuously absent, and Sam and Will were untroubled as they made their way towards the site where William Gasser's corpse awaited the coroner's inspection.

It was very quiet when they arrived at the Eagle and Child, and the building stood dark and seemingly spiritless in the absence of its evening patrons. The two men had been prepared to break into the main building but found that force was unnecessary. The landlord had hung a sign on the front door directing those attending the inquest to the rear yard where there was a large stable block.

Sam was a little worried that there might be a dog to warn of their intrusion, but when the two men stopped at the entrance to the yard, nothing moved except a startled rat which scuttled down a drain.

Around them, there was complete silence. Sam nodded, and they stole into the yard which was bathed in the light of a half-moon. The entrance to the disused stable had been left unlocked, although entry was said to be prohibited according to a small sign hanging from the latch and bearing a court seal. They would not be needing tools on this night, Sam realized, as they ignored the court notice and entered the old stables through the unlocked front door.

It was dark inside, and Will lit a candle. The flame flickered into life, and they could see that tables and chairs had been laid out ready for the court proceedings which were now only a few hours away. It was clear from the ring stains that most of the furniture had been borrowed from the main bar in the public house.

'In here,' Will whispered, and he disappeared into a small room to one side. The room had previously been used to store animal feed, and a few sacks were still piled up along one side. There was a strong smell of horse manure although the floor looked as though it had recently been scrubbed clean. In the centre of the room, two of the Inn's tables had been brought across from the public house and pushed together. On top, there was the ghostly outline of a human form covered in a white shroud. Sam lifted the end nearest the feet and confirmed that in this case 'feet' was actually 'foot'. He immediately recognized Gasser's amputation from the unusual position of the surgeon's cut.

'This is definitely Gasser,' he told Will. 'Help me with the shroud.'

Will set down the candle on a nearby shelf, and the two men folded back the white cloth. Gasser's dead body looked grey and slightly inhuman with its waxy skin and the puffiness of early decomposition. A postmortem examination had already taken place, and the man had a long line of stitching down the front of his torso. Strangely, though, the surgeon had not bothered with a craniotomy, despite an obvious injury to the side of the man's head.

Sam had to smother his anger when he saw the extensive facial bruising; it was quite clear that Gasser's assailant had beaten the valet ruthlessly before killing him. Sam briefly wondered what information the valet had been forced to disclose, but he knew it was not the moment for speculation, and he turned his attention to Gasser's head injury which he studied carefully. The injury lay just behind the ear, but there was something odd about it. The skin was broken, and Sam could feel that, beneath the surface tissue, the skull was soft and broken into several pieces. Gasser had clearly been struck with sufficient blunt force to cause a depressed fracture, but where was the blood? If the man had been alive when his head was struck, Sam would have expected to see a lot of blood around the wound and matted in the man's hair. But there was nothing to see apart from a small amount of clear fluid leaking from the lining of the brain. It looked as though the man was already dead when he was struck on the head.

Sam was about to call time on his examination when he remembered what Cleobury had said about checking both sides of the body.

'Help me roll him onto his side so I can examine his back,' he whispered. Together, they gently rolled Gasser towards them and Sam peered over the man's side. And there it was.

'Look, Will. This is what killed him.' Will

peered over at the man's back. Gasser had been stabbed in the back by a thin sharp object, possibly a sword or a long knife.

The entry wound looked innocuous because the blade had been very slender. However, around the entry hole the skin was quite bruised indicating that the man had been alive when he was stabbed.

Sam used one of Matron's screwdrivers to measure the depth and angle of the hole. It extended from just below the left shoulder blade all the way through to the heart. It had continued straight through the organ and had only stopped when it struck one of the man's front ribs. There could be no doubt that this was a fatal wound, and it seemed likely that it was the stab wound that killed him, and the blow to the head was applied afterwards. As a decoy or deception perhaps? Sam was certain that he was correct, but they would have to consider it later as a dim light was already starting to pierce the night sky from the east, and it was time to leave before they were observed by early risers. They rolled Gasser onto his back, replaced the shroud, and left the building as they found it. Fifteen minutes later, they were back in Sam's room.

'He was dead before he was struck on the head,' Sam told his friend. 'I would wager that this has been done to avoid a verdict of unlawful killing. I predict the stab wound will go unmentioned. Instead, there'll be a suggestion that the man might have been struck on the head accidentally. There'll be just enough doubt to ensure that the jury declares an open verdict.'

Will nodded. 'And that judge will prevent Cecil getting to the bottom of it should he suddenly develop a conscience and be tempted to open an investigation.'

Sam became thoughtful. 'Listen, Will. We need

to observe this inquest and record what happens along with our own findings. Would you mind going to do that in my place? There are likely to be several people attending who would know me, and I think my presence there would be a bit too suspicious. If you're worried, then you could go in disguise. What do you think?'

Will laughed. 'What do I think? I think the House Surgeon has been getting all the fun and it's about time the Apothecary had a go! I'll have to make some arrangements with my new assistant, but I'm sure he will cover me for two or three hours, though I doubt the inquest will take that long judging by what we've discovered.'

Sam smiled. Will's enthusiasm was infectious, and he felt his mood lift a little. His friend was observant too, as he discovered when Will returned later that day.

***

The Inquest into William Gasser's death was quite an event, and, as Sam predicted, it made a complete mockery of the law. Will had arrived at the Eagle and Child early, pulled his hat down over his eyes, and settled into a corner chair at the opposite end of the room to the top table. Nobody seemed to notice him as the disused stable filled with a noisy mixture of jurors, witnesses and inquisitive observers. Many carried pots of beer from across the yard, and one or two staggered inside and were clearly suffering from the effects of overindulgence. The unruly atmosphere was not helped by a thick pall of tobacco smoke hanging in the air, adding to the sense that the room was more like a rowdy public bar than a solemn venue for upholding the law of the land. Eventually, the Coroner, Mr Cecil, arrived along with a robed judge. Everyone in the room stood up and then returned to their seats once the two officials had taken their places.

'Good morning,' Cecil announced, indicating the start of the proceedings. 'This is High Court Judge Lord Brontley KC. He is undertaking a study of the Coroner's Service in England and will be observing today. Now, I understand that this is a relatively straightforward matter so we shouldn't be too long. Have the jury been sworn in yet?' he asked breezily. The clerk nodded. 'Good, then let's view the body.'

The judge and coroner rose and were followed by the jury who formed a queue waiting for entry to the side room where Will could just make out Gasser's body. He could see a man standing next to the corpse. He was pointing at the head wound and saying something to the coroner that was unintelligible but looked like it might be a description of the injury. As Sam had predicted, there was no attempt to inspect the rear of the dead man, and the stab wound in Gasser's back remained unseen. After a cursory inspection, everyone returned to their seats and waited for the witnesses.

The first to stand was the man who Will had seen in the side room standing next to Gasser. He was Lord Vane's personal physician, Doctor Cedric Herbert. He was a short, portly individual for whom lying was evidently second nature. Will thought that the man had probably been paid handsomely. His evidence was shamelessly false, and he delivered it as though he was the lead actor following the script of a well-known play. Yes, he had examined the victim. Yes, the man had died of an injury to his head. No, there were no other injuries that were relevant. And finally, no, he could not be certain that the injuries were sustained deliberately, and it was quite possible that they could have happened accidentally. Cecil then asked for an example, and Herbert pretended to think for a moment before answering a question he had previously been told to expect. It was cleverly done. He sowed a seed of doubt by stating that the injuries were not necessarily by foul play and might have been caused by a passing coach. He then cultivated the seed by casually reminding the jury that the victim had been found at the side of the road.

When Herbert sat down, Will could see several of the jurors already nodding at each other in agreement. The doctor had performed his role to perfection, and it looked like an open verdict was already uppermost in the minds of at least half the jury and that was without any intervention by Mr Cecil.

The remainder of the proceedings were over very quickly. Lord Vane identified the man and told the court that he had known Gasser for many years and that he had employed him as his valet. He said that Gasser had behaved normally in the days leading up to his death, and that he was unable to explain why the man had travelled to central Oxford. The judge nodded at Vane as he returned to his seat. It was a brief exchange of eye contact, but Will could see the complicity that lay within the unspoken exchange.

The final witness was the nightwatchman who had found Gasser lying in the gutter. He told the court there had been nobody else about, and he had seen nothing suspicious. That just left the coroner to sum up. Before he did, however, the Judge nudged him and there was a whispered exchange. Was it advice or instruction? Will was unable to say, but it did appear that Judge Brontley was attempting to influence Mr Cecil who shuffled uncomfortably before addressing the jurors.

'It is for you to judge the facts of the case and to arrive at a decision on how Mr Gasser met his untimely end. Your choices are death from unlawful, accidental or natural causes. If you cannot be sure, then you may also return an open verdict, and I will decide whether to initiate an investigation.'

Will had attended inquests before and knew that Cecil's words usually marked the end of the coroner's summary, but on this occasion, there was more guidance to follow.

'It is not for me to influence your decision, but the law allows me to point you to the relevant evidence, and it seems that in this case you should consider carefully how Mr Gasser's head wound occurred. You have heard expert opinion from Doctor Herbert that it can be explained as an accidental injury rather than necessarily by foul play. The most important thing that you must remember is that, if you are at all unsure, then you should deliver an open verdict.'

It was as close to judicial direction as decency would allow. Judge Brontley clearly thought so as he beamed at Mr Cecil as the Coroner sat down looking uncomfortable. The jurors trooped out and went across the yard to the rear room of the public house to drink some more beer while they discussed their decision.

Once they were gone, Will saw Lord Vane walk over to Judge Brontley and shake his hand. There was a whispered exchange, and then Vane returned to his seat with a look of satisfaction on his face. They clearly knew each other. In the other corner of the room, a scruffily dressed man noticed the exchange and went over and sat down next to the peer. Will had seen the man scribbling notes during the proceedings and assumed that he was a reporter. A quick enquiry to his neighbour confirmed that he had guessed correctly, and to his surprise, he also learned that the reporter was from the Oxford Journal and was called Henry Lipscomb.

Now this is interesting, he thought as he watched the two men. Lipscomb began questioning Lord Vane whose face darkened as the reporter tried to probe more deeply as his interview progressed. There was a good deal of head shaking and angry gesticulation, but just as Will was about to try and get closer to listen, the foreman of the jury returned to notify the Coroner that they had reached a verdict. As the clerk called the room to order, Vane looked relieved that the resumption of court proceedings had forced his inquisitor to abandon his questioning and return to his seat.

What followed was the predictable end of a perverted and entirely corrupt inquest. The Foreman confirmed an open verdict, and Cecil told the court that on the balance of probabilities he thought the injury was caused accidentally, and therefore the case merited no further investigation. With those final words, the hearing ended, and the jury was discharged. During the shooting party, Gasser had told Sam that nobody of any importance would notice if a valet disappeared, and in a way the hearing had effectively proved him correct.

***

Sam grew despondent as he listened to Will's account. It was not that the hearing had turned out to be corrupt - that had been entirely predictable - it was the thought that he might have caused William Gasser's death by bringing Lipscomb into their confidence. As he sat listening to Will describe Lipscomb's interview with Lord Vane, Sam wondered who else the reporter had been questioning. Lipscomb had promised Sam that he would keep out of the way, and yet here he was interrogating one of the main protagonists. If he had been blundering around asking the wrong questions, it was quite possible that the conspirators were now aware that their plans had been compromised. Sam had been careful not to reveal the valet's name to the reporter and had merely stated that his source was on the domestic staff. However, if Lipscomb's line of questioning had even hinted at this, then it would not have taken the conspirators long to identify the valet as a likely suspect. Sam thought of Gasser's bruised face and the beating he had received before he was murdered. It would have been a strong man indeed that could resist such violence without eventually submitting to his interrogator.

As Sam reflected on his decision to involve Lipscomb, he realized that their own situation had become perilous, and further enquiries would have to be carried out covertly. The investment meeting seemed crucial and was probably their last opportunity to get the facts before the conspiracy was activated. Sam knew that their best chance of a successful outcome would be to ensure they were thoroughly prepared for it. Will's suggestion of a prior visit to

Christ Church College was a good idea, and Sam desperately hoped that it might herald an improvement in their fortunes.

Sam remembered a Latin proverb that Wingfield had once tossed at him, and he threw it to Will to reinforce his friend's resolve: '*Ubi vita, Ibi Spes*,' he stated gravely and was surprised when Will started laughing. 'Yes, my friend: "Where there is life, there is hope." But note, there is a condition within that proverb. We only have hope while we live. And after today, are you so confident that we have such long-term prospects?'

Will was joking, and it made Sam laugh. But when Sam later considered the danger awaiting them, his friend's graveyard humour no longer seemed quite so amusing.

Chapter 20

The Proposal

As the clock ticked down towards the date of the investment meeting, Sam and Will busied themselves at the infirmary and made their preparations. Will sent a message to the porter at Christ Church College asking if they might visit on a confidential matter. The man was called Robert Drury, and he had once been treated by Will after a minor workplace cut to his hand had developed into a nasty bout of erysipelas. Will had treated the condition with an ointment that his family had developed over many years, and the man's hand had eventually recovered. Drury knew he was lucky to have remained under Will's care as erysipelas could quickly become a serious matter requiring the brutal attention of the surgeon's knife. As a result, the grateful man did not seek any further explanation for the doctors' unusual request and sent a message back arranging for them to visit one evening during the following week.

In the meantime, there was plenty to keep the two doctors occupied. The casework was relentless, but there was also an amusing domestic drama to enjoy. It concerned a lewd and highly embarrassing event that had Absalom Whiting scurrying around for two days as he tried desperately to prevent the story reaching the enquiring minds and active pens at The Oxford Journal. It was one of those episodes where, after a while, nobody could be certain of exactly what had transpired, as the facts were gradually transformed into a story which turned into a myth. Future historians might look to the minutes of the Governor's Weekly Board Meeting for an accurate record of events, but even these were subject to careful censorship to ensure that only the *right* stories were made public. And so, it was into this historical washing machine that the case of Nurse Bradley ended up. It took only one week before the matter was firmly in the category of hospital myth.

It was said that Matron had been patrolling the wards when she heard a noise coming from the storeroom where Sam and Anne had hidden some weeks earlier. When she opened the door, she was shocked to find Nurse Bradley in company with a male patient. There were many versions of what they were doing when the door opened, but what seems certain is that Matron was scandalized and walked the corridors for a week wearing a traumatized expression and clutching her bible for comfort as she searched unsuccessfully to find suitable words to describe the scene to The Reverend Thomas.

While Matron struggled to find her voice, there were no such inhibitions amongst the staff, and the details swept through the infirmary becoming more lurid with each telling. However, the end of the story seemed to have more substance when Nurse Wallace reported that she had seen her ex-colleague leaving the infirmary for the final time. Bradley had been in a cart driven by a man half her age who had been a convalescing patient on Bagot Ward at the time that Matron made her unspeakable discovery. Patient and nurse had both been dismissed, but Catherine Wallace said that neither of them appeared to care very much as the cart disappeared through the gates.

Will and Sam laughed when they heard the story and took heart from the thought that the governors were too busy shoring up the infirmary's reputation to worry about two house doctors.

***

It was not long after Nurse Bradley's storeroom adventure that Sam experienced a welcome distraction of his own, and it arrived in the form of a letter delivered in the mail. He immediately recognized Anne's handwriting and opened the envelope in the privacy of his room. She started by apologizing for her lack of contact since their brief encounter at Blenheim Palace, and she said that she had learned of his shooting accident and hoped that he was not badly injured. The main point of her letter, however, was to arrange another clandestine meeting. She explained that she had arranged to visit her dressmaker on Broad Street, and that she would be chaperoned by her brother, Thomas, who had taken a week's leave from his post in London to visit the family. She explained that her brother had agreed to make a convenient visit to his tailor, leaving her free to walk with Sam in the parkland around Trinity College.

It was another plot arranged between brother and sister, and Sam was excited by the idea because he had something to discuss with her. He had decided to make Anne a proposal of marriage, but by necessity it would be an unconventional arrangement, and he was not entirely certain that she would say yes.

***

As Sam waited impatiently for his illicit assignation, time seemed to slow, and after a few days the waiting became excruciating as he dwelled on the possibility that Anne might decline his offer. By the time his afternoon off had arrived, his anxiety was at fever pitch, and even Will asked him several times if he was feeling quite normal.

The problem Sam faced was that the engagement would have to remain a secret until they could get the blessing of both of Anne's parents. However, Sam was concerned that his relationship with Anne's mother seemed to be beyond repair, and he was worried that Anne would eventually tire of waiting or, even worse, she might suspect Sam's intentions and decide he was attempting something unsavoury that would damage her reputation. Eventually, the day of their meeting arrived, and by the end of the afternoon the waiting was over, and Sam had his answer.

They had planned to meet outside Anne's dressmaker on Broad Street, whereupon her brother would take his leave for an hour while they walked in the park. As soon as Sam rounded the corner, he saw them waiting for him. Anne smiled and gave him a small wave as he approached. He shook her brother's hand, kissed Anne's hand and expressed his gratitude to her chaperone.

'This is very kind of you, Thomas,' Sam said.

'Well, I am trusting you completely,' he replied. 'My mother thinks that you are a monster who will take advantage of my sister's affection and then abandon her, leaving her reputation in tatters. However, I think that is a harsh assessment. I can see that you are an honourable man, and I do not see that an unescorted walk in a public park is anything of concern.'

Beside him, Sam saw Anne nodding furiously. 'Mother is such a prude,' she exclaimed. 'But I'm sure you'll win her around, Sam.'

Sam was not so certain of that, but by then Thomas Kirtland was looking at his watch. 'I must attend my tailor's shop now. Shall we meet back here in an hour?'

Sam nodded and shook the man's hand again. He liked Thomas, but as Sam watched him set off down Broad Street, he thought the man appeared to be a little downcast and preoccupied. Anne took Sam's arm as they walked in the opposite direction towards the park. She seemed to read his thoughts.

'I'm worried about Thomas. In fact, I'm worried about my father too. Both seem to be weighed down by something, but neither of them will explain what's going on.' She dabbed her eyes with a handkerchief and Sam took her hand and squeezed it.

'I know one thing,' she continued after returning the pressure of his touch. 'The situation seemed to get much worse after that man, Lord Vane, came to stay with us following the shooting party.' She paused as she remembered her conversation with Sam at the Temple of Diana. 'You didn't discover anything else while you were at Blenheim Palace, did you?'

Sam had been dreading this question. Should he lie or should he tell her what he had unearthed? If he revealed his suspicion that her father was being manipulated, then he would also have to explain the nature of the conspiracy. That knowledge could easily place Anne in danger if she acted precipitously. Could he trust her to remain silent while he and Will tried to work out precisely what was going on? As he wrestled with his conscience, she studied his face and settled the matter for him.

'It's no good, Sam. I know you well enough to recognize that you're about to deceive me. You are a terrible liar. Whatever it is, you must tell me.'

'Very well, he replied, 'but not here. I don't want you to worry, but there is a man following us.'

It was the man's clothing that made him stand out. Earlier in the week, a powerful summer heatwave had developed over the whole of the British Isles, yet the man was dressed in a thick overcoat that looked wholly out of place in the roasting heat of the afternoon. At first, Sam had been uncertain that he was following them, but after the man continued into the park behind them, Sam became sure of it.

'We must try and lose him,' Sam announced as he saw a possible means of doing so. Ahead of them, the path passed by an extensive patch of huge rhododendron bushes that extended for several hundred yards. The path initially remained on the outside of the wood before it entered the leafy gloom. Sam had previously walked there and knew that once the path was inside the woods it forked several times.

It was easy to lose your sense of direction unless you had been there before, and it made a good place to lose a pursuer. Sam did not want to alarm Anne, so he did not tell her that he was armed. However, he suddenly felt reassured by the two pistols he had tucked into his waistband under his jacket at the back.

In the event, the pistols remained concealed. The path had just bent around a thick group of shrubs when Sam spotted a gap between them.

'In here,' he directed quietly and helped Anne to dodge through the bushes to the other side. There, he spotted a large fallen tree, and the two of them hid behind it just as the man came up the path behind them. He was breathing heavily, and Sam watched him as he went past the gap in the hedges and then stopped a little further on when he realized he had lost sight of the couple. Sam heard him mutter a curse before he hurried along in a fruitless attempt to catch up with his quarry who were, in any case, safely behind him and well hidden.

Sam looked down at Anne who was looking a little scared.

'Are you all right, Anne?' he whispered and offered his hand to help her stand. She nodded as she stood up and brushed herself free of dried leaves and twigs. Fortunately, the ground was dry, and her skirts were still clean, otherwise they would be facing a difficult explanation when they met Thomas again.

'I hope you have a good reason for dragging me into the bushes, Samuel Ansell,' she said as the fear drained away from her face and was replaced by a smirk.

'I assure you I did, upon my word as a gentleman,' Sam replied laughing. 'But look, I know you probably have a lot of questions, but we need to retrace our steps and put some distance between us and that man. We cannot be certain that he won't return once he realizes we're not in front of him.' She nodded, and they took the path back towards the entrance to the park. On the way, Sam saw a small group of bushes. They had once formed a leafy glade for a bench that somebody had left as a memorial to a deceased relative. The bushes had almost consumed the seat, but it was still accessible and almost invisible to anyone that was not standing right by it.

Sam looked at his watch. 'We can hide in here if it's not too uncomfortable for you. We still have half an hour which is enough time for me to tell you what I know.' He paused. 'And I have to ask you a very important question.'

He gestured to a small gap in the undergrowth and wondered if she would go through it. It felt like an important decision, and Sam was relieved when she nodded. He had no need to worry, though, because Anne wanted to hear his question so much that she ignored the stinging nettles that stood guard over the entrance to the glade and went inside. The seat was intact, and there was just enough room for the two of them. The sweet smell of leaf mould and wild garlic hung in the air, and Oxford suddenly felt a great distance behind the two lovers.

Anne smiled at him once they were seated in their hidden world. It seemed a wholly appropriate place for what she thought was about to occur. She understood Sam's nerves and looked deeply into his eyes to inject resolve into his purpose.

'Go on, my dearest Sam,' she whispered to encourage him. 'Please ask me your question.'

Sam felt the warmth of her gaze and knelt in front of her. It suddenly seemed like a simple question to ask. He took her hand and made his promise. Looking into her eyes, he said, 'I will tell you everything, Anne, but I will start by telling you that I love you, and that I want to marry you if you'll have me. It will have to wait until after I have gained your mother's approval, and there is the matter of your father which we can discuss in a minute. But a promise between us has no less meaning just because we are the only two people who know of it. It is our promise which one day I would like to seal with a ring, but in the meantime Anne Kirtland, will you marry me? One day? When we can?'

Tears filled Anne's eyes. She loved this mild-mannered man, and he had proposed so movingly. 'Yes, Samuel, of course I will marry you. One day. When we can.' She took his hand, and they both stood up. They looked at each other for a moment without a hint of shyness and their faces gradually converged before their lips came together and sealed their promise.

Eventually, their faces parted. 'That was lovely, Sam,' she said. 'I will always remember this moment. I will treasure it. I was hoping so much that you would ask me.'

'I really wasn't certain that you would say yes,' he admitted to her. 'It's been a tense few days.'

She laughed. 'Of course I was, silly. I was minded to ask you myself, but I decided that for such an important matter, I should leave you something traditional to do. We now just need to work out how to get my parents' agreement, but I'm certain we will win them over in the end.' At the mention of the parental obstacles that lay ahead, Anne's smile faded, and it dropped further when she remembered her father's troubles.

'Do you know what's worrying him so much, Sam? What is this mystery that seems to be casting such a shadow over my family?'

'I will tell you,' Sam replied, 'but you must swear that you won't take any action before discussing it with me first. As you'll hear, two men have lost their lives in this conspiracy, and if you act without careful thought, you'll endanger yourself and possibly others like me and Will. Do you really promise?' She looked taken aback by Sam's vehemence, but she swore an oath and later understood why he was so worried.

It took Sam twenty minutes to explain what had transpired since he had amputated John Crosley's leg. Anne listened carefully and asked questions sparingly. When he had finished, she was astonished.

'This is very serious,' she exclaimed. 'Is there nobody you can tell?'

'There is nobody we can trust in Oxford. The police are corrupt, and the conspirators include representatives from all the civic sources of power - even a high court Judge. I'm also worried about the Duke of Marlborough. He always seemed like a moderate man to me, but he's been taking a lead role as far as I've been able to discover.'

Anne was shocked. 'There must be someone, Sam,' she said.

'Well, I've been thinking about that, and I wondered whether Will and I should contact someone senior in the Metropolitan Police Force in London once we've been to the investment meeting. Surely, we can find someone there who would be interested and could be trusted.'

'That sounds like a good idea, Sam, but what about my father? I can't picture him being involved in anti-Catholic intrigue and treasonous plots. What on earth is he doing?'

Sam looked at her. 'I don't think he's acting willingly, Anne,' he said gently. 'I think he's under some kind of duress. Gasser told me that they were positioning him to take the blame if it all goes wrong, so it's important we find out how they are blackmailing him, even if there is a degree of embarrassment involved.'

She sniffed as tears started to form. 'Poor Papa, he is so easily taken in. I'm sure Lord Vane has been sent to keep an eye on him.'

Sam looked at his watch. 'Our time is up, Anne. Your brother will be waiting for us, and we must go.' She nodded and kissed him on the lips.

'Be careful Sam. You can't do this all on your own. And I don't want to be a secret widow without becoming your wife first.'

***

Will was delighted when Sam told him of his secret engagement to Anne, and he shook Sam's hand warmly. He agreed to be the best man, and they laughed when Will said he would take personal responsibility for Sam's safety when Lady Kirtland discovered what had happened. He became more solemn when Sam described his visit to the park and the stranger who had followed them. It brought back into focus the task that lay ahead, and uppermost in their minds was the visit to Christ Church College.

Chapter 21

The Porter

Robert Drury was a hefty man who had retired as a Chief Petty Officer after distinguished military service in the Royal Navy. He made an impressive college porter because he was not only physically imposing, but he observed everything and wielded his authority in a manner that was perfectly tailored to the situation.

From his vantage point in the porter's office, he religiously guarded access to Christ Church College and imposed military style admonishments to any of the undergraduates that he caught misbehaving. He was unable to help with their academic studies, but he assumed a personal responsibility for developing the young students as gentlemen. Usefully, Drury had a particular talent for recognizing the difference between youthful exuberance and more serious misdemeanours that he judged to be ungentlemanly such as boorish or illegal behaviour. His principal demand was that the young men always behaved with good manners - no matter the situation or how drunk they felt. It was a matter of self-discipline he told them. The students respected him, yet they always felt a little unsure in his presence which is exactly how Drury wanted it.

He had thought carefully before agreeing to Will's request, and he had only agreed to show the two doctors around on account of Will's previous medical care. However, as a man of great integrity, he guessed that the two men were planning something clandestine, and that made him uncomfortable especially if they were planning something that would embarrass the college.

'In here, Gentlemen,' he said to the two doctors as he unlocked the door of one of the meeting rooms at the College. 'They always come here for their meetings. I know this because Professor Dinsmore has to book the room, and I run the diary. The next one is in a week's time, I believe.'

Inside, the room was unremarkable. There were several rows of seats facing a long table at the front to one side and a central podium. Will pointed to a door at the end of the room in the far corner.

'What's in there?' he asked.

'That's another small room that visiting speakers can use to prepare for their presentations. I'm always asked to unlock it.' Drury looked a little sheepish. 'I don't like to snoop, but I've noticed that the same two or three people always gather in there after the main presentation has finished. There are two men called Lords Vane and Kenyon, and an army Colonel who I don't like very much.'

'Fairman?' Will asked.

'Yes, that's him. He may be a senior officer, but

he has the manners of a navvy.'

Will looked at the door. 'May we see inside, please?' he asked. The porter started to look a bit uncomfortable as his conscience began to gain the upper hand, but eventually he nodded and selected another key. Inside, the room looked just like any other university office. There was a partially full bookcase, a desk and four chairs. There was certainly nowhere for an eavesdropper to hide. Sam glanced up and saw a small glass skylight. It was grubby from years of neglect. Drury followed Sam's gaze and then turned to Will. He had agreed to show the two doctors the meeting room, but he had reached the limit of his forbearance.

'Dr Perks, I owe you a great deal, but I've always been loyal to Christ Church College. I can guess that you wish to observe this meeting, perhaps in secret. When you sent your message to me, I thought it best not to ask too many questions, but can you at least reassure me that your intentions are honest? The investment business is crooked and corrupt, and I wouldn't want to encourage something that would later reflect badly on this college.'

Will looked at Sam, and they both knew they would have to dispel the man's doubts or risk him reporting their activities to the university authorities.

'It's a secret, Mr Drury,' Will replied, 'but it has nothing to do with the investment meeting. It's what happens afterwards that we're interested in. We believe there is a treasonous plot underway, and we want to find out what it is and report the matter to the appropriate authorities. It is a plot that extends to the very highest level in the land. We just can't tell you what it is, but please help us. Our monarchy may be at great risk.'

Drury fell silent and looked at the floor deep in thought. 'I wondered why Joseph Ackers was brought in,' he murmured. 'I knew it must be something serious when I saw he was part of it.'

'Joseph Ackers?'

'Yes. Ackers is a boxer. He is well known in the worst areas of Oxford, and he often appears before the magistrates for crimes involving violence. He is known to be available for hire when someone needs a bit of muscle. I was surprised to see him attending these meetings. He acts as some kind of security guard and even stands outside the door to this office when the three men get together. The very fact that Ackers is involved lends credence to your story so, yes, I will help you.' He pointed up at the skylight. 'If you're looking for somewhere to listen, that's the spot you want, Dr Perks.'

Ten minutes later, the two doctors were heading back to the infirmary; their visit had been extremely worthwhile. Dury had explained that the roof of the small office was easily accessed from the street outside. There was a drainpipe that could be easily shinned, and a ledge around the perimeter of the roof where someone could stand. From there, it was possible to lean against the roof slope and look through the skylight into the office below. He knew it was secure because he had once caught two undergraduates trying to break in through the roof when they had arrived back at the College after the gates had been locked. It was a perfect spot for eavesdropping, but it had one problem: there was room for only one person on the ledge.

The arguing started as soon as they were back

in Sam's room. Will was adamant that he should be the one on the roof and supported his claim by stating that it was his idea in the first place. Sam felt responsible for his friend's safety, but he was unable to support his case with a convincing reason. However, he pleaded with Will to settle the matter with the toss of a coin. Will was reluctant, but eventually capitulated, and then won the toss anyway.

It was a good-natured exchange, but Sam was left with a great sense of foreboding. He told Will that he would try to join Wingfield inside the main meeting room where they could observe events and be close-by to offer help if Will was discovered. They felt their plan had only a half-chance of success, but both men were excited that their investigation seemed to be nearing an end.

Chapter 22

The Meeting

On the evening of the investment meeting, the weather was still uncomfortably hot. The air was heavy with moisture, and in the absence of even a whisper of a breeze, it felt like a thick blanket had descended over the city, trapping the sun's daytime energy and compressing the stink of Oxford's overpopulated yards. Most of the city's inhabitants had retreated home early to escape the heat. Many prayed for rain. It was urgently required as the water table had fallen, and the remaining supplies in the city's wells had started to assume the same unhealthy aroma as the surrounding atmosphere. The city was ripe for disease and another outbreak of cholera.

As they approached the Tom Tower entrance to Christ Church College, the two men went their separate ways. Will went around the side of the college to position himself close to the drainpipe that he would climb to reach the perimeter of the roof. It was too early to make his ascent, so he found a nearby passageway and lurked like a footpad in the lengthening shadows.

Meanwhile, Sam met Wingfield under the clock tower. They signed in with the porter who nodded at Sam as he recorded their names but otherwise gave no indication that they had met before. He handed them a prospectus for the railway project and pointed to the door of the meeting room.

'In there, gentlemen, please.'

As they went through the doorway, a huge man with a broken nose asked for their names and added them to his own list without making any further comment. He looked like a boxer, and Sam assumed he was Joseph Ackers, the hired thug. Sam thought it would be a foolish individual indeed that tried to tackle this huge beast of a man, and he avoided making eye contact. Instead, he looked around for some seats and found two together near the back.

'In case we need to leave quickly,' he explained to Wingfield who nodded and started reading the prospectus. When they entered, the room was nearly full, and Sam could sense the greedy anticipation that seemed to hover above the audience, mingling with a thick haze of tobacco smoke. All around him, there was the excited chatter of men clutching papers and speculating wildly on the profits that they might make on their investment. As he surveyed the audience, Sam noticed that Colonel Fairman was sitting at the table at the front. He saw Sam, and for a moment Sam thought he was going to order Ackers to eject him from the meeting. However, he seemed to change his mind, and he leered at Sam instead. Sam looked away and remembered Fairman's shotgun and the wounds the

Colonel had inflicted on him at Blenheim Palace. Sam's shoulder was mending nicely, but it still ached a little and was a useful reminder of the danger they faced. He was reassured to feel Wingfield's pistols in his belt, but he was nonetheless looking forward to returning to the relative security of the infirmary.

Five minutes later, Lords Vane and Kenyon entered the room with the Duke of Marlborough and sat down at the table with Fairman. Kenyon looked around at the audience and seemed pleased with the turnout. He nodded at Ackers who closed the door. Kenyon then stood up and introduced his guest who was sitting next to Professor Dinsmore on the front row near the podium.

'Gentlemen, thank you very much for attending this evening which I'm sure you will find most illuminating and…shall we say…extremely profitable.' There was a murmur of expectation around the room which Kenyon went on to exploit.

'We are very pleased to introduce Mr Bartholomew from the Great Western Railway Company. As you know, these railway projects are attracting a lot of attention at the moment, and for those lucky enough to invest at the outset, they can end up being quite profitable. That is to say, *highly* profitable,' he repeated to stir the greed that was bubbling away in the audience.

Sam admired the skill that Kenyon deployed to manipulate his audience. He thought that many of those present had probably been invited not just for their wealth but also for their susceptibility to the most powerful motivators of them all: speculation and greed. However, Sam knew that such emotions made a potent elixir for rash behaviour, unwise decisions, and financial impoverishment. He looked at Wingfield studying the prospectus and hoped that his mentor would not be suddenly overcome by the feverish atmosphere.

Sam might have had his reservations, but the rest of the audience feasted on the Company's financial projections and the expected profits, and there was loud applause when Mr Bartholomew finished his presentation twenty minutes later. He had explained that the railway company was hoping to build a branch line to Oxford and needed capital for the venture. He told the audience that the new line would encourage trade and transport to and from London, and that it was expected to be highly profitable. At the end, Lord Kenyon thanked his visitor and asked those who were willing to pledge their investment to form a queue with Mr Bartholomew who would sort out the necessary paperwork. At this, there was a bit of a mass scramble to get to the front. It was the perfect distraction to allow the conspirators to move quietly into the side office. The heart of the conspiracy was about to meet, and Sam was surprised that only three men went through the door: Vane, Kenyon and Fairman. Even the Duke of Marlborough remained in his seat. Could it really be just three men behind all of this? Sam felt Wingfield stir beside him. The surgeon looked at him and waved the prospectus.

'I don't think I'll be investing, Sam,' he said, discarding the document onto the empty seat next to him. 'But this has been an interesting exercise in human behaviour.' He lowered his voice. 'Have they retired?' he whispered.

'Yes, they've just gone inside that door over in the corner. We should wait a while in case Will needs our help.'

It did not take long. They had been waiting for about five minutes when a muffled shout came from inside the office. Joseph Ackers went straight over to the door which opened to reveal Fairman. The Colonel looked extremely angry and pointed to the roof. There was an urgent exchange, and Ackers tried to rush out of the building. However, most of the men queuing to see Bartholomew thought the man was trying to jump the queue, and despite the boxer's intimidating appearance, several sets of elbows came out to impede his progress. Ackers was shouting furiously and had to push men out of the way as he fought to reach the exit. Fairman watched Ackers with undisguised frustration and rage, and he was about to return to the side office when he saw Sam sitting at the back of the room. He glared at Sam as though he was to blame, and for a moment it seemed as though he might confront the two surgeons, but then Drury appeared at Sam's side, and Fairman changed his mind and retreated into the office.

Drury had news of Will. 'I think your friend needs some help,' he told Sam. 'They heard him up on the roof, and now Ackers has gone after him. God help him if he's caught.'

Sam thanked Drury for letting them know, and the two men quickly left the college in the direction he had indicated. As they entered the bottom end of Fish Street, Wingfield fell behind. Sam rushed on a little further and could hear shouting. At first the noise was indistinct, but as he got closer, he could hear that a physical struggle was taking place just inside one of the passageways leading away from the street. One of the voices was Will's but it only lasted a moment before there was a loud thud and everything went quiet.

Sam was reaching for one of his pistols when Ackers burst out of the passage. He looked at Sam and then ran off towards the High Street. Sam advanced slowly into the shadows, and as his eyes adjusted to the darkness, he saw Will crumpled up on the soiled floor of the passageway. He was barely conscious, and blood was seeping from an injury to his head. He looked at Sam and tried to sit up.

'Don't, Will. Stay down until we can get you back to the infirmary.' His friend flopped back and then tried to speak. Sam could barely make it out, but he leaned over to let Will whisper into his ear. The apothecary's voice was weak, and his breathing was becoming laboured. He was failing fast.

'The Princess,' he whispered. 'It's an assassination.' He tried to say more, but could only manage a croak, and then he slipped away into unconsciousness. Wingfield caught up, and his face fell when Sam told him what he had just heard. He looked even more troubled when he saw the extent of Will's head injury.

'I'll look after him, Sam. You go and catch the brute who did this. Use your gun if you must but be careful.'

Sam nodded and ran up the street. When he got to the junction with the High Street, he looked both ways and saw Ackers. He was about 100 yards away and heading towards the castle. Heavyweight men can stand and fight well, but they are often poor runners, and Ackers was no exception. As Sam raced after him, he could see that the man was already fatigued and had slowed markedly. It took Sam only a few minutes before he was just behind him. He could hear the man's laboured breathing as his heavy muscles ran out of oxygen and made demands on his lungs that they were unable to satisfy. Eventually, Ackers was forced to stop, and it was then that Sam saw that he was carrying a bludgeon. It was covered in blood, and Sam was in no doubt that it was Will's. Ackers looked scornfully at Sam and laughed.

'Go on then, let's see if you can do any better than your friend. I'm going to enjoy this.' He crouched and adopted a fighter's pose. It was the posture Sam knew the boxer would adopt every time he went into the ring, but it was not one Sam was willing to honour physically. Instead, he drew a pistol from his waistband and cocked the hammer. Ackers looked shocked; he hadn't considered that the doctor might be armed. Further down the street a shout pierced the dusk. Ackers glanced towards it and assumed that Sam had help.

'You won't use that toy gun,' he bragged. 'You haven't got the guts.' With that, he turned to run across the street.

The problem with moments of extreme stress is that they produce high doses of adrenaline which cause the brain to telescope time and focus attention solely on the most existential threat. For Ackers, that threat was Sam's gun, and he was oblivious to anything else around him. He was still laughing at Sam when he stepped out into the path of the ten o'clock coach to London. He did not hear or see it, and he had no inkling that he was about to lose his life.

There was a sickening crunch as the boxer was thrown forward by the horses followed by two dull thumps as both nearside wheels of the four-ton coach ran over Ackers' torso and crushed his vital organs.

Sam had no need to perform an examination to know that Ackers was dead. Nobody could survive trauma like that. He thought of his friend and desperately wanted to know how he was faring. Sam certainly did not want to get embroiled in a long police investigation, and so he replaced the gun and dodged into a backyard just as two constables arrived. It was a rash decision that Sam would come to regret, especially as the accident had been observed by someone else. As the coach stopped, and the driver rushed to join the constables standing by Acker's body, Colonel Fairman was watching from the shadows on the other side of the road. He had seen enough and slipped away into the evening gloom.

Chapter 23

Imprisonment

Sam had never seen so many constables on the streets. As he made his way back to the passage where he had left Wingfield with Will, he ignored the potential dangers lurking in the shadows and decided to keep to the backyards. He could hear police whistles, and they seemed to surround him as he threaded his way through the alleys towards Fish Street.

The police activity did not seem to deter Oxford's footpads, however, and as Sam entered a particularly narrow passage, he was threatened by a man hiding in the gloom. He looked unkempt with a dirty beard, and he wore clothes that smelled as though they had never been washed. The thief was the perfect caricature of a creature of the night who thought that he had come across easy prey. It was not often that a foolish gentleman appeared on his patch after dark.

'Hold on there, Mister,' he said from the

shadows as he waved a knife in Sam's face. 'You're a little bit off your usual path, aren't you? I'm afraid those that come down this alley must pay a toll. And after dark, the price goes up a very long way indeed - especially for a well-dressed gentleman who seems to be in a hurry to get somewhere.'

Sam looked at the footpad and his anger ignited. He did not have time for this. 'Put the knife down and all will be well,' he told the man who laughed in Sam's face.

'Or what?' he asked. 'Every time you delay, the price for safe passage increases.'

Sam's heart was hammering, but he forced himself to stay calm and allowed a brief period of silence to increase the tension in the gloomy passageway.

'As I told you, put the knife down and all will be well. I don't think you heard me,' he repeated.

The man glared at his victim's obstinacy and gestured with the knife again. 'I'll be needing all of your purse now,' he snarled. 'And don't think about running or I'll slit your throat like a Christmas turkey.'

'Very well, but I'm afraid there isn't much money inside it,' Sam told him and calmly reached around to his coattails. It was not for his purse, of course, and when Sam cocked the hammer and pointed his pistol at the thief's face, the man was astonished and immediately held up his hands in surrender. The well-dressed gentleman was speaking to him in the language of the street, and he did not need to see Sam's face to sense his opponent's resolve. He knew he had no choice but to comply.

'Drop the knife and back up,' Sam told the man who allowed the blade to fall and then retreated backwards to a point where the narrow passage widened into a yard. It was covered in a foul-smelling layer of mud and human faeces. Sam waved the pistol at the man.

'Get down,' he ordered. 'Face down and arms outstretched.'

The man did as he was told, and as Sam ran into the next passageway, he felt strangely elated. It seemed like poetic justice to leave the footpad face down in the dirt where he belonged. Sam's heart was pounding from the confrontation, but he was determined to reach his friend whatever obstacles were placed in his way.

Unfortunately, the city itself becomes an obstacle in the darkness, and it took Sam longer than he expected to reach his destination. He became a little disorientated in the maze of backstreets, and at one point he had inadvertently started to retrace his steps before he recognized a derelict building and was able to correct his path. When he finally arrived at Fish Street, the road was empty, and the only sign of his friends was a pair of broken spectacles lying beside a large pool of Will's blood where he had lain in the entrance of the passageway. Sam forced himself to ignore the implications of such a sizeable stain and decided to return to the infirmary. If Will required surgery, he reasoned, it seemed most likely that Wingfield would have taken him there rather than to his house.

Sam set off to find them. He kept to the backstreets and was relieved when he finally arrived at the front gates of the infirmary a few minutes later. However, as he stepped through the entrance, Sam was taken by surprise when he discovered that Whiting was waiting for him in the shadows.

'That's him, Constables!' the secretary shouted, as he stepped forward pointing at Sam. 'That's the man you're looking for.'

Sam was initially confused but then was stunned when two constables hiding behind the gateway appeared at his side and seized him. They forced him, facedown, onto the ground and handcuffed his hands behind his back before removing the guns from his belt. As he was led away, Sam saw Whiting. The man was watching with a treacherous smirk on his face, and he gave Sam a theatrical wave to send him on his way.

***

Sam was taken by cart to a local magistrate's house. The justice was clearly annoyed at being disturbed, and he gave no quarter in his treatment of Sam. The University Sergeant had been summoned to present an outline case for the prosecution which began as soon as Sam was brought into the magistrate's office.

'What is the charge here, Sergeant?' the magistrate asked wearily.

'Murder, your worship,'

The magistrate's face darkened. 'Go on.'

'This man is called Samuel Ansell. Earlier this evening, he tried to assist with a break-in at a private meeting at Christ Church. He absconded and was pursued by a man called Ackers who had been hired to provide security. A witness has come forward and will give evidence that Ansell fought with Ackers and deliberately pushed him into the path of a coach, killing him instantly. The witness will say that Ansell was aware of some approaching constables but chose to run away into the backstreets rather than waiting to explain himself. The prosecution will say that the push was deliberate, and that Ansell knew the consequences were likely to be fatal. The charge of murder therefore seems appropriate, and we ask that the prisoner is incarcerated pending an appearance before a judge and jury at the quarterly assizes next week.'

Sam listened and realized that he was being set up. Fairman was behind this, and Sam knew he would be supported by a formidable array of officials who would line up to ensure that Sam was found guilty. The magistrate looked grave.

'Do you have anything to say, Mr Ansell?'

Sam shook his head and said, "I am not guilty, your worship, but I wish to reserve my defence until I am able to get legal representation.'

The magistrate nodded. 'Very well. You are to be imprisoned and will appear before the quarterly assizes next Monday. I believe that His Lordship Judge Hector Brontley KC will be sitting.'

Brontley? Sam's heart sank as he remembered the Judge's voice at the shooting party. This was getting worse by the moment. He tried to banish his previous image of Brontley's black cap, but it remained obstinately at the forefront of his mind as the gravity of the situation dawned on him. As he was led away, Sam was bewildered by the speed of his descent from respected surgeon to suspected murderer in the space of a single day. The situation was looking hopeless, and his growing despair overwhelmed any spark of remaining optimism.

***

When Sam was led into his cell at the prison, the gaoler recognized the prisoner's dejection. Sam was wearing a face that was typical of those in his situation. It was one of abject misery and hopelessness, and it was especially common amongst those that faced an untimely end at the end of the hangman's noose. The gaoler felt sorry for this gentleman who seemed to be out of place in the dank surroundings of the prison cell. As he fastened some leg irons around Sam's ankles, he tried to make light of the situation with some gentle small talk, but like all the other condemned men, Sam did not really listen and was too preoccupied with his own thoughts to answer.

After the gaoler had departed, Sam took stock of his surroundings. Oxford Castle was first built in Norman times and had housed the county prison since the fourteenth century. Sam knew that in the past it had held captive some notable individuals including, ironically, some royal prisoners. Over the last hundred years, it had gradually fallen into a state of poor repair, and the prison had gained a reputation for its harsh conditions.

This decline was immediately apparent to Sam as he inspected his cell. He felt fortunate to be given one to himself, although one wall consisted entirely of bars and a large iron gate making the cell fully visible from the corridor beyond. In one corner there was a horsehair mattress. It was filthy and looked like it was probably infested with lice. There was also a blanket that looked no cleaner. On one side, there was a small table on which the gaoler had kindly left him a small candle and a bible. Finally, there was a bucket toilet in the corner furthermost from the bed. It was unspeakably dirty and filled the cell with unpleasant fumes that seemed to emphasize Sam's terrible predicament. He sat on the chair and waited for someone to come so he could try to arrange a lawyer.

After twenty-four hours, Sam received his first visitor. It was Anne and when he saw her, his heart leaped. 'Oh Anne, I'm so glad you've come to see me.' She looked at him through the bars and squeezed his hand. Her face was full of pity, and she looked so sad that Sam was compelled to reach out with his other hand. 'It's not so bad, Anne,' he said, 'Something will turn up, it always does. That's what Will says, anyway.' He paused when she started sobbing. 'He is alright. Will, I mean. He is alright?' Anne drew a breath and tried to gather the strength to tell him what she had learned.

'I must break some terrible news to you, Sam. I went to the infirmary today, and I was informed by the Reverend Thomas that Will was brought into the infirmary with a head injury last night. Mr Wingfield attempted an emergency operation, but Will never regained consciousness and passed away in the early hours of this morning. I'm terribly sorry; he was a lovely man, and I know he was your close friend.'

Sam was stunned and as his grief took hold, his despair deepened further. He stared at the floor. It was hard to accept that his friend had gone. Will Perks had been so full of life and so selfless. He thought of the men who had murdered the apothecary. Although it was Ackers that had dealt the fatal blow, they were all responsible, and Sam felt his anger rise. He looked up at her

'You know I didn't do it. Kill that man, I mean. Fairman is behind this false accusation, and I expect this witness of his has been paid well for his lies. The truth is I was chasing the man after he bludgeoned Will, and he just stepped out into the path of the coach. It was a mistake to run because they now think I was trying to abscond from a crime scene. In fact, it was an accident, and I just wanted to see if Will was alright.'

'You are no murderer, Samuel Ansell,' she said firmly. 'I know that for certain.' She paused as she realized that it would be others that would need to be convinced of Sam's innocence. 'Do you know when your case will be heard?' she asked nervously.

'I'm not sure, but I believe it will be in two days' time. By then, I must find a reputable lawyer to represent me if I am to have half a chance of avoiding…well…you know the penalty I face here.'

She nodded. 'I do, Sam. It's all my fault too. This only happened because I told you about my father and encouraged you to pry.'

'It's not your fault, Anne. We would have investigated it without your encouragement. Please don't blame yourself.' Sam then realized that she was alone and unchaperoned. 'Nobody is with you,' he observed.

'My father brought me, but he refused to come and see you. I think it's guilt, but I still don't understand his involvement in all of this. Anyway, he said he had to return home to collect my mother. They are going to London for a few days to some social event. I wish I was going too because my father has also allowed Lords Vane and Kenyon to hold another one of their meetings at our house while my parents are away. Actually, it's all a bit strange. My father was very firm, and he directed that I was to remain at the house until he returned home. He told me I am to avoid the visitors by feigning illness and taking to my room.'

Sam was alarmed by the idea of Anne being alone in the house with the three conspirators and came to a decision.

'Listen, Anne, we don't have much time, and I need to tell you something vitally important.' He lowered his voice to a whisper. 'This is not about a regency. This is a plot to assassinate Princess Victoria and make the Duke of Cumberland the first in line to accede to the throne after King William dies. The story about a regency is a diversion to entice people of power to donate money and use their influence to help the conspirators. The problem we face is that we don't know when and where the assassination will take place, and we don't know who we can trust.' There was a noise in the corridor, and Sam paused until he saw that it was just a rat going about its usual prison business.

'Now listen, you must send word to your father to come home urgently. When he does, confront him with your knowledge. Tell him what is about to happen and persuade him to go to the authorities in Westminster. I am certain that he is being blackmailed, although I don't know what they want from him. I'm also sure that he has no idea that an assassination is being planned, but he must face down these men otherwise he may end up taking the blame for the murder of a member of the royal family. I feel sure that when your father is told the full facts he will agree to act - whatever damaging information may eventually emerge. Do you understand, Anne?'

She nodded just as the gaoler opened a distant door, and the clank of iron signalled that the visit was at an end. Sam had just enough time for one final instruction.

'Anne, please do not under any circumstances try to take on these men by eavesdropping or confronting them. Look at my situation. They are ruthless. Promise me!'

The gaoler's shadow appeared on the wall as he approached keys jangling. They were out of time.

'And Anne. I love you. Please forgive me for leaving you like this.' A tear fell from her cheek, and she squeezed his hand. 'I will come back' she promised.

The gaoler was gentle; it was a scene he had seen many times. 'I'm very sorry, Miss, but your carriage is here, and it is time for you to leave.'

She nodded as the tears started to fall again. She released Sam's hand and then swept down the corridor towards the daylight, cheeks wet and unconsolable. She sobbed and felt helplessly alone as she wondered whether she would ever see Sam again.

***

After Anne had gone, Sam worried whether he had done the correct thing by telling her about the assassination plot. He would have been a little more confident if there was somebody Anne could confide in, but Wingfield seemed to have disappeared, and Sam's friend had died at the hands of a murderer. He sighed. Poor Will. No doubt someone like Whiting would be tasked to inform Will's family of his death. A story would be fabricated, and unless Sam was released, nobody would know of his friend's selfless bravery and the sheer evil of those that Will had tried to confront.

Sam knew he had to get out, for Will, for Anne, and also for the Princess and the Infirmary. But where was Wingfield? He desperately needed the man's help, and he was worried that something was amiss. Perhaps Wingfield had been targeted too? Sam wondered whether he could persuade the gaoler to allow him to send a message, and he decided that if nobody visited on the following day, then he would at least ask the man.

In the event, Sam did receive a visitor the following day, but it was not someone offering help. It was Judge Hector Brontley KC who had come to gloat and to bargain. Sam heard him coming before he saw him, and the gravelly voice sounded even more malevolent as it echoed off the whitewashed walls of the prison. After two doors had clanked their notice of the judge's arrival, he finally appeared outside Sam's cell and looked in.

'Ansell,' he intoned. 'How far you have fallen.' He gazed without pity at Sam and gave a hollow laugh. 'And you will fall yet further when the executioner opens the trapdoor beneath your feet. And he surely will, Samuel. I will ensure that it is so when you appear before me tomorrow.'

If he expected Sam to wilt, he was mistaken. 'You are a disgrace to your office, Brontley. The worst felon within these prison walls has more morals than you,' Sam observed bitterly.

The judge just laughed at him. 'That may be so, but I am not the one languishing behind bars. You need to consider your own position. The trial will probably last two days, and an execution normally takes place a day or two after that. Not long, Ansell. Less than a week. However, I haven't come here just to enjoy your predicament; I want to make a proposal.'

Sam's survival instinct stirred. 'What proposal?'

'You have a notebook, and we want it back. If you tell me where it is, I will sentence you leniently after you are found guilty. There is a big difference between the noose and transportation.'

Sam's spirits lifted a little. Perhaps there was a deal to be struck. He had forgotten about the notebook, and he wondered what was in it that was so important to the conspirators. He closed his eyes trying to remember what he had seen when he had discussed it with Will. There was more information in it than just the canal shares fraud. He remembered that several of the names had been familiar, but he could not recall who they were or the reasons they were recorded.

'Very well,' he said to the Judge eventually. 'You have left me no choice, but I will only surrender the book after the trial has finished and you have sentenced me.' Brontley looked irritated by Sam's proviso. 'You didn't really expect me to tell you beforehand, did you?' Sam added.

The judge shrugged. 'It makes no odds, Ansell' he said, turning to leave. 'I'll see you in the dock tomorrow. You'll be taken to recover the book and then onwards to a prison hulk to await transportation. You should make your farewells before the trial because there will be no time afterwards.'

Brontley summoned the gaoler by rapping on the bars with his cane, and he left Sam alone with his thoughts. Uppermost in Sam's mind was the realization that he had probably said his final farewell to Anne. It was a depressing idea that dampened his mood despite the welcome discovery that he was not going to be hanged after all.

***

When the shackled prisoner was brought into Courtroom Number Four, a close observer might have concluded that this was a gentleman who had fallen on hard times. They would have seen that the crumpled clothing had once been respectably cleaned and pressed, and that the man's dirty and unshaven face was a temporary aberration rather than a façade of habitual scruffiness. But that would have required some careful deduction, and the baying mob in the public gallery had no time for informed deliberation. They were present for one purpose only: to see a guilty verdict and the judge's black hat. The fact that the prisoner looked unkempt only added to the excitement and the sense that the prisoner must be guilty otherwise he wouldn't have been standing there.

For Sam, the courtroom felt like a Roman amphitheatre where the public gallery had gathered for gladiatorial enjoyment but first needed warming up with the spectacle of one or two unarmed Christians being fed to the lions. Sam stood helpless in the dock and tried to look like a doctor rather than a murderer which was hard to do after several days in prison.

At the last moment, a small weaselly man had appeared at Sam's cell and announced that he had been appointed by the court to represent him. Sam was initially excited until it became clear that the lawyer was one of Brontley's stooges. The man confirmed that the court would accept a guilty plea to the lesser charge of manslaughter, and that Sam would be transported to the colonies. He would not be permitted to address the court, and his plea for mitigation would be submitted on his behalf by his legal representative.

As Sam waited for Brontley to appear, he

looked around the courtroom. Up in the gallery, Anne was sitting between Wingfield and Sam's father. She smiled at him and gave a small wave. Wingfield looked solemn and nodded in a manner that suggested he feared the worst possible outcome. Sam was pleased that his father was well enough to attend, although he was still prone to outbursts of coughing. He looked down sadly at his son, and Sam felt wretched as he imagined his father's disappointment. The conspirators had gathered at the other side of the public gallery. The Duke of Marlborough was sitting next to the man wearing the heavy coat. Behind them, Lords Vane and Kenyon looked on, enjoying the spectacle. They were all here to gloat, Sam thought, and he looked away quickly, determined to avoid eye contact and any appearance of fear.

He looked down into the well of the court. Amongst all the gowns and wigs, he saw that Lipscomb was sitting alongside the other reporters with a notebook on his knee. He nodded at Sam, but his look suggested that Sam had become the story and that he was no longer useful as a co-investigator.

Sam was about to face the front when a sudden flash of red up in the gallery caught his attention. Fairburn had arrived and had taken a seat at the front where he had his feet propped up on the railings. He wore a nauseous expression of self-satisfaction, and he laughed when he saw Sam chained to the dock. It was an unbearable humiliation, and Sam let his gaze return to the floor as misery and helplessness threatened to overwhelm him.

After a few minutes, the waiting was over, and the courtroom rose as Judge Brontley came in and took his seat. He looked even more menacing in his robes and wig, and his voice was sombre and threatening as he banged his gavel and brought the court to order. He looked down on Sam with hooded eyes and made no effort to disguise his disdain. Sam began to worry that Brontley might renege on their deal, and the realization made his legs weak as he tried to stand up straight.

In the end, the prosecution barrister stood up and informed the court that the prisoner had pleaded guilty to the lesser charge of manslaughter which the prosecution had accepted. There was a groan of disappointment from the gallery which was only silenced when Judge Brontley picked up his black cap and twiddled it thoughtfully. There was a brief murmur of renewed expectation as the gallery realized that it was not over yet, and there was still a fair chance of some high drama.

With the plea accepted, Brontley dismissed the jury, and the court listened as the prosecutor outlined the facts of the case. Sam stopped listening after a while because the facts were interwoven with half-truths and outright lies, and he could do nothing to influence what was said anyway. The same sense of resignation hung over him when his representative stood up and made some inane remarks on his behalf. Sam was relieved when the storytelling was finally over, and he looked up at Brontley to hear his sentence.

The Judge was in no rush, and he stared at Sam for a whole minute without speaking. The courtroom was absolutely silent, and the atmosphere became heavy with expectation. Brontley looked down at his black cap and slowly picked it up again. For a few horrific seconds, Sam thought the deal was off before he realized that it was all a cruel act designed to torment the prisoner and to tease the gallery. After allowing the atmosphere to ferment, Brontley returned the black cap to the bench in front of him. He had extended the drama to the fullest extent possible, and it was time to give his pronouncement.

'Samuel Ansell, you have pleaded guilty to the charge of manslaughter which has been accepted by the crown. You should consider yourself lucky because the facts of the case suggest you acted with a degree of intention when you pushed Joseph Ackers and then tried to abscond.' He paused to let his words sink in.

'However, we have heard that you are a doctor who has worked hard at the infirmary on behalf of your patients, and, with that in mind, I am going to act mercifully today.'

'Murderer!' a shout interrupted. 'Hang him!' came another. Realization had struck the mob, and angry disappointment burst out into the courtroom. Brontley allowed the drama to continue for a moment and then banged his gavel until order was restored.

'With this in mind,' he continued over the final residual shouts, 'I am sentencing you to transportation to the colonies for a period of twenty-five years. You will leave this court immediately and be taken to Portsmouth docks to a prison hulk and thence to the New World. There are no grounds for appeal, and your goods will be sold off and the proceeds awarded to the family of Joseph Ackers.' He leered at Sam. Brontley always enjoyed the drama of the final words. He banged his gavel. 'Officers, take him down.'

Sam looked up to the gallery for one last sight Anne, and he ignored Fairman and the other conspirators. He wouldn't waste precious seconds observing their predictable satisfaction. Anne was sitting, transfixed by the enormity of the sentence, with tears streaming down her face. Sam tried to smile, conscious that this was the last time they would see each other. He was still looking into her eyes when two constables wrenched him from the dock and took him down to the cells where a secure carriage was waiting to start Sam's long journey to the other side of the world.

***

There were three other prisoners chained to the seats inside the prison wagon. They all looked as dirty and bedraggled as Sam, and they looked at each other with mutual mistrust, wondering about their neighbours' crimes, and whether they would pose a danger during the long voyage ahead. Sam was dreading the next part of the agreement he had struck with Brontley. He was expecting to be taken to the infirmary where he would lead one of the guards to secure Crosley's notebook from Will's hiding place. Sam was certain he would be seen by Moss, and he fully expected Whiting to be nearby, gloating at his downfall, but Sam hoped they would be the only witnesses to his disgrace. Even though he would soon be lost in the New World, his reputation would linger at the infirmary, and he did not want it further sullied by someone's memory of a doctor once respected, but seen chained, dirty and disreputable.

It took Sam nearly an hour of contemplation of life in the colonies before he was jolted back to the present. The infirmary was only a few minutes from the court and yet nearly an hour later they had still not arrived. It was unexpected and rather worrying. What if the book had already been found and he had become expendable? It would be so easy to arrange for him to be killed and his body disposed in some lonely ditch. As Sam worried, he thought about the prospect of escape and decided that he would make a run for it if he was granted an opportunity.

Eventually, the wagon stopped, and he heard approaching voices. One sounded familiar and confirmed his worst fears. It was the Duke of Marlborough. Moments later, the door opened, and an officer unchained him from the bars at the side of the secure compartment. Sam looked out. Marlborough was standing next to a small carriage with the man from the park. They were outside the city in the countryside, and the road was quiet and devoid of witnesses. The Duke's colleague looked at Sam and decided that the prisoner was about to run.

'Hold him,' he shouted, and the officer grabbed Sam's arms. Sam went limp; any opportunity for flight was now lost. 'Bring him here,' the man instructed.

Sam was led over to the other carriage. The Duke looked at him. 'Don't be alarmed, Sam, all will become clear shortly. You have nothing to fear from us. In fact, you're being released.'

Sam looked at him with distrust and started to interject, but the Duke held up his hand. 'Not here, Sam. I know what you think of me, but you are mistaken about my intentions, and you need to hear my explanation before you make a judgement.' He turned to the constable and gave him a hefty purse.

'Thank you, officer, you may go on your way.' The man nodded, and after closing the rear door, he sat by the driver and the wagon resumed its journey to the sea.

Sam watched as it disappeared into the distance and tried not to fan a spark of hope that had started to smoulder. Beside him, the Duke gestured to the waiting carriage and Sam climbed in. He was free, but for how long?

Chapter 24

The Lost Notebook

There was silence in the carriage as it set off back towards Oxford. Sam was still unsure whether he had left one danger only to face another. He had assumed that the Duke of Marlborough was a key member of the conspiracy but now he was not so sure. And who was the man with the heavy coat? Did he work for the Duke? As he looked out of the window he had plenty of questions, but the Duke had indicated that any discussion should take place privately, and so Sam waited to see where he was being taken. He allowed hope to catch fire, and he started to enjoy the possibility of freedom. Perhaps all was not lost.

The coach travelled west for only fifteen minutes before it came to a stop. Sam could see that they had pulled into the yard of the Britannia Coaching Inn on the New London Road in Headington. He recognized it because it was a regular coach stop, and it was on the route between Oxford and the Kirtland's home at High Cross Manor. The man in the heavy coat spoke for the first time. He had a voice of understated authority.

'Wait here, gentlemen. I will check that everything is clear.' He left the coach and then returned after a few minutes and instructed them to follow him inside. The three men entered the Inn and went up the stairs to a small room on the first landing. Sam sat down on a chair and waited for an explanation.

The Duke started it. 'Now, Sam I need to start by introducing you to Inspector Alan Pound. The Inspector is a member of the Metropolitan Police Force in London. He is highly respected, and the two of us have been selected for a very important and confidential task. You see, we work directly for the Palace. We don't answer to anyone except His Majesty the King's private secretary.' He sat down on an armchair while Pound stood at the window, seemingly deep in thought.

'For some time, we have been aware of a political plot to engineer a regency if King William died while Princess Victoria was still so young. The conspiracy seems to have originated in Parliament, which is why I was asked to assist the Inspector. Together, we have been observing a few individuals to determine who is involved. I have been trying to infiltrate the group as a supporter which is why you thought I was acting so suspiciously, whereas the Inspector has been conducting clandestine surveillance of the main suspects.'

Sam remembered the park and nodded, 'Yes, I know. I was one of the targets for a while.'

The Duke looked a little self-conscious. 'I must

apologize, Sam. When you appeared on the scene, we thought initially that you were a party to the plot until the shooting party. At that stage, we realized that you and your friend, William Perks, had been investigating the matter for yourselves.' The Duke looked at Sam sympathetically. 'By the way, I'm very sorry that your friend has lost his life over this.'

Sam nodded and was suddenly relieved that he had at last found someone to help. He looked at the Duke.

'There is much more to this than you know, Your Grace, and I think there may be only a little time left to prevent a disaster.'

Across the room, Pound seemed to stir from his deliberations. 'Go on, Mr Ansell, please tell us what you have discovered.'

Sam nodded. 'This may take a little time,' he said, 'but I will start by telling you that this is not about a regency. That is a cover story designed to conceal the real intention which is to assassinate the Princess so that the Duke of Cumberland becomes the next in line. They've been raising money for the political aftermath. It's almost a kind of royal coup d'état.' The Inspector walked over from the window and sat on the bed. He took out a notebook and started scribbling furiously.

'Go on, Mr Ansell. We seem to have made a breakthrough in the case.'

It took Sam twenty minutes to explain everything that he had learned over the previous six weeks. The two other men sat quietly, and the astonishment on their faces grew as the scale of the corruption within Oxford's civic structures became apparent. Eventually, Sam finished, and there was silence as the two other men considered what they had been told.

Eventually, the Duke looked up. 'This connection to the Orange Order makes complete sense. The debate in Parliament has been ferocious. When the Bill for Catholic Emancipation became law, we all hoped that the matter would gradually subside, but there are clearly a fanatical few who are determined to use any means necessary to restore protestant influence at the highest levels. I don't think there's been anything like it since the Glorious Revolution in 1689.'

The Inspector consulted his notebook. 'We need to discover the full extent of the conspiracy and remove those who have abused their positions of authority. But knowledge is not enough; we need evidence.'

Sam looked at him. 'I can help you with that, Inspector. The reason I escaped the noose today was because I did a deal with Judge Brontley: my life in exchange for Crosley's notebook. It clearly contains incriminating evidence, and that might be enough for your purposes. I was told to recover it from its hiding place at the infirmary while I was on my way to the port. I presume the prison guards didn't take me there because you had diverted the prison wagon to go elsewhere.'

The policeman nodded. 'When we bribed the officer he said he had instructions to take you via the infirmary, but we didn't understand why. We really need to know when and where the assassination will take place and who is involved. I don't suppose that's in your hidden book, Sam?'

Sam shook his head. 'I don't know, we only gave it a cursory look because at the time we were only looking for information about the canal shares. It's possible there is more.'

The Inspector nodded. 'Well, we'd better go and take a look at it. Where is it hidden?'

'It's in Will's room at the infirmary,' Sam replied as the two other men started to rise.

'When we get there, I think I'll also be speaking to the chairman,' the Duke declared. It's time the administration of the infirmary had a clean out.'

He looked at Sam who had remained seated and was looking uncomfortable. 'What's the matter, Sam?'

'Before we go, I need to ask the Inspector something.' Sam paused as he marshalled his thoughts. The policeman sat down again and could sense Sam's reticence.

'What is it, Sam,' he asked. 'Tell me.'

'Do you have any men helping you?' Sam asked.

'I had three but now there are two with me. The other man went missing a fortnight ago. Why? Do you know something of this?'

Sam nodded. 'Yes, I'm afraid I do. Was he a balding man with an unusual pair of spectacles?' The Inspector nodded. Sam sighed and described how the nameless man had been shot and brought to the infirmary with a terrible wound to his lower jaw. He explained about Fairman using the widow's address to collect embezzled funds, and that Pound's man had probably been killed by the Colonel after he had questioned the widow.

'I'm sorry, but there was nothing I could do to save him; he was just too badly injured. He was buried in the infirmary burial ground. I'm sure the chaplain would remember where his grave is located.' Pound listened carefully and made some notes. Eventually he looked up.

'Constable James Edrington was married with two young children,' he announced, closing his book. 'We now have an excellent reason for dealing with Colonel Fairman, don't we?' The question was asked rhetorically, but it ensured that when the three men rose to leave the inn they did so with renewed purpose and a grim determination for justice.

***

Less than an hour later, the three men arrived at the porter's desk at the font of the infirmary. The foyer was empty, but Sam knew that it would not take long before their presence became common knowledge. The Duke of Marlborough ordered Moss to unlock Will's room, and when they trooped up the stairs, they encountered only one individual and that was Nurse Wallace who smiled recognition at Sam and then hurried on her way to another ward.

As they passed by the Dead Room, Sam asked them to wait as he peered in. There was a coffin standing on one of the tables. The lid was screwed down, and the nameplate recorded the occupant as William Perks, Apothecary. At the foot of the coffin Sam noticed the infirmary's Burial Register had been left open. The final entry had been filled out with Will's details, and Sam recognized the chaplain's handwriting. He looked at Moss, who nodded.

'There was an inquest this morning, Mr Ansell. A verdict of unlawful killing by persons unknown was declared.'

Sam nodded. 'Well let's see if there's anything in Dr Perks' room.' Moss unlocked the door. He looked quizzically at Sam who knew that everyone at the infirmary would have heard of his imprisonment and would now see him as a fugitive or a murderer rather than the respected house surgeon. Sam pretended not to notice the porter's expression and decided to let the man draw his own conclusions. The Duke thanked Moss and dismissed him. When the three men went inside, they found the room had already been cleared of Will's possessions which were stored in a wooden crate on the floor, awaiting collection and return to the family home in Banbury.

'Where is the notebook hidden?' Pound asked quietly.

''I'm not sure,' Sam replied. 'It was Will that concealed it, but he told me that it was behind one of these wooden panels.' Sam began tapping on the cladding. He started by the door and was halfway around the room near the fireplace when a knock resonated deeply with the sound of a concealed cavity in the wall behind. He placed a hand flat down onto the wooden panel and rocked it. It was loose, and after a few more movements, Sam was able to get his fingers under the bottom of it and slide it up to reveal the cavity in the wall. There was nothing in it, and nothing to suggest there ever had been.

'Someone has been here before us,' Sam remarked glumly to the three men. 'I'm afraid that like my friend, the book is lost.'

The room darkened as a figure filled the doorway. He was silhouetted by the sun which was streaming in through a window opposite the door.

'We need to talk about both of those matters, Sam,' a familiar voice called. Sam looked over and smiled as Charles Wingfield strode purposefully into the room.

Chapter 25

Trephination

Wingfield closed the door behind him and allowed Sam to introduce Inspector Pound. He already knew the Duke of Marlborough who had supported his election as a consultant to the infirmary, and the two men shook hands. Wingfield looked at the expectant faces and saw the empty void in the wall.

'I expect you will want to know about the notebook, but first I feel I must tell you about Will.' He looked at Sam. 'You will remember that you last saw me in Fish Street. I need to explain what happened after you gave chase to that thug…'

***

As Sam disappeared into the darkness, Wingfield applied a clean handkerchief to Will's head. It looked as though he had been struck by a cosh, and he was bleeding heavily from an injury just behind the top of his ear. Wingfield studied the unconscious man and concluded that the blow had not only fractured Will's skull, but it had also caused internal bleeding which was raising the intracranial pressure and pressing dangerously onto Will's brain. He knew that if the internal pressure was not released soon, then Will could easily die or be left severely handicapped with brain damage. The apothecary needed urgent treatment, including a dangerous operation that was best conducted at the infirmary rather than at his own surgery. As he wondered how to get Will there, a constable ran up and asked if he had seen a man fitting Sam's description. Wingfield told the policeman that he had been walking home and had come across a man with a bleeding head wound who needed his urgent medical attention. He explained that he had been there ten minutes and had seen nobody else during that time. He asked the constable to arrange transport and was pleased that it took only ten minutes of whistle blowing before a carriage arrived, and he was able to move Will off the street.

When they arrived at the infirmary, Moss was just handing over to Littleworth for the night. He winced when he saw Will's white face and blood-stained clothing. He was surprisingly squeamish and had applied for the position of porter believing that his duties would exclude him from close contact with the patients. It had therefore been an unpleasant surprise to discover that the porter was usually the first point of contact for accident cases which could appear unpredictably at any hour of the day or night. He looked away from Will's bloodied face, but managed to set aside his discomfort to help carry the injured doctor upstairs to the operating room.

Wingfield took off his coat and washed his hands. He turned to Moss. 'What staff do we have on duty this evening?' he asked.

Moss shuffled uncomfortably. 'There are no doctors here except you, Mr Wingfield. Both house doctors were meant to be on duty this evening, but Dr Perks is laid before you now, and nobody knows where Mr Ansell is. He went out earlier and hasn't returned. The assistant apothecary was given leave, and he is away in London.'

Wingfield sighed. 'Well, I need somebody to help, and I need them quickly otherwise Dr Perks is likely to die. Find me someone, a nurse even.' Moss ran off and returned with Nurse Wallace. She looked at Will and gasped.

'I need your help, Nurse Wallace,' Wingfield told her. 'I know you're not trained, but Dr Perks is going to die unless I operate soon, and there is nobody else to help me. I will tell you what to do if you are willing to try.' Nurse Wallace nodded and washed her hands. Wingfield prepared to conduct a trephination while Moss escaped back to the safety of his nighttime accommodation.

The object of the trephination procedure was to release the pressure that the internal bleeding was applying to Will's brain. Wingfield chose a scalpel and made an incision across the area of the fracture and down to the bone. He then selected two sets of retractors and used them to part the incision to reveal the skull underneath.

'Hold these, Catherine,' he said to the nurse hoping that the use of her first name would offer encouragement and bolster her resolve. He turned to the trolley and selected a one-inch trephine. It was an instrument with a T-shaped handle at one end and a circular barrel on the other. The barrel had saw teeth at the bottom. Wingfield lined up the instrument on one edge of the fracture and started to twist it. The teeth dug in, and after a several turns, the trephine had cut through the skull, and Wingfield was able to lift away a disc of bone to reveal the membrane beneath.

'See here,' he explained to Wallace, 'this is called the Dura. It is a lining between the brain and the skull. There is very little blood on the outside, but I can tell that there is a significant quantity of blood underneath it. This means that the bleeding has occurred inside the brain itself which can be very dangerous. In moment, I will release the pressure and there will be a significant quantity of blood so don't worry. If the bleeding persists, then there is little more that I can do for him, but if the bleeding stops, then we can replace the disc and sew him up.'

Wingfield positioned some clean dressings near to Will's head and held up his scalpel. 'Ready?' he asked. Wallace nodded and held the retractors open a little wider. Wingfield looked down, chose a spot on the Dura, and then nicked it. The accumulated pressure beneath the membrane was released, and blood flowed rapidly through the hole he had created. As they watched, the river seemed to increase initially, and Wingfield wondered if he was about to lose his patient. However, the flow eventually stabilized and after a few nervous minutes it stopped altogether. The operation had succeeded, at least in the short-term. Wingfield's only remaining concern was whether he had reduced the pressure quickly enough to avoid irreparable brain damage. That would take a day or two to discover.

'Right,' he said, 'let's get his head put back together.' He put a single stitch in the Dura and then wired the disc of bone back into position. Finally, he relieved Nurse Wallace of the retractors and sewed the skin back over Will's skull. After a further five minutes the job was done, and Will was still breathing.

Nurse Wallace looked down at the unconscious doctor. 'Will he live?' she asked.

'Oh, I think so,' Wingfield told her. 'But Dr Perks will have to die first.'

***

Two days later, Wingfield looked at the confused faces of the three men.

'You see, gentlemen, popular belief has it that Dr William Perks died in the early hours after surgery failed to save him. However, I am pleased to tell you that our apothecary is alive, well, and currently recovering from his operation at Mrs Crosley's house.'

Sam was confused and then he saw it. 'You faked Will's death,' he exclaimed, as relief flowed through his veins for the first time in several days. 'Will's alive.'

Wingfield smiled. 'Yes, I decided that he was extremely vulnerable and might be killed to prevent him recounting what he heard up on the roof of Christ Church College. I thought that the best way to protect him was to stage his death and then move him secretly to somewhere suitable for him to convalesce. I had to enlist the chaplain, Reverend Savage, to help me. You see, another patient recently died of a head injury, and because he had no family to claim his body, he was due to be interred in the infirmary's burial ground. We just renamed him: William Perks. The Reverend Savage helped by ordering some coffin furniture with Will's name on it, and by filling out the Burial Register with Will's details. The only other thing I had to do was to give evidence at the inquest this morning that the corpse belonged to Will. Aside from us, the only people who know that Will is alive are Nurse Wallace and the Reverend Savage who have both pledged their silence. For the moment, the conspirators will think Will is dead and stop looking for him.'

Inspector Pound was impressed. 'That's an ingenious deception, Mr Wingfield; I will arrange for some of my men to guard Mrs Crosley's address, but in the meantime, what has happened to Crosley's notebook?'

'Well, I remembered that Sam told me it was hidden in Will's room behind a wall panel. I thought that it would be safer with Will, so the book went with him to Mrs Crosley's house.'

Sam was elated that his friend was still alive. For the first time he felt that they were starting to get the upper hand. They needed to go to Mrs Crosley's and recover the book for the Inspector, but there was some infirmary business to attend to first. He caught the Duke's eye, and the two men made their excuses to Pound and Wingfield and told them they would return within a few minutes. There was no sign of Whiting as they approached the chairman's office and knocked.

The Reverend Vaughan Thomas opened the door and was surprised to see the Duke of Marlborough with one of the house surgeons. 'Your Grace…Samuel. Come in, come in. This is a surprise. What can I do for you?' The Duke looked at Sam and nodded.

Sam decided to be direct. 'Sir, you remember that you asked me to watch for any financial irregularities, well, I have uncovered the reason that the infirmary funds have been leaking away. You see, we can prove that the secretary and the treasurer have been embezzling funds to support a political plot that extends to the highest levels in the land. There is a policeman downstairs who has been charged by the King's private secretary to work with His Grace here to thwart the conspiracy. In the meantime, you will want to restore the infirmary's good name by removing the secretary from his post and the treasurer from the Board of Governors. The sooner we get an honest Board, the quicker we can turn around the infirmary's accounts and get back to our main purpose which is treating patients.'

The chairman was speechless, and turned to the Duke who nodded and said, 'this is all true, Vaughan. We must act immediately, or our reputation will collapse.'

The chairman frowned as his anger finally sparked into life. 'Bring them to me, Samuel, please. They are both down in the secretary's office.'

Sam rose and left the room. He collected Pound and found Littleworth and Moss. There had to be no possibility of escape. He knocked on the secretary's door and entered without waiting for a reply. Whiting looked up from his desk, and Sam enjoyed watching the man's expression change from confusion to fear.

'Aren't you meant to be…'

'in prison,' Sam finished for him. 'Yes, which is where I think you'll be going very soon. And you, Roach,' he added to the treasurer who was standing at his desk and looked as though he might try to abscond. 'We know you've been diverting infirmary funds to Colonel Fairman, and we know the reason too.' Behind Sam, the Inspector blocked the doorway.

'This is Inspector Pound from the Metropolitan Police. He will help you up the stairs to see the chairman. Don't think about running. Moss and Littleworth are here too. I'll be along shortly,' he added, glancing at the filing cupboard.'

Whiting saw where Sam was looking and recognized the significance of his gaze. 'There's nothing in there to concern you,' he began.

'Oh, but I think there is,' Sam smiled. 'You are so arrogant that I doubt you had the presence of mind to cover your tracks. Let's see if I'm correct, shall we?'

He walked over to Whiting's desk, removed the key from the draw, and unlocked the cupboard. The file on canal investments was exactly where Will had left it. 'Oh, I wonder what this is,' he said picking up the file, feigning surprise.

'It wasn't me,' Whiting declared as Sam flicked through the document to confirm all the papers were there. 'Roach told me to do it.'

Roach glared at him. 'Be quiet, Whiting, you whining gibface. They have no evidence.'

'We'll see about that,' Sam laughed. 'But I think there's enough material here to ensure that you are both removed from the infirmary as a starting point. We can find out later whether the magistrates wish to proceed against you for embezzlement… or worse,' he added.

The two conspirators fell silent and looked resigned as they were led upstairs to the chairman's office. The Reverend Vaughan listened as Sam outlined what he had uncovered, and then formally dismissed the two men, explaining that his decision would be confirmed at the next quarterly meeting of governors.

Once the chairman had completed his statement, Whiting turned to Sam. His face was full of spite, and he had one final retort.

'Don't think you've heard the end of this, Ansell,' he spat. 'You'd better watch your back. And your friend, Perks too.' He saw Sam's expression change and knew he had scored a hit. 'Oh, your secret? Poor you,' he mocked. 'Did you really think that we wouldn't find out that Perks is alive? We know exactly where he is; the chaplain made sure of that.'

From the doorway, Inspector Pound had heard enough. He had ordered Littleworth to summon three constables who were waiting just outside. The inspector stood back and pointed inside the chairman's office.

'Take those two men there,' he ordered, pointing at Whiting and Roach. The officers went in. There was a brief scuffle, and moments later the two disgraced men were handcuffed and on their way to the prison and the magistrate's judgement.

'I doubt they will face charges of treason,' Pound said after they had gone. 'But they will at least spend some time locked up while the magistrates decide what to do with them.'

The chairman looked at Sam. 'What did Whiting mean about Dr Perks? The inquest on his death was only held this morning. How can he be alive?'

Sam thought the chairman had heard enough surprises, for one day. They were short of time, and they needed to get to Will quickly now that his location was compromised.

'Sir, would you mind if I explained this later? We need to go to Dr Perks. He is indeed alive but may now be in great danger. In the meantime, it seems that The Reverend Savage is also part of the conspiracy, and you will need to consider how to deal with him too.'

The chairman glanced at the Duke who nodded. 'Very well, Samuel. Go to your friend. I seem to have misjudged him so it's the least I can do. We can discuss the chaplain later.'

Sam thanked the chairman for his patience, and they left him shaking his head in astonishment at what had transpired.

Chapter 26

Crosley's Widow

The woman that came to the door looked very different to the one that Sam remembered from his previous visit to Mary Crosley's house on New Inn Hall Street. The black clothes of mourning had been replaced with a brightly coloured dress chosen to match the sunny weather, and the grief that had previously corrupted Mary's natural beauty had faded away. Sam smiled at her and was relieved that they had arrived there before Fairman and his men.

'Mr Ansell,' she cried when she saw him. 'You've been released. The newspaper said you'd killed a man, but Will and I didn't believe it for one moment. He'll be so pleased.'

Sam smiled, and noted her use of the term, 'Will and I'. His friend really was a charmer, he laughed silently to himself. Even when he was badly hurt.

'Hello, Mary. I'm very sorry to arrive

unannounced, but we need to speak urgently with Will.'

Mary looked at the three men at Sam's side. 'You have company,' she observed.

'Yes, this is the Duke of Marlborough, and this is Inspector Pound of the Metropolitan Police. And you know Mr Wingfield already.'

'A duke, a detective and two surgeons. What will my neighbours think?' she laughed. 'You'd better come in quickly before somebody comes round to ask.'

The house seemed larger and better appointed than Sam remembered, and as she showed then into her sitting room, the light shone through the rear window revealing that there was ample seating space for the four men. Wingfield remained standing and asked Mary if he could examine Will before they went up to see him.

'He was still very weak when I last saw him,' he explained. 'I should check to ensure he's well enough to answer our questions.'

Mary nodded approvingly, and as Wingfield climbed the stairs, Sam related everything that had happened since Will had been brought to her house. She looked a little alarmed when Sam revealed that her address was now known to the conspirators, but she seemed reassured when Pound told her that he had arranged for two of his men to guard her house for as long as it took to resolve the matter. Moments later, Wingfield called down to tell them that his patient was ready to receive visitors.

'First room on the left, gentlemen,' Mary called out as Sam led Pound and the Duke up the stairs. 'And please don't tire him out,' she added.

While Mary Crosley made tea, the three men

joined Wingfield in Will's room. Sam looked at his friend and grinned.

'Hello, Will. It seems you will do anything to escape work and fall into the arms of a beautiful widow!'

Across the room his friend smiled. He looked pale and tired from his injury, and Sam knew that it would take a few days for his body to regenerate the blood he had lost. He went over to the apothecary and saw the neat stitches on the side of his head where Wingfield had completed the trephination.

Will tried to laugh. 'Hello, Sam. I heard that they'd finally put you in prison for all your misdemeanours, yet here you are again like a bad penny. Did you dig an escape tunnel?'

Sam laughed too. 'I cannot recommend the prison accommodation, but fortunately I've had some help.' He turned and gestured at the other visitors. Will noticed the Duke of Marlborough and his face started to darken.

'It's alright, Will. The Duke is with us. Let me explain.'

Ten minutes later, Will's suspicion had subsided. Sam's account seemed to rejuvenate him, and some colour returned to his cheeks. He tried to sit up, but Wingfield intervened.

'Lie still, Dr Perks,' he warned theatrically. 'We don't want the bleeding to start again.'

Will collapsed back onto the pillow. 'Very well, who am I to argue as a mere apothecary? It seems I am once again outnumbered by the surgeons,' he grumbled.

Sam was glad to see his friend becoming his old incorrigible self. He was about to say more when

Pound shuffled uncomfortably at his side, reminding him that time was short.

Sam looked at his friend and wondered if he had lost any of his memory. 'Will,' he said, 'We need to ask you some questions about the other night. Are you absolutely certain about what you heard up on the roof of the college?'

'I am, Sam. I may have suffered a bump on the head, but I recall it quite clearly. There was just the three of them, and they were gloating over the success of the investment meeting. Fairman told them that they had raised enough money for him to pay a gunman and for the political campaign that would follow, but he needed to know about the Princess's movements so that he could make the final arrangements. Kenyon said that he would find out, but then he stopped talking when one of the roof tiles next to me slid down the roof and alerted them to my presence.'

Pound spoke for the first time. 'So, it was Kenyon who seemed to be the one who was able to find out about the Princess's movements?'

'It was, Inspector, but I'm afraid he didn't explain how.'

Pound nodded, 'I need to get my colleagues to investigate Lord Kenyon's links to the King's household. We must discover who's providing the detailed information they need to complete the plot. However, that still won't tell us when the assassination will take place. It sounds like it might be quite soon now that they've raised sufficient money. Perhaps there's something that would help us in John Crosley's notebook. Do you have it, Dr Perks?'

Will nodded. 'Yes, it's over there in the top drawer.' He pointed at a chest of drawers which the

Duke opened. He lifted out the book and passed it over to the inspector who placed it in his coat pocket and immediately rose to leave.

'Time may be short,' he told the group as he moved towards the door. 'Thank you all for your help, but I think it's best if you now leave this to me and my colleagues. Please don't interfere, but if you do think of anything else then you will find me at the Britannia Inn at Headington. In the meantime, Dr Perks, I wish you a speedy recovery.'

The others sensed that the visit had reached its natural conclusion and started to follow the inspector. Sam stayed behind for a moment and whispered to his friend, 'I'll be back in a few minutes, Will. Don't go away!'

He followed the men down the stairs. Pound departed immediately after apologizing to Mary for leaving without taking the tea she had prepared. He explained that the situation was urgent, and he promised her that his men would arrive soon to protect her. The others took tea, but eventually the Duke of Marlborough looked at his watch and made his excuses too. He offered Wingfield a lift in his carriage, and the two men left after Sam indicated that he wished to stay a while longer. As soon as the door closed, he returned to Will's bedroom and sat on the bed.

The apothecary had been waiting for him. 'So, is that it, Sam? Is this the end of the story?'

Sam nodded at his friend. 'It certainly appears that way, and in truth I think it's for the best,' he replied, gesturing towards Will's injured head. 'Anyway, you seem to have made the most of your stay here. Swift work, some might say.'

Will was indignant. 'How do you mean?' he

demanded, knowing precisely what lay behind Sam's remark.

'I was referring to the nursing care here. As you know full well.'

Will smiled. 'She's a lovely woman. I think she might have captured my heart.'

'I think you are in luck, my friend. Mary is very protective of you and seems very different to the last time I met her. Goodness knows how you've managed to charm her so quickly; I find it quite incomprehensible. Perhaps I need to tell her all about you and bring her to her senses.'

They both laughed, and then Will asked after Anne. Sam's face fell as he realized that she would be unaware of his release. He considered her visit to the prison and the events that had followed, and suddenly her position seemed quite precarious.

'Actually, Will, I'm a bit worried. Anne doesn't know that I've been set free, and her parents are away in London. She visited me in prison and told me that Lord Kirtland has agreed to let the conspirators meet at his house while they are away. Not only that, but he told Anne to remain at the house until he returned. I should have told Pound, but I forgot all about it after the excitement of discovering that you were still alive. Anne is at home and except for the servants, she's alone.'

'What does she know?' Will asked.

'Everything. I made her promise that she wouldn't confront the conspirators, but she's headstrong and determined to protect her father. I'm certain they're blackmailing him, but I don't know what they have hanging over him. If I knew that, then we might be able to save his reputation. I feel like the answer may be in Crosley's notebook, but now that's gone off with Pound.'

Will smiled. 'I think I can help you with that, Sam. When I regained consciousness, Mary told me that when Wingfield brought me here, the book came with me. I had a good look at it this morning, and I could see that Lord Kirtland is deeply indebted to Kenyon and Vane. It looks as though they have lent him a great deal of money to invest in several investments that have performed very badly.

'No doubt it wasn't their own money to lend either,' Sam observed angrily. 'It was probably cash raised from gullible people like the men we saw at the investment meeting the other evening.'

'Exactly!' Will replied. 'But I'm afraid it gets worse, because Lord Kirtland used High Cross Manor as collateral against the loans. When I examined the book, I found a letter tucked into it at the back. It was from Lord Kenyon to the solicitors instructing them to call in the loans. It seems that the letter was lodged with the Mayhew brothers, but it has not yet been activated. I'm sure this is the lever they are using. If the loan was called in, the Kirtlands would be ruined financially and would lose their home.'

Sam's heart sank. 'It's a powerful thing to hold over somebody,' he replied, 'but we still don't know what they want him to do. Lord Kirtland doesn't know the Princess's schedule or travel arrangements, and he surely wouldn't be the actual assassin. Remember also, that Gasser heard them boasting that Kirtland would take the blame if the plot went awry, so either way, Anne's father is in a difficult position unless we can find a way to defuse the blackmail.'

'What will you do?' Will asked.

'I need to go to High Cross Manor. I'm concerned about Anne's safety, and if there is anything to implicate her father in an assassination, I need to find and destroy it. While I'm there, I'll see if I can discover anything about the timing of the plot and try to alert Pound.'

Will started to get out of bed, and Sam held up his hand. 'No, Will. Not this time. You heard Wingfield. You could end up bleeding again and losing your life. Even moving about is dangerous, never mind a further blow to the head.' Sam heard a noise at the door. 'Besides,' he whispered, 'you now have a very good reason to stay safe.'

Mary walked in carrying a box. The two men quickly learned that she had the hearing of a cat.

'I agree with your friend, Will,' she told him. 'It would be foolish to go out in your state. And yes,' she added blushing, 'there are some that care deeply about your health. Please, Will. Go back to bed.' Will looked at Sam who nodded. In his heart, he knew they were right. He sighed in capitulation and sat back against the pillows.

Mary Crosley told them that Pound's men had arrived and were outside at the front of the house. It was time for Sam to leave. He shook his friend's hand. 'Get well, Will Perks,' he said. 'Use one of the men to send word to Pound about my intentions. I will find a horse and ride to High Cross Manor.' He turned to leave.

'Wait, Sam.' Mary called. 'I have no horses, but if you're going off into the night, you might want to take these.' She set the box down on the end of the bed and opened it. There were two guns inside that looked rather old. They were flintlock pistols.

'They belonged to John's father,' she explained. 'He was a naval officer. They've been up in the loft for years. There's these as well.' She held up a powder horn and some lead balls. 'I don't know if the powder will still work, but it's dry in the loft.'

Sam looked at the guns. They had been well oiled before they were put into storage, and there were no signs of corrosion. He tried the hammer on each weapon and was pleased that the flintlock was still capable of generating a spark. He loaded each pistol and thrust them into his belt. He could not be certain the powder would ignite until he tried to fire one, but they were better than nothing. He bade Will and Mary a final farewell and left the house. Two of Pound's men were outside in uniform, and they looked alert and competent. He warned them both that one of the men would soon be required to take an urgent message to the Inspector and walked off to find a horse. As he made his way towards the High Street, he noticed the sky had darkened and there was the flicker of lightning on the horizon. The heatwave was finally about to break.

Chapter 27

The Storm

Samuel Young Griffith was the proprietor of the Angel Inn and Hotel located on the High Street. It was Oxford's foremost coaching inn and the main point of departure for the city's coach services to London and beyond. The previous year, Queen Adelaide had paid a visit there, and this had enhanced the reputation of the inn which Griffith guarded jealously. He was quick to judge and slow to concede which made Sam's task a little tricky when he banged on the door of Griffith's office seeking to hire a horse.

The proprietor was at his desk studying some papers. He looked up when Sam knocked on the open door, and waved him in. Sam had been wearing the same clothes since the evening of the investment meeting, and he felt a bit dirty and dishevelled. Griffith seemed to think so too as he wrinkled his nose in obvious distaste and frowned at the intrusion. Sam explained that the receptionist had directed him to Griffith's office and told him that he wished to hire a horse.

'It's a bit of an odd time of day to be hiring a horse,' Griffith observed. A rumble of approaching thunder seemed to emphasize his point.

'Yes, I need to ride on a matter of great urgency,' Sam replied. 'And I will pay you well.'

Griffith was unconvinced. 'What's so important to merit such haste?' he asked. 'This inn is not just some common livery and bait stable. Our horses are the best in Oxfordshire, and I wouldn't want one of our mounts being flogged to an early demise or injuring itself in the darkness. How far are you going?'

'I have urgent business with Lord Kirtland at High Cross Manor. It is of crucial importance.' Sam lowered his voice and leaned forward. 'It's a Palace matter. Something that you wouldn't wish to impede if you expect to continue using royal patronage to enhance your inn's reputation.' He left the gentle threat hanging in the air as Griffith started to reconsider his position.

'I presume the animal would be stabled overnight at the Manor?' he eventually asked.

Sam nodded. 'It will.'

'Very well, the hire fee is two pounds for twenty-four hours and a pound for every four hours thereafter. During its time with you, the animal must be fed, watered and rested. If it is injured, you will have to settle any veterinary fees.'

They were expensive terms, but Sam had no choice. With every minute that passed, the danger to Anne seemed to grow, and he was desperate to get to the Manor to secure her safety. Sam reached for his purse and hoped it contained enough to settle the bill. As he withdrew it, he realized that he had exposed the two pistols in his waistband. Griffith was watching, and his eyes narrowed when he saw the weapons. For a moment, Sam thought the innkeeper was about to change his mind, but Griffith seemed to decide that the weapons were in keeping with the urgency of Sam's explanation, and the suspicion on his face subsided. He remained silent and took Sam's money before picking up a small bell and summoning the head groom.

It took fifteen minutes for the groom to saddle a horse and bring it to Sam who was waiting impatiently in the yard. It was a few years since he had last ridden, and he hoped the animal had a good temperament. His father believed that riding was an important skill that every man should learn if he was ever to be regarded as a gentleman. Sam had always thought it was a strange assertion, but he was now grateful for his father's foresight and for the riding lessons he had been forced to attend.

The groom handed him the reins. 'She's an intelligent horse, Sir, and not one to give you any trouble. Please be careful with her as it's going to be a bad night.'

Behind him, lightning flickered, and there was a crash of thunder which seemed to prove the man's point. Sam promised he would look after the horse, and he felt reassured that the mare seemed untroubled by the approaching storm. She stood patiently as he swung himself into the saddle and responded promptly as he gently tapped her sides with his heels. As they trotted through the archway onto the street the groom ran for cover as the first drops fell. It really was going to be a difficult journey.

The storm that raged over Oxfordshire that night was one of the fiercest that many of the County's inhabitants could recall. High pressure had been sitting over the country for several weeks, producing a heatwave that had left water supplies dangerously low, and residents desperate for relief. Eventually, the anticyclone shifted to the east, allowing air from the south to flow up over the southern half of England. This air was heavy with moisture drawn up from the Atlantic, and as the pressure fell sharply, unusually large storm clouds started to form. The atmosphere boiled with excess heat, and the sky grew black as the clouds thickened and fierce updraughts carried the moisture to ever greater altitudes. Eventually the elements could hold back no longer, and the accumulated energy was released in a series of powerful storms. These lashed the countryside with huge forks of lightning and a deluge of rain that swept away bridges and created flash flooding that threatened to carry off the unwary.

The streets of Oxford were deserted. Nobody was foolish enough to remain outside in such a meteorological apocalypse. Nobody, that is, except a brave house surgeon and his horse who fought the appalling conditions in a desperate journey that took nearly three hours to complete. It seemed like a battle against nature itself, and Sam's mount seemed to sense it too as horse and rider drew strength from each other in a shared contest against the elements. The journey was relatively easy while they within the city limits, but once they entered the countryside, it became increasingly hazardous as the ruts in the road filled with puddles of water and threatened to trip up the mare as she tried to keep her step between flashes of lightning.

After two hours, Sam was on the verge of stopping to seek shelter in a barn, but the rain subsided a little, and the mare picked up the pace slightly. It seemed as though the rider was wavering, but the horse remained resolute, and so Sam decided to persevere a little longer. Ten minutes later, the mare's intuition proved correct. The rain gradually stopped, and the thunder and lightning began to trundle off to the north. A thin moon appeared, and Sam risked a trot. The mare responded happily, and it took only a few minutes before they were approaching the outer perimeter of the Kirtlands' estate.

They turned in through the entrance, and Sam was pleased to see that the gatehouse was in darkness and seemingly unoccupied. When they were about a hundred yards short of the manor house, Sam dismounted and led the horse up the drive. He kept to the grass verge to mask the sound of their approach as the night had become deathly still, and the clatter of shod hooves on the cobbles would be unmistakable.

Sam was uncertain about where the conspirators might be meeting, but in the absence of Lord Kirtland, he guessed that they would probably choose to use the main sitting room at the front of the house. He had no idea where Anne might be and decided to enlist the help of the servants once he had gained entry. The stables were at the rear next to the tradesman's entrance. As he led the horse around the edge of the house, Sam heard an approaching carriage coming up the drive. He paused and watched from the corner of the building as it pulled up at the front. The carriage door opened, and Lord Kenyon stepped out. He rang the doorbell and was shown in by one of the servants. The conspirators were still arriving, Sam noted before quietly leading the mare around to the back of the Manor and the stable yard. He found an empty stall and patted the horse in gratitude for their safe arrival before leaving her feeding on a sack of hay.

Sam studied the rear aspect of the Manor. It was in darkness except for one window on the ground floor. He crept up to it and looked inside. Three servants were sitting around a table and seemed to be having a heated discussion. Sam recognized one as the housekeeper. Next to her, was the footman who had delivered Anne's secret letter to him on the evening of the ball. Finally, there was the groom, John Sheffield, who had brought him news of Gasser's murder. He tip-toed up to the window and tapped on it. Inside. there was instant concern before Sheffield recognized Sam and rushed to let him in.

'Mr Ansell, Sir, thank God you've arrived. His Lordship is away, and there are foul deeds afoot.' He looked at Sam and took in the surgeon's appearance. Sam was soaking wet, and his clothes were not only several days old, but covered in wet mud from his journey. The two pistols completed the image which told the story of his ordeal far better than Sam ever could. The groom was astonished.

'You haven't ridden here in that storm?' he asked.

'I have, John. My horse is in the stable in the yard,' he replied. 'You could help me with her later but first take me to the others.' He followed the groom to the servant's parlour where the others looked at him with relief as he entered the room. The footman took charge.

'Mr Ansell, I wish we could welcome you back under better circumstances but thank goodness you've now arrived safely despite risking injury in that storm. My name is Dennis Heycroft. This is the housekeeper, Mrs Birchall, and I think you already know John Sheffield,' he said, nodding at the groom. 'His Lordship and Lady Kirtland are away in London, and there is only Mistress Anne here from the family.' He paused.

'Go on,' Sam encouraged him.

'Well, we have other visitors here as well. Lord Vane has been staying with us for some time, but he has been joined by Lord Kenyon and Colonel Fairman. The thing is, Mr Ansell, they caught Mistress Anne eavesdropping and threatened her with violence before locking her in the reading room. We've been told to stay here while they conduct their business.' He noticed Sam's weapons. 'All three men are armed,' he added, unable to conceal that he was quietly weighing up Sam's odds. Sam looked at their expectant faces and tried to look more confident than he felt.

'I can't explain exactly what this is about, but the family's safety and good name are at stake. These are evil men who are plotting a serious crime which is of national importance. We need to rescue Mistress Anne and get her to safety. Others will deal with the plotters. Now, where are they meeting and where is Mistress Anne?'

Heycroft was encouraged that Sam seemed to have a plan. 'The reading room is on the first floor above the sitting room where the men are gathering to talk. You can access the first floor by a servants' staircase.' He grinned and handed Sam a key. 'There is always a spare key.'

Sam looked at the three servants. 'I don't want any of you to get hurt, so I think this is best done by me. If you hear them capture me, then John, please will you ride to the Britannia Inn in Oxford and tell Inspector Pound what has transpired. And John, before I go to find Mistress Anne, please will you prepare the gig with a fresh horse. While you're out in the yard, there's something else you could do.' When Sam explained what he wanted, the young man nodded enthusiastically, and everyone else laughed.

Chapter 28

The Hole

Sam waited fifteen minutes for John Sheffield to prepare the gig and to complete his extra task. When he returned, Sam clapped him on the back and then nodded to Dennis Heycroft. The footman led him along the corridor to a door that opened to reveal a staircase leading to the upper floors of the house.

'Only a few of the oil lamps have been lit,' he whispered, handing Sam a candle. 'The reading room is on the first floor, along the corridor, and third on the right. Be very quiet while you're in there as those three men are in the room directly below you. Good luck, Sir.'

Sam thanked him and crept up the staircase. Heycroft closed the door behind him, and Sam could hear the man's footsteps recede as he returned to the servant's parlour. After climbing a dozen steps, Sam found a small landing where a door opened out onto the first floor. He opened it a tiny crack and listened. There was the faintest chatter of voices drifting up from the sitting room below, otherwise the corridor was silent. He stepped through and closed the door behind him. From the corridor, the door had been built to look like a bookshelf and there were few other clues that it provided an access to the lower part of the house. Towards the end of the corridor, he found the door to the reading room. He took out the key and then hesitated. What if she called out? Anne thought he was still in prison and would not be expecting him to enter the room. He considered talking to her through the door before unlocking it, but then decided there was too much risk of being heard by the men below. Instead, he knocked as softly as he could, turned the key, and went inside. The figure beside him was strangely tall, and when he looked up, he saw Anne standing on a chair and about to hit him on the head with an iron poker.

'Anne, No! It's me, Sam. Put it down!' he whispered. She lowered the makeshift weapon as she recognized him.

'Sam! Is it really you? How did you get here? How did you get out of prison?'

He helped her down, and she hugged him tightly as a loud laugh drifted up from the room below, reminding them both to keep quiet.

'I'll tell you quickly, and then we have things to do before we leave. I have a gig waiting at the back. First of all, Will is alive and is being cared for. Second, I know what they are holding over your father. He is indebted to Kenyon and Vane, and they are threatening to ruin your family by calling in the loans. I don't know what they want from him, but I do know that if the plan to assassinate the Princess goes wrong, they have made plans to ensure that it is your father who will take the blame. I can only think that they would achieve that by planting something incriminating.' Anne smiled and put a finger on his lips to quieten him.

'Sam, it's alright. I know their plan,' she whispered. 'I was being held here as surety to make sure that my father doesn't warn the authorities while he's away. At first, I did as my father instructed, and I went to my room and pretended to be ill. However, after they started drinking, I crept downstairs and listened to them discussing their plans. It worked very well until a floorboard creaked, and they caught me. Anyway, look at this.' She picked up a copy of Jackson's Oxford Journal from a small table and passed it to him. Sam looked at the newspaper and noticed that in the Court and Social section there was an article announcing that the King was celebrating his birthday with a party to be held at Windsor Castle on 21st August. The reporter said that there would be a large guest list of the country's well-known families, and that Princess Victoria would attend as the King's guest of honour along with her mother, the Duchess of Kent.

Sam groaned. 'This is it,' he whispered. 'I'm sure they will attempt to kill the Princess when she travels from her home at Kensington Palace to Windsor. You know how much her mother likes to parade her daughter; they're bound to be in an open carriage if the weather is fine. It's a perfect opportunity for an armed man to shoot at her. But we have plenty of time, don't we? The party is not until tomorrow, on 21st?'

Anne shook her head. 'Unfortunately, not, Sam. I heard them say that the Princess and her mother are travelling to Windsor today and will spend the night before the party at the Castle. Kenyon said that they will leave Kensington Palace at eleven o' clock.'

Sam looked at his watch. 'We are well past midnight,' he said, 'and we still have more to do before we can go and raise the alarm.' He looked at Anne and asked. 'Do you know how they got all of this information?'

Anne looked down at the floor. 'It's Thomas, Sam,' she whispered. 'Thomas gave it to them. You see, they blackmailed my father for something that he was unable to provide but my brother could. He's the one on the Duchess of Kent's staff with the information on the Princess's movements, and it seems as though the fool has given in to their threats. I heard them talking about a letter from Thomas to my father, and I wondered why they were discussing where to leave it. It's somewhere in my father's office.'

'Oh, Anne, I'm so sorry,' Sam whispered, taking her hand. 'Did you manage to get a message to your father asking him to return home?'

She shook her head. 'My parents seem to have disappeared, and nobody knows where they're staying. I think it's also possible that they are attending the King's birthday party.'

'No matter, we'll have to solve this ourselves. At least your parents will be safe at Windsor Castle. The Metropolitan Police are now involved, but they don't know that the assassination is planned for today. If we can get word to their man in Oxford, Inspector Pound, we might be able to prevent the Princess from coming to harm. We could then take some credit and plead on your brother's behalf.'

She sniffed and her eyes turned glassy. 'Do you

think that might work? My brother is a good man really; he has clearly acted under duress and out of loyalty to my father.'

Sam gave her hand a squeeze. 'We can only do our best, but we must hurry; there is very little time remaining to prevent this taking place. We need to alert Pound and leave him with enough time to send word to London to divert the Princess before she leaves for Windsor. Before we go, though, we must quickly search your father's office before he gets tied into the plot as a willing conspirator. Where is it?'

'It's next door,' she said pointing in the direction of the final room on the corridor.

Sam led her to the door. He opened it and listened. From lower down, the sound of laughter again drifted up from the ground floor. It was louder than before, and it sounded as though the three men might have made a start on Lord Kirtland's Madeira. They certainly sounded overconfident. Sam listened for a moment, and when he was satisfied that they were undetected, he squeezed Anne's hand and led her into the corridor. He locked the door behind them, and together they crept along to the next room.

Lord Kirtland's office was unlocked, and Sam's candle was redundant as an oil lamp had been left burning on a low setting. The room was lined with shelves of books that were interspersed with family portraits framed with gilt. Between the shelves, the walls were clad with dark wooden panels that matched the furniture. At the end of the room, an impressive desk covered in green leather stood in front of a window and dominated the room. The light was dim, and the oil lamp threw long shadows which added to the sense that the study was a place of careful consideration and studious endeavour.

'Where do we start?' Sam whispered. They looked around. The desk was an obvious place, and Anne started there by opening the drawers and rifling through the contents. Sam saw a cupboard at one end of the desk. It was unlocked and contained a few old ledgers, but nothing that might incriminate Lord Kirtland and his son. After ten minutes, they were still empty handed, and Sam was starting to become nervous. He had good reason too, because Fairman had decided to check on his prisoner and had just discovered that Anne was missing. There was a shout from along the corridor, followed by the sound of the other two men running to help their colleague.

'Where the hell has she gone?' the Colonel roared. 'She must have had help because the door was locked when I got here.'

'The servants?' Lord Vane suggested.

'Possibly, but perhaps we have an intruder,' Fairman replied. 'We need to search the corridor. I'll start with the study. I want to check that nobody has removed the letter. You two search the other rooms. She can't have gone far. Use your weapons if you must.'

Sam sighed. He hated violence, but it sounded as though it was going to be unavoidable. He reached for the pistols and prepared himself mentally to confront Colonel Fairman. As he did, there was a tug on his sleeve and Anne shook her head.

'No, Sam. This way.' She led him across the room to the wall that the study shared with the reading room next door. She fumbled with the beading on a section of the oak panels. There was a click, and the panel swung open to reveal a hidden compartment with just enough space for the two of them. 'Get in, quickly,' she whispered as Fairman's approaching footsteps echoed in the corridor. Sam did as she instructed, and moments later she joined him and closed the hidden door just as the Colonel stopped outside the study.

Within the close confines of their hiding place, the click of the secret mechanism sounded deafening, and Sam worried that it would betray their presence. However, as he forced his breathing to slow, he heard the study door open, and then footsteps as Fairman walked past them into the room. Beside him, he felt Anne move. He was about to stop her when light streamed in though a small hole that she had exposed by raising a small wooden flap just in front of her face. It was a peephole. Sam kept very still as Anne put one eye to it and watched Fairman. He could hear the man moving around in the office, and after a few moments, Anne let the flap slide back. They stood in darkness again and heard Fairman walk past and leave the study. This time his footsteps receded as he went to help his colleagues complete their search.

After five minutes, the voices of the three men began to fade, and eventually it sounded as though they had returned to the sitting room below. There was a click as Anne opened the hidden door and they both climbed out.

Sam smiled at her. 'That's a useful hiding place. How did you know about it?'

She laughed. 'We're not sure whether it is an old priest hole or something that was designed for use during the civil war, but we've always known of it, and I used to play in it when I was a child.'

'Did you see where they hid it?' Sam asked.

'It's not hidden at all,' she said and walked over to a small table on one side of the room. On it was a silver tray bearing an unmarked envelope which she handed to Sam. 'They left it where it could be easily found,' she said. 'You read it; I can't bear to.'

The envelope was unsealed. Inside was a brief letter from Thomas Kirtland to his father. It bore the letterhead for Kensington Palace and contained the entire details of Princess Victoria's route to Windsor along with the expected timings. It was factual and contained no expressions of filial love which made Sam think it was probably written under duress. The letter was signed by Anne's brother.

'Is this your brother's handwriting and signature?' Sam asked her.

She glanced at it and nodded. 'It looks like it, but I can't think that he wrote this letter willingly.'

'No, I don't believe so either. And I'm certain that neither of them understood that it was for a plot to assassinate the Princess.' He walked to the oil lamp and set fire to the letter before dropping it into the grate of the unlit fire. 'There,' he said, 'It's gone. That puts your father beyond reach of any blame, although he will still have the debts hanging over him, and we'll still need to plead for your brother. First though, we must get to Pound and quickly.' He looked at his watch. 'It is now two o'clock in the morning, and according to your brother's letter, the Princess leaves in nine hours' time. Depending on the weather, it will take two or three hours to get to the Britannia Inn which leaves Pound six hours to get word to Kensington Palace. It might be a close-run thing, but it should be possible so long as we're not delayed.'

Anne nodded, and Sam went to the door and

listened carefully before waving her through. The conspirators were in the sitting room below, and as Sam and Anne crept along the corridor towards the servant's door, they could hear the men arguing about what to do next. Sam opened the concealed door, and moments later they were downstairs in the servants' parlour. When Sam led Anne into the room, there was genuine joy and relief that she was unharmed, and the three workers gathered round her to express their good wishes. Eventually, Sam called them to silence.

'We must leave quickly,' he explained. 'Please don't put yourself at risk by trying anything foolhardy. Just pretend that you haven't seen or heard us, and then all will be well.' He turned to John Sheffield, 'Are we all set outside?'

The groom nodded. 'We are, indeed, Sir. The gig is waiting for you with our best stallion, Hercules. I have made sure that you will get a good head start.'

Sam smiled his thanks, and they left the servants and went to the rear yard where the gig was waiting for them. Hercules looked to be a full seventeen hands high, and he was all solid muscle, power, and attitude. The stallion eyed Sam and tossed his head impatiently as though he was itching to get started. Sam untied him and looked at Anne as she clambered into the open compartment.

'Are you ready?' he asked, climbing in after her. 'I'm afraid I have to inform you that I've never driven one of these before so it could get a little rough.'

Anne laughed and grasped his arm. The prospect of imminent freedom fuelled her euphoria and seemed to diminish the risks they might encounter during their race to find Pound and save the young Princess.

'Drive me away, Samuel Ansell,' she cried theatrically. 'Take me where you will.' Her joy was infectious, and Sam laughed too, as he cracked the whip, and the horse shot off like a greyhound.

Chapter 29

The Chase

John Sheffield performed a crucial task for Sam that night. It was known only to a very small number of people, but all would agree that it materially affected the outcome of what followed. After Sheffield had finished hitching the stallion to Lord Kirtland's gig, he made sure the horse was secure and then went into the workshop to find an iron wrench. There was almost total darkness as he approached the corner of the house and peered out at Lord Kenyon's carriage which was waiting by the front steps. Sheffield was unable to see Kenyon's driver, but he could hear him; the man was fast asleep inside the carriage and snoring like a drunkard after a long night out. It could not have worked out better.

Sheffield approached the carriage from the rear. The horses were blinkered and unable to see him, but they could sense his presence, and they shifted uneasily. Sheffield paused, but the coachman's snoring continued undisturbed, so he stooped down and started crawling on his stomach. He wriggled his way to the offside wheel and discovered that fortune had smiled on him for a second time. The wheel was secured to the axle by a single linchpin which was orientated head down and in a perfect position for removal. He used the wrench to unscrew a locking nut and gripped the head of the pin and pulled it downwards. The wheel hub had recently been greased and the pin slid out effortlessly and without any noise. Sheffield grinned to himself. On the first left-hand bend the offside wheel would slide off the end of the axle and the carriage would crash. Sheffield thought about Sam and laughed to himself. He was a crafty one, that surgeon.

***

Though John Sheffield admired Sam's guile, he would have been less impressed with Sam's efforts to drive a single horse and gig.

After Sam cracked the whip, the stallion accelerated rapidly into the darkness, and Sam and Anne fell back into the seat. Sam just managed to hold onto the reins and steer the horse around the edge of the house. The gig lurched dangerously to one side, and Sam worried for a moment that it might tip over. His concern lasted for a second or two before fear of toppling was replaced by fear of collision as they raced past Kenyon's carriage, missing it by inches. Sam heard a shout behind them. The hammering of fast hooves on cobbles had alerted the three men who rushed out of the front door. He glanced back and saw Fairman raise a pistol. There was a flash, and Sam felt a breath of wind as the ball passed by his cheek and lodged in the wood of the front panel. He breathed out his thanks. If the ball's trajectory had differed by only a few inches, it would have resulted in serious injury, if not to one of the two passengers, then certainly to the stallion. Beside him, Anne clung to the edge of the seat as the euphoria of her escape gave way to fear. She had seen the ball hit the wooden fascia and tried not to imagine the damage that would be caused if it had hit human or equine flesh.

Sam saw her face and smiled to reassure her. They had made a good start and had escaped the immediate threat uninjured. Fairman had been granted only a single firing opportunity, but he had missed, and despite their erratic departure, the gig was undamaged, and the horse was unharmed. It could have turned out far worse. Sam looked behind, and as the manor house faded into the darkness, he got a final glimpse of the Colonel. He was pointing at the coachman and shouting instructions as the three men prepared to give chase. Sam smiled at the thought of what they were about to discover. He would have paid good money to see Fairman's face when the wheel fell off Kenyon's carriage, but he needed to exploit the advantage it would provide. The sabotaged wheel would give him a 30-minute lead at best so there was no time for delays. He flicked the reins, and the stallion picked up the pace. After a few minutes, the driver and his horse had gradually calmed themselves, and an uneasy truce had developed. Sam told himself that he was the one that was now back in control, but he was unable to shed a nagging suspicion that the stallion probably felt the same way. He was called Hercules for a good reason.

The gig settled down to a fast trot, and Sam began to work out if they could make it to the Britannia Inn before they were caught. He calculated that they were travelling at about eight miles an hour, and that it would take them roughly two and half hours to cover the twenty miles to the Britannia Inn. It would be quite a task for their horse, but he was a strong animal who could probably out-stay most other coach horses. He thought of the two-horse carriage behind them and guessed that it might manage 12 miles an hour with extensive use of the whip. At that speed, his pursuers could complete the journey in less than two hours so even with a thirty-minute head start, it looked like the gig might be overhauled before they could get to safety. Much would depend on how long it took Fairman and the others to replace the wheel on their carriage, and how hard they were willing to drive their horses. He glanced behind the gig, but it was still dark and there was nothing to see.

Beside him, Anne noticed Sam's concern. 'They're going to catch us, aren't they?' she said.

Sam nodded. 'Maybe, but I have taken some steps to swing the odds in our favour.' He told her about the linchpin, and she laughed. It was partly an expression of relief, but it was also the kind of shared laughter enjoyed by two people completely at ease with each other, and Sam loved her for it.

'I had no idea you could be so devious,' she joked and snuggled up against him. The wound in his shoulder protested, but Sam remained silent and uncomplaining. He valued Anne's proximity far more than the need to relieve a little discomfort.

***

After nearly two hours, there was just the hint of greyness in the east. It was still too dark to call it dawn, but it held the promise of a new day, and Sam's spirits rose in concert with the approaching sun. Beside him, Anne stirred and stretched. She had fallen asleep next to him, lulled into unconsciousness by the rhythm of the stallion's hooves as they beat the drum of safety and carried the two fugitives away from danger.

However, their shared optimism did not last for long. A few minutes after Anne woke up, Sam glanced behind and saw a rider racing after them. It was at the extreme limit of what could be discerned in the pre-dawn light, and if it had not been for the man's red jacket then Sam probably would not have seen him. It could only be Fairman, however, and Sam waved the whip and jiggled the reins to encourage the stallion to go faster. The animal was tired but nonetheless responded to Sam's encouragement. Anne sat up and looked behind to see what Sam had spotted.

'Fairman,' she observed. 'Is he gaining on us?' Sam looked back again and nodded. The figure was getting closer, but only marginally so since Sam had increased their speed.

'We are about four miles from the inn,' he said. 'I was hoping that we might get a little closer to safety before he caught up. Fairman must have grown tired of waiting for Kenyon's carriage to be repaired and decided to take a horse instead.'

'That's some journey for his mount,' she said. 'It's one thing to pull a small gig, but it's quite a different matter to carry a rider over so many miles at such speed. Fairman's horse will be tired, and I would fancy our stallion in any contest of stamina. Can we go any faster?'

Sam looked behind them. Fairman was definitely gaining ground; he had seen the gig ahead of him and had brought his mount to a gallop. However, Sam could also see that the Colonel was having to make extensive use of the whip, and so Anne was correct: Fairman's horse was tired, and it was a gallop that could not be sustained for long. It had become a race where the stakes could not be higher, yet the outcome depended on the relative strength of two horses. He had no other choice but to respond and put the matter to the test.

He looked ahead. 'Right,' he shouted, 'Hold on tight, Anne. Let's see if Hercules can live up to his name.' He cracked the whip above the stallion's head and shouted 'Hah!' The horse was tired, but still willing. He was a powerful beast, and Sheffield had chosen him for the task knowing that he had a big heart. It seemed almost as though the stallion had been waiting for this moment. He whinnied and broke into a canter that soon became a gallop. Sam had no need to provide any further encouragement; the horse knew what he wanted.

As the stallion accelerated, Sam stood up to drive the gig. He had the reins in one hand and the whip in the other. It was a precarious stance as the road was badly rutted and full of puddles from the earlier storm. The gig was not really designed for cross-country use, and it rocked and swerved as the stallion raced across the uneven ground. After a few minutes, Sam looked back again and was astonished to see that Fairman was only twenty yards behind them. He could hear the beat of hooves and the slap of the man's crop as Fairman used brute force to ensure that his exhausted mount did not slow. It was cruel treatment and typified the man pursuing them. However, that cruelty had brought Fairman within yards of the gig and close enough for a shot. Sam glanced back and saw the Colonel produce a pistol from his jacket and take aim.

'Get down, Anne,' Sam shouted just as there was a loud crack of exploding powder and a plume of blue smoke belched from Fairman's pistol before being carried away in the slipstream. Sam flinched as the ball crashed into the side of the gig, and he shook the reins to encourage Hercules onwards.

It was then that the outcome became one of manmade engineering rather than equine stamina. As they approached the outskirts of Headington, the road surface became even more treacherous, and the gig swayed alarmingly as Sam tried to navigate it from one waterlogged rut to the next. Eventually, Sam saw a puddle in the road that was seemingly innocuous. The horse seemed to sense otherwise and managed to avoid it, but the gig fared less well. The puddle concealed a deep rut, and when the gig fell into it the near side wheel fractured, and the axle dug into the ground causing the gig to topple sideways. Sam was thrown out onto the side of the road. He lay there, momentarily stunned. He felt a sharp pain at the top of his chest which suggested several cracked ribs and even a fractured collar bone. He glanced back. The gig had travelled several yards on one wheel before the stallion had been able to stop. He could see the vehicle was upright but leaning heavily to one side. It was still attached to the horse which stood patiently nearby, with foam-flecked flanks and heavy breathing. Sam was relieved that the gig was still upright, but he was alarmed by the sight of Anne's arm which was hanging motionless over the side of the arm rest.

As he worried about Anne, Sam heard the crunch of approaching boots and knew they belonged to Fairman. He fumbled for a gun and found that only one of the pistols remained in his waistband. He withdrew it and carefully cocked the hammer. The sound was imperceptible, but the boots stopped, and Sam heard Fairman prepare his own weapon. When Sam had been thrown out of the gig he had landed just over a bank where the road fell away sharply towards lower ground. It was pure fortune that he was concealed from the view of anyone walking along the road. As he waited for Fairman to appear on the top of the bank, Sam glanced at the gig. Anne's arm had disappeared, and he was heartened that she must still be alive. He hoped that she would run away to fetch help and would not attempt to confront the Colonel. Just before the crash, Sam had noticed a farm close by, and he could now hear a dog barking. The sound seemed to be getting louder, and he hoped that it signalled that help was at hand. Above him, beyond the bank, the Colonel was puzzled that he was unable to see his quarry.

'I know you're here, Ansell,' he said softly. 'It's pointless to hide.' Sam pointed his pistol in the direction of the voice, and when Fairman appeared he did not hesitate for a moment; he just adjusted his aim and squeezed the trigger, hoping that the old flintlock pistol would not misfire or explode in his face.

When John Crosley had stored his father's pistols, he had been especially careful to ensure that the powder would remain dry. However, he had not foreseen that, over the intervening years, the saltpetre in it would surrender most of its potency with disastrous consequences for the next user. When Sam pulled the trigger, the hammer on his gun fell and the flintlock sparked. The priming charge even managed a feeble splutter, but the main charge refused to fire. It was the classic flash in the pan, and the weapon was useless. Sam dropped the pistol to his side. His gun had failed, and he had failed too. He had not only failed his future monarch but also the love of his life. He knew that Fairman would silence anyone who knew of his role in the plot, and that Sam and Anne would be at the top of the man's list. He looked up at Fairman and waited for the man's vengeance. The Colonel was now standing at the top of the bank and seemed to tower over Sam as he looked down at him with a contemptuous sneer.

'Oh dear,' he mocked. '"They always tell you to keep your powder dry. But did you really expect to get away from me, Ansell? Your trick with the carriage wheel was impressive but you are a useless horseman.'

'Get on with it, Fairman,' Sam replied, 'but there's no need to harm Anne Kirtland.'

The Colonel shook his head slowly. 'I'm afraid she will have to join you in a minute, but you are correct in one regard: there really is nothing more to be said.'

He slid the safety catch off and raised the gun towards Sam. There was a loud retort, but Sam felt no impact. Above him, Colonel Fairman looked surprised, and then a red stain started to spread across the front of his tunic. He seemed unwilling to accept that he was the one who had spoken their final words, and he opened his mouth and tried to utter a few more. However, his words were swamped by a river of blood, and he managed little more than a gurgle. His heart stopped, the gun slipped from his hand, and he toppled forwards onto Sam.

Sam winced as Fairman's body compressed his fractured collar bone, but then someone rolled the dead man away from him. Inspector Pound looked down on him with a smoking pistol in his hand.

'You are fortunate, Mr Ansell. Very fortunate indeed.'

'Anne…' Sam began.

'Don't worry, I'm here,' she shouted as she scrambled down the bank towards him.

Sam remembered the urgency of the information that they carried and looked back at the policeman.

'You need to move fast, Inspector. They plan to assassinate the Princess today when she travels to Windsor. There is very little time.'

Chapter 30

A Ride in the Park

Sergeant Jenkinson was the final rider in a relay of six horses and policemen that galloped from Oxford to London in a frantic race to prevent the attempt on Princess Victoria's life. As soon as he arrived in London, Jenkinson assembled a troop of cavalrymen in an unusual alliance of police and army. They rushed to Kensington Palace but arrived too late to prevent the Princess's carriage from setting off on its planned route.

Jenkinson looked at the officer in charge of the palace guard. 'Sir, I have been given orders to arrest a man on the Duchess's staff called Thomas Kirtland. He is wanted in connection with a plot to harm Princess Victoria.'

The officer looked shocked. 'I know this man, Sergeant. Are you sure of this? He is quite a senior aide.'

Jenkinson was impatient. Every second wasted increased the likelihood that the plot would succeed.

'Sir, please. I need to try and stop the royal procession. I believe the authority comes from the King's staff. This is very urgent.'

The officer shrugged. 'Very well, I will do as you ask, Sergeant. It's not for me to argue with His Majesty. You missed the Princess by fifteen minutes or so; that's time enough to catch her, but only if you ride fast.'

Jenkinson was relieved there had been no argument for the officer was correct: there could be no delays. Jenkinson's priority was the Princess's safety. He knew they had to catch up before she left the palace grounds and entered a crowded Kensington High Street where it would be difficult to reverse the procession. The cavalry troop was led by a young Lieutenant who had accepted Jenkinson's assumed command gracefully without argument.

The officer looked at the policeman and nodded. 'We can do this, Sergeant.' Jenkinson hoped so and dug his heels hard into his mount's sides as the troop galloped out of the yard and into the grounds. Ten minutes later, they raced around some shrubs, and Jenkinson was relieved when he looked ahead and saw that the small column of royal coaches and carriages was still just inside the park. He was less impressed when he saw that the palace guards had allowed some of the public to enter the grounds and stand either side of the narrow road. They were almost within touching distance of the open carriage containing the Duchess and her daughter. Jenkinson ordered the men to fan out and to search the crowds for anyone behaving suspiciously. He brought his mount forward to the royal carriage and went to speak to the Duchess.

As the policeman's horse drew alongside, she stopped waving at the crowds and looked at him. She was clearly irritated that someone was coming between her and the spectators.

'Yes, what is it?' she snapped.

'Begging your pardon, Your Royal Highnesses. My name is Sergeant Jenkinson from the Metropolitan Police. I apologize, but we will have to turn you around and find an alternative route. We have received intelligence that there will be an attempt on the Princess's life this afternoon, and I have been ordered to divert you.'

The Duchess face darkened. 'Turn around? Look at them, Sergeant, there's no danger here.' She waved her hand at the public which prompted more cheers and the waving of hats.

'Please, Madam, this is a serious threat. I can't protect you in these crowds.' Jenkinson squirmed as he wrestled with the dilemma. Whose orders should he follow? Inspector Pound's or the Duchess's?

Beside her mother, Princess Victoria observed the policeman's discomfort and intervened. 'Please, Mother. He is here to protect us; we should listen to him.'

The Duchess looked angry but managed to control herself. 'No, Sergeant, we are *not* turning around. Besides, *they* will protect us.' She waved at the crowd again who seemed to be standing even closer to the two women. Jenkinson swallowed hard and made his choice.

'I'm sorry, Madam, but I have my orders, and my duty is to His Majesty the King. I was told that good men have died to bring this information to us. We cannot ignore it.'

The Duchess was about to argue when a movement in the crowd caught her attention. Jenkinson saw it too. A man was pushing his way forward and was reaching into his coat. The Sergeant raised a whistle and blew the emergency signal. Immediately, the cavalrymen started to fall back to form a living barrier around the coach.

'Get down,' he shouted at the two women. 'Get down right now or we may lose our future Queen.' The two women were startled by his directness, but even the Duchess was becoming alarmed, and they started to get down onto the floor of the carriage. 'Turn around, driver,' Jenkinson ordered. 'Fast as you can.'

The driver nodded. He had seen the man too. As the carriage started to turn, the crowd parted, and Jenkinson prayed that nobody would fall under the wheels. He glanced at the man on the other side of the road. He was close now and starting to pull something out of his coat pocket. It was a gun.

Jenkinson pointed at him as his horse started to prance in alarm at the proximity of the crowds.

'That man there,' he bellowed at the crowd. 'The blue coat! Save the Princess! Arrest him.' The men in the crowd began to understand what was at stake and turned to see who the Sergeant was pointing at. Some saw the man's pistol and shrank back as the man began to take aim. One man was braver and threw himself on the Princess's assailant and wrestled for control of the weapon. Another man joined in, and then another. The assassin disappeared under a pile of helpers, and his gun thankfully remained silent. Jenkinson stayed with the Princess and her mother, and as the coach finally emerged from the crowd of onlookers they accelerated away back towards the Palace. Once he was satisfied that the two women were safe, Jenkinson ordered some of the escort to return and take the man into custody. He allowed the procession to slow, and as they made their way back to the palace, he allowed himself a moment of reflection. He was worried about the repercussions of his treatment of the Duchess and the Princess, but he was reassured when he glanced into the carriage and was rewarded with a smile of gratitude from the young heir to the British throne.

For Sergeant Jenkinson, Victoria's smile was sufficient reward. He was a modest man who expected no public acclaim for doing his duty. And it was just as well, because there would never be a full account of what took place that day, only a small piece in the paper describing a minor public disturbance involving a drunk protestor who had been dealt with in the usual way by the authorities. It was an official cover up that was never revealed to Jenkinson but was explained to Sam sometime later.

***

The following night, the King welcomed his guests to his party at Windsor Castle and the only mention he made about the assassination attempt was an oblique remark expressing his gratitude for the safe arrival of his niece. During the meal, the King glanced down the central table and saw Lord Kirtland and his wife. The peer looked drawn and preoccupied, and the couple were not engaging with their neighbours. The King came to a decision and beckoned to an aide who was standing against the wall. The man leaned over, and the King lowered his voice.

'Tell Marlborough that I agree to his request, but with some conditions. Come closer.' The aide leaned in, and the King whispered his instructions.

Chapter 31

Lunch

A month later, the Duke of Marlborough was sitting in the chairman's office, peering over the desk at Sam. He decided that the surgeon was recovering well. There was still a faint scar on Sam's forehead from the incident at the front of the infirmary, but his fractured collar bone seemed to be healing, and there was no sign of the sling that had supported the injury following his crash on the London Road.

'The attempt on Princess Victoria's life will never be made public,' the Duke told him. 'The Palace has decided to keep it a secret to avoid any possibility of someone else copying the idea.' Sam nodded. Pound had warned him that there would be a cover up so the Duke's statement came as no surprise. However, there was something that Sam had been particularly anxious to hear, and he looked expectantly at the King's messenger. Marlborough smiled; he knew what Sam wanted.

'I have been instructed to inform you that no action will be taken against Lord Kirtland or his son who, it is accepted, were acting under duress and had no knowledge of the planned attempt on the Princess's life. Thomas will have to leave his employment at Kensington Palace, but he will be allowed to do so with his reputation intact. I am told that Lords Kenyon and Vane have decided to forego any repayments on the loans they made to Lord Kirtland, and so he is financially secure once again. I informed Lord Kirtland of this yesterday, and when you next meet the Kirtlands I think that you'll find they are both grateful to you for saving the family's home and reputation. It is most uncommon that someone foregoes a reward to plead for leniency on behalf of others.'

Sam was relieved. 'I'm glad that Thomas Kirtland has been spared,' he remarked; 'I never believed that he was a willing partner in the plot. But what about the actual conspirators? What about Lords Kenyon and Vane?'

The Duke laughed. 'They have been dealt with in a most peculiarly British way. Did you not read what happened in parliament last week?' Sam shook his head.

'Well, they were exposed publicly and forced to defend themselves in the House of Lords. An MP called Joseph Hume stood up in the House of Commons and accused the Orange Order of plotting to place the Duke of Cumberland on the throne after the King dies. Hume produced a letter from Fairman encouraging the two Lords to support the plot. However, once the scheme had been revealed, the House of Commons voted to disband the Order. The

King supported the proposal, leaving the Duke of Cumberland no choice but to dissolve the lodges. Vane and Kenyon both made statements in the House of Lords decrying the plot and trying to distance themselves from it. However, everyone knew it was a public humiliation, and politically they are damaged beyond repair.'

Sam smiled. 'And all without any mention of an assassination attempt. Very subtle.'

'Yes,' the Duke agreed, 'It's the way the King wanted it. Now,' he said, changing the subject. 'I hope you don't mind, Sam, but I have arranged a bit of a surprise lunch for you with some of your friends. They are waiting for us in the conference room.'

Sam followed the Duke down the corridor. He recognized some of the servants from Blenheim Palace who had been seconded to serve the meal which was spread out on the board room table. All of his friends were waiting there, with one surprising addition. His father was standing opposite the doorway talking to Wingfield. Sam went over to them. In all the excitement, he had only had the opportunity for a brief word with his father. However, it did not seem to matter because it soon became apparent that he knew everything about it.

'Father! I'm so glad to see you here. Are your lungs recovered?'

His father laughed. 'Yes, I'm fine, Doctor. I was invited by the Duke of Marlborough who explained what you've been up to. I must say, I'm impressed: dukes, princesses, palaces…whatever next?'

Sam laughed. 'Well, it has certainly been an eventful time.'

His father gestured at Wingfield. 'I was

chatting to Mr Wingfield before you arrived; I believe he has something to tell you.'

Wingfield beamed at them both and got straight to the point. 'I was telling your father that the quality of your work is first class, Samuel,' he began, 'and that you are an excellent colleague to work with. Now, my private surgical practice is growing rapidly, and I have been wondering whether my work colleague would be interested in becoming my partner. We can work out the details of the financial arrangements later, but I am offering you a fifty per cent share in the partnership. You don't need to answer now as these things are best considered in slow time, but I really hope that you will accept my offer.'

Wingfield paused and glanced across the room to where Lord Kirtland was standing with his wife and Anne. He looked back at Sam and winked.

'A partnership would mark a significant improvement in your prospects. And that might help you with other matters too,' he added, nodding towards the Kirtlands.

Sam understood and smiled. Wingfield was right, and Sam thanked him for his kind offer and told him that he would respond to it very soon. His father looked overwhelmed, and Sam was about to speak to him about it when Henry Lipscomb sidled up to them and coughed to attract Sam's attention. Sam wondered what the reporter was doing there and was about to express his anger at the man, when Lipscomb spoke first and started to explain. It soon became clear that the reporter wanted to clear his conscience of the death of William Gasser, Lord Vane's valet.

'Mr Ansell,' he said, 'Might I have a quick word? I believe that I owe you an apology.' Sam did not really feel inclined to speak with the man, but he excused himself from Wingfield and his father and followed the reporter to a quiet corner.

'What is it?' he asked Lipscomb when they were alone.

The reporter looked anguished. 'I want to apologize. I promised you that I wouldn't break your story, but I asked some questions that I thought were innocent enough but turned out to be too close to the mark for that infernal Colonel. I did not intend to betray your source, and I deeply regret that he was murdered because of my enquiries. I know it is poor recompense, but my paper will seek to compensate his family or donate to charity if he had no relatives.'

Sam nodded. Lipscomb had shown some courage by attending the lunch to make his apology, and Sam decided it was not a day for recriminations.

'I accept your apology, Mr Lipscomb. My source was called William Gasser, by the way. He was Lord Vane's valet, and I don't believe he had any family.'

Lipscomb looked relieved but seemed to have more to say. 'I am very grateful for your understanding, Mr Ansell. You have lived through a very interesting story, but it is not one that I can ever report, and my article about all of this is now firmly on the editor's spike.' He lowered his voice. 'However, there is one piece that will be run because the editor has received instructions from the highest authority in the land.' Lipscomb paused and looked around to confirm that they were not overheard. Sam looked at him and was intrigued.

'Go on, Henry,' he said, 'I take it these instructions came from the Palace?'

Lipscomb nodded. 'Yes. We have been told to write a sympathetic report about a brave surgeon who took on an Oxford footpad called Ackers after he had assaulted one of the infirmary's other doctors. We have been asked to emphasize that you were later subject to a reprehensible miscarriage of justice, and we have been told to hold nothing back in our praise for you. I am told that it will improve your chances greatly.'

'Chances?' Sam began to ask, but was interrupted by the Reverend Vaughan who had rushed over after spotting that Sam had entered the room. The chairman was generous in his praise.

'Samuel, I am so glad this has turned out well. You have not only performed a service for the nation, but you have saved the reputation of the Infirmary.' He looked at Lipscomb who was nodding. 'Now, this is a little bit indiscreet of me, but I wanted to let you know that we are considering the appointment of a third consultant surgeon, and I was hoping that you might apply. The other two consultants think highly of you, and I'm sure your public reputation will help when it goes to a ballot.'

Sam looked at Lipscomb. 'Chances?' Reputation?' Sam repeated.

'Exactly, Mr Ansell,' the reporter grinned. 'A little bit of good publicity never did any harm when it comes to an election for a consultancy at the Radcliffe Infirmary.'

Nearby, Wingfield had watched The Reverend Thomas rush over to Sam and came to the rescue with Sam's father who Wingfield introduced to the effusive chairman. As they chatted, a loud laugh came from where Lord Kirtland was joking with his wife and daughter. Sam looked across the room, and Anne waved at him. Wingfield saw her gesture and offered him some encouragement.

'Go on, Sam, they're waiting for you. I'll look after your father for the moment.' Sam's father nodded his approval, and Sam went over to the Kirtlands.

As he joined them, he knew something important had changed but he was unable to identify what it was. Then he saw it: that infallible bellwether of mood - Lady Kirtland's jaw - was fully retracted. Not only that, but she was smiling, and there was no sign of the scornful glare that she usually deployed when faced by her daughter's unacceptable suitor. It was quite a transformation. Sam bowed and kissed Lady Kirtland's hand, causing her to blush.

'Mr Ansell,' she said. 'Our family owes you so much. In fact, we owe you everything. When we first met, I was…well...shall we say, I was hardly welcoming, and I wonder if you would now forgive me for my rudeness?'

Sam took her hand. 'Lady Kirtland, there is nothing whatsoever to forgive, but only if you promise to dance with me at your next ball.' The woman blushed and was grateful that Sam had the grace to make light of the situation and spare her from further embarrassment. She tittered.

'I most certainly will, Mr Ansell, but only if you promise not to stand on my toes!'

They all laughed, and then Sam remembered his father. He turned to Lord Kirtland. 'My Lord, may I introduce my father to you.'

'Of course, Samuel, ask him over.' Sam waved his father across and introduced him. Lady Kirtland was polite, and Lord Kirtland immediately engaged him on the possibility of purchasing some of the yellow silk that Taylor had used to make the waistcoat Sam had worn at the ball.

After a while, Sam felt Anne at his side. She looked up at him with a flicker of excitement burning in her eyes and took his hand. Sam worried for a moment that she was being too forward, but her parents kept smiling as she turned to her father.

'Go on Papa, tell him. It's time.' Lord Kirtland nodded and looked at Sam carefully.

'As I'm sure you have realized by now, my daughter takes an unconventional approach to life, and this moment will be no exception. She came to see me this morning and turned tradition on its head by asking for my permission for her to marry you. I of course said "yes" as we cannot think of a son-in-law that we'd rather have.'

Beside her husband, Lady Kirtland nodded in agreement as her eyes became glassy. 'Go on, Anne,' she said. 'Ask him. You have our blessing.'

Anne looked up at Sam and smiled nervously. The room had fallen silent, and it was just as she had planned. She took his hand.

'Samuel Ansell, I love you very much. Will you marry me and make me your wife?'

Sam smiled down at her, and despite the drama of the moment, he felt the tension of the previous weeks ebb away. He kissed her hand.

'Of course I will marry you, Anne Kirtland. I would be honoured to be your husband.'

There was silence and then somebody clapped. A familiar voice shouted, 'Oh Bravo, indeed!' and the applause spread and became prolonged and enthusiastic as it reverberated off the walls, down the corridors, and onto the distant wards. Sam looked for the familiar voice and saw his friend. It was Will who had come in unobserved, and he shook Sam's hand vigorously.

'My dear friend,' he said. 'Many congratulations.' He looked at Anne and could not resist himself. 'I warned Sam that you were a feisty one,' he laughed, 'but he never listens to me.'

'Are you well, William?' Anne asked looking at the scar on Will's head.

'Well, no worse than usual,' he grinned.

Anne laughed too and then noticed a woman standing quietly behind the apothecary. She wagged her finger at him.

'William Perks, I declare that you've been hiding a secret from us. Where are your manners, Sir? Must we do everything for you?'

The woman standing behind Will stepped forward and smiled shyly at them. Will became serious; he too had an important announcement to make, and he cleared his throat.

'My good friends, I'd like to introduce you to Mary Crosley, who has foolishly agreed to become Mary Perks by marrying me. And I couldn't be more fortunate,' he added, taking Mary's hand. Will's announcement caused quite a commotion, and the small group all began talking at once. Sam looked across at his friend.

'Where will you live, Will?' he asked.

'A house doctor is no job for a married man, so I've decided to return to my father's apothecary's shop in Banbury. He needs a partner who can take over the practice once he retires. We intend to find somewhere to live close by, but we'll make sure we have rooms spare for visitors,' he added, nodding at

Anne and Mary as they chattered away.

Sam congratulated him, and they were about to ask a steward to open a bottle of celebratory wine when the porter, James Moss, appeared in the doorway. He tapped a spoon against a glass; it was a day for announcements.

'Gentlemen, I'm sorry to interrupt, but an emergency case has been brought in. May I ask which doctor is on duty?'

The room fell silent, and Wingfield shrugged. 'It's sounds like a job for a house doctor to me.'

Will looked at Sam. 'Well, I think it sounds like a job for a surgeon.'

Sam sighed and looked apologetically at the Kirtlands and his father as he made to follow Moss.

'It's always the same,' he told them. 'You can never get an apothecary when you need one; I must be in the wrong job.'

He followed Moss down to Bagot Ward. A workman had been struck by a falling stone and was seriously injured. Sam could see immediately what was required and set about it. He knew the patient might not live but he would do his best for him. After all, he told himself, that was the whole purpose of the Radcliffe Infirmary and those that worked there.

*****

Historical Note

The Oxford Conspiracy is a novel rather than an historical record, but I created it by taking certain historical facts, timings, and personalities and embellishing them in an effort to make an enjoyable story. The true historical record is rather interesting and occurred in 1836 during a period of British history that perhaps receives less attention than other, better-known periods. The following note covers the issue of a regency and finishes with some interesting facts about the infirmary's burial ground.

During her reign, Queen Victoria would face seven assassination attempts of varying sophistication, but none of them occurred while she was still a princess. The attempted assassination in *The Oxford Conspiracy* is therefore fictional. However, history does record an unsuccessful attempt by the Orange Order to install their Grand Master - The Duke of Cumberland - as Regent. The main parliamentary protagonists in the plot, Lords Vane and Kenyon, really did exist, and I have tried to use their biographies and portray their political views as accurately as possible within the limits of artistic licence. The plot was exposed by the MP John Hume who laid a letter before the House of Commons which was said to be from the Deputy Secretary of the Order, Lieutenant Colonel William Fairman. The letter asked the two peers to voice their support for a Cumberland Regency although there is little detail on how it was expected to be achieved. The Duke and the two Lords were forced into making humiliating statements decrying the proposal, and the lodges were disestablished. For Kenyon, at least, the episode resulted in the political wilderness. There is an extensive parliamentary record of the matter in Hansard.

During Victoria's teenage years, the issue of a regency was very much a live discussion especially as William IV was in quite poor health. The debate centred on Victoria's youth and childhood health issues, but I wonder if there was a touch of misogyny about it too. I have mentioned the Duke of Cumberland and the Orange Order plot, but there was another proposal - originating from Kensington Palace - that suggested that Victoria's mother, the Duchess of Kent, should be named as a regent in waiting. In many respects, the Kensington proposal was more realistic than the Irish plot in the novel except for one crucial fact: it was totally opposed by the King.

The Duchess's chief proponent was her advisor, Sir John Conroy. I find him interesting because Conroy was such a schemer and self-obsessed character, and for a novelist that alone makes him worthy of study as a potential model for future fiction.

Conroy worked tirelessly behind the scenes to promote the Duchess as the nominated regent. He tried to develop an alternative seat of power, centred on Kensington, with himself at the helm as the undisputed advisor. Within well-informed circles, this arrangement even become known as the Kensington System. To make his position unassailable, Conroy isolated the Duchess by gradually sidelining many of her close friends and advisors and anyone else who might have offered different, and more measured advice than his own.

Beyond the Duchess, Conroy also tried to control access to Princess Victoria. He achieved this by fuelling the Duchess's paranoia over Victoria's safety which he encouraged by informing her of frequent plots to harm her daughter. As a result, the Princess's movements and security became strictly monitored. It kept Victoria safe, but it also allowed Conroy to control who could influence the development of the young girl. Consequently, whilst the Princess was not a prisoner at Kensington, her movements were tightly controlled, and she was kept well away from the King's court and any influence he might bring to bear on his niece.

The King was furious about this, but he was also irritated by the way the Duchess seemed to court public opinion. Once again, the driving force was Conroy who tried to harness the public as a means of building up the Duchess's popularity and reputation. His favoured tool for this was Victoria who was paraded in ever more extravagant ventures. With his encouragement, the Duchess took personal control of Victoria's journeys and adjusted them to ensure that as many people as possible could see her travelling alongside her daughter. She devised ever more extravagant trips including several grand tours between 1832 and 1835. These were on a scale that might be enjoyed by a reigning monarch rather than an heir, and they were also extremely expensive. Not one of the tours was cleared with the King beforehand.

By 1836, the King had run out of patience. He was fond of Victoria and wanted to introduce her to court. He was also angered by the attempt to set up a rival court at Kensington Palace. The final straw came after the King invited the Duchess and his niece to his party at Windsor. It was to be a celebration of the King and Queen's birthdays which occurred within days of each other. The Duchess replied that she was unable to attend on his suggested date of 17th August because she was too busy celebrating her own birthday. However, she informed the King that she could attend on the 20th for a party on 21st. He agreed to the new date, but he decided he would not overlook her snub when it came to writing his speech which I have included at the end of this note because it was so direct and, I confess, it made me laugh.

In discussing the truth, it is worth mentioning a little about Oxford and the Radcliffe Infirmary. The characters in the outer layer of my conspiracy were all fictional, and I drew a mental picture of their personalities from some of the history of Oxford that I encountered during my research. I am not a resident of the City, so I tread warily when suggesting that during the first part of the Nineteenth Century there was a degree of competition for civic power between the University, the Diocese and those civic structures that were enhanced by the Municipal Corporations Act of 1835. This tussle is apparent from some of the articles published by Jackson's Oxford Journal during the period, which provided a source of inspiration for some of my fictional characters and their corrupt behaviour.

Last of all, we come to the Radcliffe Infirmary

and the patients that were treated there. These were the subject of my wife's academic research which I supported as her assistant. We spent hours in the Oxford Family History Centre studying the hospital archive, and I was privileged to gain access to original source material such as the Governors' Minutes, Account Books for Matron and the chaplains, the Secretary's Minute Books, and a host of clinical material including Admissions Registers and an original Operations Book.

The Infirmary burial ground was excavated by Oxford Archaeology in 2013/14 prior to redevelopment of the site, and a special licence was granted to allow the skeletons to be studied for academic purposes. The remains are currently stored at Durham University under the care and study of the Department of Archaeology, for a limited period, and before they are reinterred in Oxford.

It is true that all the graves were unmarked, and that they were positioned rather haphazardly. The only record of the burials is a partial list of 196 names in a Burial Register recording interments from 1815 until the graveyard was closed in 1855. However, the burial ground was in use from 1770, and there were many more individuals buried at the Radcliffe who have no burial record at all. Only one skeleton has been identified out of more than four hundred. I found that rather sad, and so I have attempted to bring some of these individuals back to life by choosing the first and second names of all my fictional characters from people listed in the one surviving Burial Register. Hopefully the spirit of Mary Wallace, 40, of Dorchester (buried on 3rd February 1815) will not object to me using her surname for my fictional and rather flirtatious infirmary nurse.

In closing, I will end by pointing out that some of the infirmary characters were real individuals including the chairman, the Duke of Marlborough, Charles Wingfield and some of the others. Of note is Absolom Whiting who really was a crooked secretary who was dismissed for embezzling infirmary funds.

Finally, Samuel Ansell and William Perks are both fictional characters who I tried to portray as caring and thoughtful doctors. I like to think that the real patients at the Radcliffe Infirmary were served by doctors with the same caring attitude, though I doubt they would have enjoyed the same kind of adventures.

****

Annex

King William IV Dinner speech 21 August 1836 - Excerpt.

'I trust in God that my life may be spared for nine months longer, after which period, in the event of my death, no Regency would take place. I should then have the satisfaction of leaving the royal authority to the personal exercise of that young lady [he pointed to the Princess], *the heiress presumptive of the Crown, and not in the hands of the person now near me, who is surrounded by evil advisers and who is herself incompetent to act with propriety in the station in which she would be placed. I have no hesitation in saying that I have been insulted – grossly and continually insulted – by that person, but I am determined to endure no longer a course of behaviour so disrespectful to me. Amongst many other things I have particularly to complain of the manner in which that young lady has been kept away from*

my court; she has been repeatedly kept from my drawing rooms, at which she ought always to have been present, but I am fully resolved that this shall not happen again. I would have her know that I am King and that I am determined to have my authority respected.

The King concluded his speech with expressions of affection for the Princess who burst into tears. The Duchess of Kent rose silently and left the table.[1]

[1] Victoria, A life, Wilson A N, Page 69

About The Author

I was born in Tanzania, but I have lived most of my life in the United Kingdom. At various times I have sold motor spares, served as an RAF fighter pilot and farmed the land.

Readership

To the reader, I offer my thanks for reading *The Oxford Conspiracy*. It is only my second novel, so if you have enjoyed the story please help me to improve my writing skills by leaving a constructive review.

Future Work

My next novel will be a sequel to my first book, *Dangerous Heritage,* when Michael Calvert returns and decides to research his father's side of the family tree by having his DNA tested. The results are unexpected and lead him to a 1960s world of youthful protest and Cold War intrigue. He soon discovers it is a time where personal loyalty cannot be assumed, and little of value is guaranteed by the mere presence of family ties…

Printed in Dunstable, United Kingdom

64687520R00194